IN THE BLUE HOUSE

IN THE
BLUE HOUSE

MEAGHAN DELAHUNT

BLOOMSBURY

First published 2001
This paperback version published 2002

Copyright © 2001 by Meaghan Delahunt

Grateful acknowledgement is made to the following for permission to reprint
previously published material:

Esenin, Sergei *Suicide Note, 1925* and *Wolf Nemesis* from *Confessions of a Hooligan*
G. Thurley (transl.), Carcanet, London, 1973

Mayakovsky, Vladimir *At the Top of My Voice* from *Listen! Vladimir Mayakovsky
Early Poems 1913–1918*
Maria Enzensberger (transl.), Redstone Press, London, 1987

Mayakovsky, Vladimir *To Sergei Esenin* from *V. Mayakovsky Selected Verse Vol. 1*
Victor Chistyakov (transl.), Raduga Press, Moscow, 1985

Paz, Octavia *Brotherhood* from *The Collected Poems 1957–1987*
Eliot Weinberger (ed. and transl.), Paladin, London, 1991

Every reasonable effort has been made to ascertain and acknowledge the
ownership of copyrighted text included in this volume. Any errors that have
inadvertently occurred will be corrected in subsequent editions provided
notification is sent to the publisher.

Bloomsbury Publishing Plc, 38 Soho Square, London WID 5HB

A CIP catalogue record for this book
is available from the British Library

ISBN 0 7475 5765 9

10 9 8 7 6 5 4 3 2 1

Typeset by Hewer Text Ltd, Edinburgh
Printed in Great Britain by Clays Ltd, St Ives plc

For Francis

I am a man: little do I last
and the night is enormous.

Brotherhood
Octavio Paz

CONTENTS

JUDAS AT THE CASA AZUL

THAT HOUSE: THE cradle and the grave. The colour of it – *azul anil* – a deep matt blue to keep evil away. We say it is a blessing to be born and to die in the same house. Now that she is gone I imagine the birth and remember the death. It rained much on both occasions. Rain on a coffin tells us the person is happy. Rain on a newborn tells of a difficult life. The *señorita* loved the rain, the tears of the sky. Between her birth and her death, the sky cried many times.

Without tears she journeys now to Tlalocan, the Southern Paradise. Here the god of rain, Tlaloc, watches her progress. In this land of springtime she will run through the colours, moving easily, gathering them with her skirts for a palette. The other souls will see her and smile. They will sing her arrival and the dry branch near her funeral urn will turn green.

For she wanted this journey, spoke of it often.

At her funeral, so many people. And after, the *señor*, my *patron*, presenting me to them with eyes swollen, *Señora Rosita Clemente Moreno*, he said, *the Judas-maker, the artist.* And I had to move away then. For I had looked into the flames as her body eased into the burning. At the last moment, a gust from the furnace blasted the body upright, fiery strands of hair across her face, the eyes in the centre of the blazing hair. Like the face of a flower. Like something from her own hand. As if she had painted herself, one last time, a still life that was never still, to sit upright like that, with eyes that saw through fire.

Shortly before her death, the *señorita* showed me a painting which had her face at the centre of a sunflower. She looked at this painting for a long time. As she lay in her bed, the red plaster corset supporting her spine, blankets piled over the stump of her leg, she slowly scraped the paint off the canvas. 'I am drowning inside that damned flower,' she said, and kept scraping away at it, destroying it.

Drowning inside the flower.

The flower of her own life. Brilliant and short. The energy of a flower. Even in death, an energy.

When a friend dies, what is left? The name that you can repeat so that they will not be forgotten. *La señorita Frida.* The name of my friend. She had a talent for friendship. 'I have an open door for a heart,' she once told me. And it was true. So many passed through that doorway. To feel the warmth of that heart was special. Big people, famous people, but also the small people, the *campesinos*, entered the places of her heart. All of us flowed through her. *El Viejo*, for instance. Flowing – like the story of oceans and rivers. For what is one life but the record of other lives?

The first meeting with the *señorita*, I was at my stall, the last baby at my breast, although at the time I did not know that baby to be my last. I was watching the movement of the crowd, watching the people at my stall: the extension of a hand towards the fruit, the bend of a knuckle around a pear, the line of a nose as a person bent to inhale. Each day, I memorised these lines and angles of faces and bodies, and at night I worked on my figures from the memory of them.

I looked up. There was a sudden disturbance of air, as if birds had risen from branches, and there she was, moving towards me, a pink *rebozo* over her shoulders, hair braided with red ribbon, colour everywhere, a woman in Tehuana costume coming towards me. The *señor* was with her and they spent a long time at the stall, looking at my papier-mâché figures, and I kept looking at this couple, too tired from the baby to speak, silently measuring the girth of the *señor*, how much flour and water I would need, how much wire for the jaw, how long it would take me to model a Judas on the scale of the *señor*, the biggest broadest man at the market that day. I was thinking all this when she spoke to me and asked me to make a model of her husband, a huge Judas-figure for burning, *did I think that would be possible*? As if she had looked into me and interrupted my thoughts. I nodded, yes, it would be possible, but a big work, and how much would she pay me for such a big work? I indicated the height and breadth of the *señor*, who, from that moment, became my *patron*. They laughed and offered me two hundred and fifty pesos, more money than I had ever seen. They bought some apples and prickly pear that day. As she counted out the money, I noticed the track-lines of her palm. 'You have no head-line,' I said, as she extended her hand. 'You must be careful. With no head-line, there is only the heart.' And that was the beginning of our friendship. I looked at her dress, the way other people pointed and stared as if she were a bird freed from a cage. I asked her: *What is the occasion*? For no one outside of Tehuana dressed like that then. I repeated my question. *So, what is the occasion?*

And she looked at me closely and at the baby in my arms and at the many around us, in the Mercado Abelardo Rodriguez. The pyramids of apples and oranges, the sharp cries of the vendors, the scent of bougainvillaea from the flower stalls, my Judas-figures set out in preparation for *Semana Santa*, Holy Week. '*This* is the occasion.' She spread her hands wide, taking in the whole market. She laughed, a few of her teeth slightly blackened, covering her mouth with her hand. And over the years, I learnt that for her every day was an occasion. Every time I saw her – the hair, the rings, the nails, never the same from one day to the next. It made everyone keep watching her: a walking festivity. *She* was the occasion.

Between friends, what is there not to say? 'You drink too much. You smoke too much.' I used to scold her, more so in these last years when she would limp past my stall and I would check her pockets for the silver flask of *mezcal* or rum. She tried to laugh with her mouth shut. By then there was too much pain. Although in her paintings, the pain showed rarely in her face. Many times, in her studio, after I had brought her my latest figures, I would sit and watch her moving around, arranging objects and brushes, tiny flags in bowls of fruit. Hanging my black-and-white *calaveras* from ceiling hooks. I never saw her paint. Only Diego was allowed to watch. And I would look about the studio at her portraits cooling on racks. 'The face is the same, always the same,' I said to her once, 'but these paintings are of everything beyond the face.'

And at the end, an unfinished painting of a man with a heavy moustache. 'Why paint that face?' I asked her. 'He is not so beautiful as you.'

'But his moustache is beautiful!' She smoothed the heavy down, a dark crescent over her own upper lip. 'You know I like a good moustache.' She laughed. She laughed a lot, the *señorita*. Even in the wheelchair.

I looked at this portrait and I remembered another man. With his white hair and small white beard. '*El Viejo* would not be laughing.'

Frida swung around to face me. '*El Viejo* made many errors – I see that now.'

'Errors.' I shook my head. 'We all make errors.' I pointed at the easel. 'But I am tired of this man and his moustache. This Stalin.'

La señorita was *una comunista*. People spat the word in the streets. Nuns threw holy water in her doorway as they passed. Outside the Casa Azul, bourgeois women covered their faces with rose-scented handkerchiefs. I said, 'Stalin. My husband can think of nothing but Stalin and *pulque*. He spends more time drinking to Stalin than feeding his own children.'

'But that is the nature of the struggle,' she said.

'No, no,' I protested. 'For me, the struggle is to get up every morning, to mix my paste, to fix my colours, to sell my fruit, to keep my children alive for another day. *That* is the struggle.'

'And for myself –' She paused, wheeling back a little, eyes fixed on the portrait of Stalin. 'Who cannot get up every morning, the struggle is to keep on believing.'

She swung away from me, her amputated leg hidden by the coloured mass of her skirts. She moved to pick up a brush, turned back to her easel, started to block in the heavy outline of the man's face. She was crying. This portrait hung like an argument between us. I feel ashamed of it now, how I left that day.

I sit at my stall waiting for a car with the *señor* squeezed behind the wheel and the *señorita* next to him, her coloured braids snaked around her head. In my pocket are two gold teeth – a present from Frida many years before. The teeth I lost when my husband came back from the mines, thin and tired, swinging his fists, full of *pulque* and dreams of the Revolution. And now I gape as if my mouth is the opening to disaster, my gums as bruised as a landslide. I sit here, my hands closed over the bloodied gold, and I weep. I wish she could see me, my generous friend. For the *señorita* knew what it was to suffer a husband. She told me as much herself.

Five months since her death. I stand opposite her house, the Blue House, in the Avenida Londres. I see Señor Rivera come through the doorway of the Casa Azul, brushing past my work, the huge Judas-figures arching over him, red-and-blue figures, framing his bulk in the doorway. I have come to see if he wants any works for Christmas; table decorations, toys, *piñatas* maybe. I have come also to check on my Judas-figures, those guards at the Casa Azul. And, I admit, to admire my work. To tend the colours. And I call to him, this day, from across the street, but he does not hear me, does not see. And it seems that Diego is suddenly an old man, talking to himself, his clothes flapping loose around him.

I call and he does not hear me. For these are still early days, when his mouth tastes of ashes, when grief is a furnace, forcing the feelings upright, like the blast of her cremation.

M Y WIFE HAS been up before me. The newspaper is open on the table, creased and folded as she has left it, the stain of her coffee cup in one corner. On the front page there is a photo of Diego, hat in hand, walking behind a coffin draped in a Communist flag. Frida's coffin. This flag over the coffin has caused a furore. Even in death, she makes me smile.

I unfold the newspaper. And it is the sight of that flag, and the smoothing of the newsprint which has been read before me, that recall that other time. With Frida and Diego. The time with Trotsky – the Old Man.

El Viejo, she used to call him.

The newspapers. Whenever *Pravda* or any other newspaper arrived by post, I would place it on his desk unopened. He never read a newspaper that had been opened before him. He was very exact about things. I learnt to anticipate and respect his wishes, his attention to detail. And of all the secretaries and bodyguards, I stayed with him the longest. I could balance his small furies and Natalia's wary silences. For three years this was my role.

Trotsky. For months after *she* broke with him, he spent his evenings looking blankly out on to the cactus garden, listening to the nightingales in their green cages. Natalia hovered. In the mornings, the sun over the patio of the Casa Azul, the orange trees, the red of the bougainvillaea, the pre-Columbian statues, now cast long shadows.

This was her effect on the Old Man and I tried hard to put such thoughts behind me as I waited for her that day out in the market, inhaling the charcoal from the adobe braziers, the sharp scent of the eucalypts, remembering her softness from the night before.

Frida's skirts covered my face and my tongue reached inside her. Her scent of jasmine and sex over me. And after, my tongue was sweet and bitter and every part of me alive to that taste, and the thought of the Old Man upstairs, the possibility of discovery. Everything rushed and intense.

Nights we would wander the bars in Coyoacán, the mariachi bands at either end of large rooms; the cacophony of it. Arms and legs whirling, dipping, gyrating in time to whichever band was loudest. And Frida's eyes on me as she drank *mezcal* from her hip flask and rested her bad leg on a stool. She watched me dance through every place in town, and I danced like a demon, knowing that such nights, such freedoms, were seldom. I stretched the dancing and laughing and staying out all night, I stretched them as taut as a rubber band, as if such nights contained my existence.

And then the folding home at dawn. To become again the responsible one, the organised one, the one keeping the household together, and I felt myself split: the demon dancer and the responsible comrade, and the split widened over time.

After these evenings, a pendulum of unrest would swing over the house. And if the Old Man was up already, feeding the rabbits with his tan-coloured gardening gloves, grinding the feed with a mortar and pestle, no words would pass between us because no words were needed. The Old Man resented these nights of my freedom. The reasons unspoken between us. For days after, he would be brusque and exacting. He would give me tracts to translate, would find fault with the translations and demand that I begin again. I did as I was asked because he didn't know the extent of the time with Frida. And I didn't want him to know what she had become for me.

It is fourteen years since the Old Man's death. Three days since the death of Frida. I had watched Diego at the funeral, scooping a handful of her ashes. I had watched her body flash upright in the furnace. And after her death, those of us from that time become fewer. And it amazes me, down the spasm of years, how life transforms us from participant to witness.

Myself, now a witness.

I can say that Frida was a whirlpool; everyone close to her wanted to be pulled in, wet and drowning. She liked it that way. That was her attraction. Years later I realised that this pulling-in was also a manipulation. For no matter who came close, at day's end, it was Diego's voice she waited for. Diego at the door, humming 'The Internationale' to announce his arrival. Diego, smelling of sex and paint and other women's perfume. Diego – *who liked to watch*.

When I first met Frida I was twenty-one. She was almost ten years older. We became friends after her time with the Old Man. And I had never seen anyone like her, but it was not just the way she looked, it was the way she lived. Of course, there was her talent: those exact brushstrokes that caught the gradations of a hair-line, the look behind the eyes, the jangle of colours, the shock of herself. Although it was the muralists, Diego foremost among them, who were famous at the time.

But she had a gift for people, also. Frida was fascinated by people and that was part of her fascination. For who can refuse someone who is so intensely in the moment with you? Who can refuse a person who can listen like that, who can make you feel as if your whole life has led to this conversation at this time, in this place?

Of course, like everyone else, I was in love with her. For a time we were lovers. In the period after the Old Man and before anyone else.

Trotsky had fallen for Frida and in those first six months at the Casa Azul something had been building between them. And he had carried on, lovelorn, infantile, had jeopardised the whole operation: thought only of himself. His wife Natalia grew silent. His staff chafed under the weight of it – these things they told me. Six months after the affair, after I had arrived in Mexico City, he was still enthralled by Frida. Still punishing himself for his weakness. Punishing those around him so hard that his chief bodyguard left in anger and I was pressed into service. Became a participant.

The Old Man would start up at the sound of her voice. I would find him standing transfixed before her self-portrait. She had presented it to him on the occasion of his birthday, the twentieth anniversary of the Russian Revolution. Trotsky standing helpless before this portrait made me realise: *the Old Man makes mistakes*. I remember how the thought iced through me, chilling my days with him. And the bond between us eventually started to strain. This bond of historical circumstance. Both of us yoked together, as Trotsky used to say, both of us instruments of history.

My body, the vessel.

As if history were something hot, something viscous, poured into the mould of a human being and left to cool through the ages. History, pushing the personality along through epochs and wars and revolutions and finally to the peace of the grave.

My body, the instrument of history.

In my time with Frida, I became alert to the aches in my life. The gulf at my centre: the absence of love. How, in pushing for a better future, how much easier it was to profess love for humanity, that great seething mass, than to profess love for one other person who could fell you with a glance.

At those rare times, out drinking and dancing in Coyoacán with Frida, history in abeyance for an evening, I felt another part of myself alive and longing for release. The joy of dancing and laughing and being, and the gratitude I felt. It stays with me. Now that she is gone, my last link to the Old Man, these memories return.

And it was strange, my confusion. I remember various bars, Frida at my side, the Revolution forgotten, streamers around my ankles, a glass in my hand. I would sit there consumed with a desire to offer up thanks for this happiness, to stop at dawn in a roadside chapel, sit down, light a candle, and pray.

And then, how the moment would turn, and this remnant of a Catholic childhood would recede in a haze of tequila, and the features of the Old Man, his resolute atheism, would rise before me, and I would feel shame that Comrade Marr, all discipline and rationality, could be consumed by the irrational.

But Frida had that effect on me. Frida's gift was to open me to other experiences: dancing, music, love-making. Falling into the power of a painting. And I had never felt so complete. Not in the time in Spain, fighting with the POUM. Not, I had to face it, in those years with Trotsky.

Mexico had that effect on me. I have stayed on here these sixteen years because it is here that I have learnt how to live. To embrace those contradictions. Here I have learnt that religion, faith, the spirit, announces itself in many forms. It can be shrouded and epiphanic. It can be raw and open. It can cut you with its ragged edges. It is politics and it is more than politics. It surprises me still. In Mexico, the catechisms of my childhood first came alive, everywhere I chose to look.

And how I looked. Colour, sound, form. All my senses engaged. Entering Veracruz – the stun of those first sights – a wall of heat and drizzle; the heavy scents of coffee and vanilla. And as I stepped from sea to land, at the same point where Cortes arrived centuries before me, there was the illusion of stepping from something fluid to something more solid. The earthiness of colour and heat and scent. Beguiled, as the Spanish had been. The Spanish set off from here, and it was here they were defeated.

I should have seen the signs that day in Veracruz. Mexico: a place of illusions; a place of final stands.

Those first sights from the bus window on the way to Mexico City: a white church set against the mountains; a row of cow skulls and bones in the doorway; images of the Virgin framed in tin or wood, unfinished and splintered at the edges. In the streets, tied to the base of lampposts and trees, plastic sunflowers grew – embedded in an orange or a lime. I remember a brass band blasting its way through a *barrio* at the edges of the city: men in felt hats embroidered with the tree of life, shirts rolled to the elbow, gold chains thick and heavy around their necks. A small man with an enormous tuba nodding to the bus, engulfed by the tuba and the sound it produced.

I still marvel at these things. These daily epiphanies.

Sound. Colour. Form. In Mexico, it became apparent to me that the further I moved from the faith I was born into the more tenaciously it clung. How one catechism layered upon another in this place of everyday crucifixions. For I understood discipline and self-sacrifice and penance. Discipline harnessed to faith in the Idea. My Irish father and Spanish mother had instilled that in me. The revolutionary movement had honed it.

I remember seeing for the first time the stony landscape of Mexico and a man carrying a large wooden table on his back, stumbling over the grey stones. Two children followed him with smaller wooden tables across their backs. I remember stepping over a *campesino* lying in a doorway with his arms outstretched, how, with the layering of these things, it seemed to me that there were Christ figures everywhere in Mexico. Everyone outstretched and abandoned.

How in Mexico, this place of everyday crucifixions, I started to change.

How I could never have broached this with the Old Man. For he would not have understood.

Images of life and death. I think often about the beautiful resignation and release of a Mexican death. How death in Mexico is not something separate from life, but bound to it by a million invisible filaments. The task of the living is to tease out these filaments, adorn them with coloured paper and tinsel; make them visible.

Frida knew all about these filaments and their adornments. Perhaps the Old Man, at the end, also came to understand them.

In Mexico, in the early days, another image of death often came to me. A snapshot from childhood: my father swinging from the beams in the ceiling. Myself as a child jumping up to grab my father's ankles, trying to free him from the grip of the rope around the beam. The groove marks on the ceiling where he had flailed against the wood, clawing back into his life, wondering at the end exactly why he was swinging and how he could stop. And myself keeping vigil over the body until my mother returned that day. For two hours, exhausting myself with jumping up and up. My child-self trying to drag the grown man by the ankles back into life.

And the mystery of it still. For my father had his goals, his ideals. He had my mother, he had me. But there was a restlessness in him. He was always searching.

He had marched in New York in 1921, protesting at the sentence for Sacco and Vanzetti. I could say that this sentence, the beginning of my political education, signified the end of my father. But of course that would only be part of it.

Sacco and Vanzetti. They towered over my childhood. The story of the poor shoemaker and the fish peddler: anarchists, immigrants, on trial for a murder they didn't commit. On trial for their political opinions. Nicola Sacco and Bartolemeo Vanzetti kept in cages for the three months of their trial. Their dark skin and broken English pushing through the iron bars. How it hurt to look at them. Holding my father's hand in the courtroom gallery. And later, my father outside, jostled by police while distributing leaflets: *Sacco and Vanzetti have been convicted for a crime of opinion.*

My mother lighting candles for them, for divine intercession in the lives of those men like ourselves who stumbled into history at the wrong place at the wrong time: America, 1921. Poor, immigrant, *dark-complected*, heads full of radical ideas. A fish peddler and a shoemaker. *Anarchists. Un-American.*

And my mother's response and my father's response to these events. Very different but somehow complementary. The candles and the icons, the leaflets and the men who had to sacrifice themselves for the greater good. The bloody catechisms of my childhood. With my father, it was the political. Long marches on his shoulders through the streets; below me sinewed arms and big fists and big ideas on small newsprint passing through the crowd. With my mother it was the soul. It was Sundays, all rosary beads and penance, and quiet kneeling and benediction; shaking hands with the priest and bursting from a dark church into a sunlit street: cleansed.

My earliest memories are of our life in the States. In Massachusetts. Of my father returning from work, his hair slicked back, smelling of industrial soap under his fingernails and grease on his overalls. Sometimes he took me to the machine shops where he worked. And this was something I later shared with the Old Man, who had his own memories of a machine shop from his childhood. How we both loved the assemblage of wheels and spare parts. Nails and corkscrews. Engines. Our fascination for the mechanical. Our belief in the power of the machine. In the liberating force of technology.

I remember my father would return from his day's work, and from his agitating outside the courts, trying to save Sacco and

Vanzetti, and he would slump in front of the radiogram, eyes shut, disappointment heavy about him. *Capitalism makes men comatose*, he used to say. For the men he worked with wanted nothing more than their own homes, their own families, a vacation once a year: security. They worked long and hard for this security; long after it had broken them. They were not interested in a couple of *wop Reds* on a trumped-up charge of murder. They had no energy for the bigger picture. My father failed to understand their proud individualism. He was impatient. He wanted the future – now. He was always searching for the perfect way to live. A loner in search of community. And then we left the States, under pressure, like many other immigrants of radical persuasion. By this stage he had grown sick *in the belly of the monster*, he said, his politics got him fired from more jobs than he could remember, and we went back to my mother's birthplace, Spain, where he felt that life would be simpler. And in the end, he abandoned his search. In 1925, two years before the execution of Sacco and Vanzetti for a crime they didn't commit, my father killed himself. For my father in the end, there was nothing between himself and chaos. He swung a great disappointment that day from the beams in the ceiling – a disappointment in humanity and in himself.

I was determined never to make his mistake.

The memory of those scratch marks on the ceiling. Each time my mother whitewashed that ceiling, after a month, maybe two, the groove marks would return, like stigmata, and my mother pronounced it a miracle and wanted the priest to bless the house, the least he could do, but the priest refused because my father was a sinner, an atheist and an Anarchist who took his own life.

It was harder for a poor sinner to be buried with dignity, that much was certain. My father was buried on a hill, without a gravestone. My mother planted roses in his memory. Eventually we left that house, that small village outside Barcelona. It was 1926 and again we travelled across the ocean to America, back to Massachusetts. My whole childhood there in the crossings of that ocean. My mother's fingers beading the rosary as we left, her fingers worn with the effort, her spirit worn because there are only so many times you can paint over a ceiling, whitewash a memory.

For many years, back in America, I tried to erase that last glimpse of my father. And for a long time, the Revolution helped me forget.

As I grew older, I rejected his romantic Anarchism. I felt drawn to discipline and commitment, to the paradise of a strong proletarian state. Something that was possible. I looked to politics to fend off chaos. But a different politics from my father.

Up until the war in Spain, I was a young man drifting in revolutionary currents in Massachusetts, a union man, an apprentice mechanic like my father had been. In the August of 1936, I read of the first show trials happening in Moscow – the trial of the sixteen, the first round of Old Bolsheviks – Zinoviev and Kamenev, men who had taken part in the Revolution in Russia, now on trial for treason. For the Anarchists, this was seen as the logical conclusion of Bolshevism – the strong state devouring its own. I read everything, including a copy of the *Bulletin of the Opposition*, published in Paris and written by Leon Trotsky from exile. Trotsky had another interpretation: Stalinism, bureaucracy, the isolation of Russia.

Trotsky. The Old Man.

I had read of him. We all had. How, in the year of my birth, he had helped lead a revolution. And how did I, the son of an Anarchist, come to be in his service? Those accidents of history; we bump up against our destinies many times.

Spain. That was really where it all began.

The world was in tumult then. Politics mattered. All around me, my friends – the sons of my father's old Anarchist comrades – were joining the Communist Party as an act of rebellion against their parents. The American Left was growing.

And the Spanish war gave my energies a direction, an outlet, and my mother threw up her hands at my leaving, but she was powerless in the face of idealism, she had learnt that bitter lesson, and so she waved me off on a steamer from New York to Paris, willing me God speed and a safe return.

From Paris, a train to the Spanish border and then the long march over the Pyrenees with a group of volunteers.

I was nineteen years old. It was the beginning of 1937. I was back in Spain.

I found myself fighting against Franco with a brigade of the POUM, the anti-Stalinist Left. I was accused of Trotskyite affiliations. And the irony of it, later in Mexico, the arguments I would have with the Old Man. *The POUM – no Trotskyists there*, he would say darkly. He was critical of the whole Left in Spain – no one had the correct line, he said. No one had learnt from the Russian experience: we managed without foreign help, we set up Soviets, we armed the workers, we fought to win.

There was too much against us, I said. *But there were many good people.*

But no good organisers, he countered, no revolutionary party.

And I was young, willing to learn. I suffered our differences in silence.

The Old Man. He was always so certain. Arriving that day in 1937 in the lush port of Tampico, as Frida described him to me. Walking down the gangplank, proud, as sure of his abilities to organise and educate and agitate as he had been at any point before in his political career. And hearing this story, the awe I felt, the Old Man so self-possessed and confident, after having lost so much, still so convinced of his own capacity for greatness, to feel history coursing through him.

My body, the vessel.

It is seventeen years since Trotsky and his small entourage walked down the wooden plank and into the hot brilliance of the port of Tampico and the warm, wonderful embrace of Frida and Diego, and their lives were never the same again.

I WATCH THEM move towards me. I am shrouded in the
shadows of the doorway. As they approach, a light breeze
knocks Alberto's straw hat hung over a branch. Its large flag
shadow tilts on the ground. A bony animal, a dog, arches past. A
few chickens scratch thinly in the dirt. I see these details of my life
through the eyes of this man, the famous friend of the *señorita*.
Suddenly I feel unworthy to receive them.

And then, she is at my door, with this man I have seen only in
photographs. And I step out into the sunlight to greet them. To
usher them inside. He must stoop to enter, to fold himself through
the low opening beneath the tin roof. He is not Mexican. He is a
tall man with a broad chest and high forehead. He has bright eyes
behind glasses, eyes the colour of the Casa Azul. He blinks rapidly,
adjusting to the absence of light in the room; he pauses in the
doorway. He stumbles on the buckets of paste and wire, finely
tangled. I am embarrassed by this visit. Unprepared. The *señorita*
usually visits alone. In front of her, I am not poor. But a stranger's
eyes are a mirror. In this mirror, I see the dust. I see Alberto's
workboots tumbled in one corner, the Madonna in a tin frame. I
see newspapers and tin cans and empty cement bags and the small
hammocks for my children strung from the roof. The jumble of our
life together. The man's eyes light over the hammer-and-sickle flag
thrown across the table and grow dull at the small portrait of Stalin
on an upturned bucket.

'Señora Rosita is an artist.'

Frida is excited, when introducing us, her hand is on the man's arm. She tells me that this is her friend, Señor Trotsky, that he has travelled very far to be at last safe in Mexico. That he and his wife, Señora Natalia, are Diego's guests, are her guests, at the Casa Azul for as long as they want. He clasps my hand and bows. The *señorita* points towards some white *calaveras* in a corner, exclaims over them.

Uneasy with such attention, I shrug. 'I am a maker of Judas-figures, a maker of *retablos* sometimes, of *piñatas* for children. But not an artist, *señor*, no.'

The *señorita* insists. 'Rosita is too modest, she is the finest Judas-maker in all Mexico. In all of her figures, each one different, the expressions, the range of movement . . .' She offers me a cigarette, which I refuse.

'So.' The man smiles. 'A genuine popular artist.' He looks around at the papier-mâché limbs idling in corners. He picks up a small skeleton, striped blue and white, a death figure, lying on the red-flag tablecloth, cushioned by the hammer and sickle. He walks over to a Judas, with a huge head, half completed. 'Tell me,' he says, 'tell me about the construction.' He speaks in clear, heavily accented Spanish. I hesitate at first, and then Frida nods at me and so I tell him about my friend José, the carpenter, who works to my instructions, making the form for each figure from the wood of a shade tree, the way he strips down a branch. I point to the heavy paper of the cement bags I use to cover the form. The trouble I have with those bags! I tell the *señor* how my children and I climb the refuse on the city's edge, how we forage in building sites at midnight to keep my supply of those cement bags. Then the coating of flour and water so the paper sticks to the form, how I hollow out the form and plug it up. How I let it dry for a day or two, and how, in good weather, I line the figures up outside our hut. Like a procession for carnival. How I then paint each figure with a layer of Spanish white – thick, matt white – and then, while this is drying, I let my mind feel for the colours that suit the form of the Judas. For each one is different. Each one is special. I tell him how I take my colours from the day's work at the market. The florid cheeks of a priest. The colour of the pomegranates on my stall. The pale eyes of a *gringo* tourist. All day I am studying forms and colours. At night I let the colours settle and shape behind my eyes.

I find myself talking quickly, with enthusiasm, about my work.

How I make butterflies out of paraffin wax and cardboard and the wicks of candles. How no material is ever wasted, how I use everything around me. My papier-mâché dolls with broad-brimmed hats and tiny flags in their hands, how these are placed on cakes, all over the city, each year on the anniversary of the Mexican Revolution. I tell him that I make Judases with giant heads, with feet that dance. I keep talking about my work and it takes on a shape for me, and a fear grows inside, as if in the speaking it has become more important than I ever thought. And, if I stopped my work, perhaps my life would stop also. And this is new to me, this thought. For I have lived for Alberto and the children, but now, in the speaking, I see that, maybe all along, I have existed for these figures that I shape and colour, which are faithful to me, which do not wither and die or desert me. My work, which is beyond husband and children. My work without which I am not. For the first time I feel the truth of it like a fist in my belly and I am overcome. I stop. Maybe I have said too much, have given too much away.

Frida smiles, she is a proud friend, encouraging me. She turns to Señor Trotsky playfully. 'What do you say, *Viejo*? There is nothing Rosita cannot make.'

When she calls him *Viejo*, Old Man, he laughs. He has white hair but I see that he is not really old. I see that it is a game between them.

Trotsky is silent through all this. His eyes absorb everything and I see how I am to him: the small woman with the broad cheekbones and the cut-jawed face. The green cloth turbaned around my head and over one shoulder. The thick veins in my arms. Through his eyes I see myself, my life.

When I have finished speaking, he clasps my hand and says, '*Señora*, in future, everyone will be an artist, like yourself, we will create the conditions for it. There will be no such thing as the individual artist. Homes will be decorated, murals on every public wall, figures made in celebration . . .'

I have heard it all before.

And I say to him, 'But in this future where everyone and no one is an artist, there will still be a small child who will want to carve something special from a branch, or a young girl who will pick up a paintbrush for herself, something private, because it is inside a person, and not everyone has this feeling, to make something out of nothing . . .'

'But we all have the potential,' he insists.

We look at each other, the man with his blue eyes behind the glasses, and myself wiping the dust from a *piñata* in the shape of a drum. And I feel small in the face of this future in which I am no longer special, feel myself resisting it, resisting him. 'But everyone is different,' I tell him, 'like the expressions of a *Judas*. Everyone has a different destiny . . .'

I have had this argument so many times before with Alberto, my husband.

I feel the *señor's* impatience. He tries to sweep my life into his sentences. So many words. A man accustomed to words, to being listened to. I look at his mouth, the full outline of it framed by a moustache and a small goat beard. And already I am thinking of how to use this mouth and this beard on the next figure I make, for nothing is lost, nothing is wasted. The *señorita* rolls her eyes at him, gently steers him to another subject. 'Señora Rosita knows a lot about destiny, *Viejo*. She reads palms. She has her mirror of obsidian. She can tell you things . . .'

The *señor* hmmms. And then he says, with both confidence and amusement in his voice, 'We make our own destiny. There is nothing else.'

I look at him. Such confidence and such amusement in the face of destiny! I pick up my old mirror of rainbow obsidian. How it changes in the light. I motion them to the doorway to show them the colours in the sun. I say: *Tezcalipoca, the god of the smoking mirror, would not agree with you*, señor. *I look into this mirror and I see many things*. The *señor* looks at the face of the mirror, sees himself in rainbow stripes. He looks away. I look into the mirror and I see a cone of red fire extending up to the sky. I see a comet with three heads rushing past. The same signs that Montezuma saw before the arrival of Cortes. A portent. I frown at the mirror.

What do you see? Frida asks me. *Nothing*, I say. *Today, I can make out nothing*. We move back inside and the mirror looks black again, impenetrable.

And I pray to the Madonna and to Tezcalipoca, to release the *señor* from that destiny flash on obsidian.

And then Frida forces his palms over and demands that I look at the track-lines there. And I feel the weight of his hands and I look at his left palm, the lines slowly erasing, and I look at his right palm, the many lines crossing, like telegraph wires. And he looks at me with eyebrows raised and I tell him seriously. 'This,' I say, gripping his left hand below the wrist, 'this hand is everything of you before the age of thirty-five. It speaks of your promise. And this' – I grip the right palm with both hands – 'is what you have made of that.'

'And what have I made of that?' The *señor's* voice is quieter now, less amused.

And I look at the tangle of lines on his right hand, how the life-line forks abruptly and fades and I look at the age of him and I realise what I am seeing, suddenly fearful.

'What?' he asks, looking at me closely. 'What is it?'

I hesitate. 'Much living. That's what I see. A big life.'

He nods and laughs, he is pleased with this. He flexes his palms, looks at the lines as if for the first time. 'Yes, a lot of living.' He says this proudly and he takes the arm of the *señorita* and she kisses me three times and the man shakes my hand and she gives me an order for two dozen *piñatas* for Christmas, and promises more orders to come and I watch him leave, angling into the sunlight, his terrible palms in his pockets.

I LEARNT MY history from walls. I walked around the Ministry of Education building some years after Señor Rivera had finished and I learnt more in that day of the history of my people than I ever knew. Cycles of destruction. That's what history seemed to me. The *señorita* took me to see the frescos. The three floors, the archways, the two courtyards, the stairwell panels. I saw them all. Just off the Courtyard of Labour, I stopped before the paintings of the dyers, the purple and blue flooding through me. Such colours! I moved to the south wall. The wall of work. There was a rhythm to the work, and these small men that I knew in my life were here painted as large as legend.

And this was Señor Rivera's gift. That he took us, the small people, the dark people, the Indians of Mexico, and made us as large as the walls.

In the Courtyard of the Fiestas, Frida showed me *The Burning of the Judases*. The politician, the churchman and the army man, exploding. The figures were based on my own work, she told me. And I looked up and I could see that it was true, and I wept. The Judas of the army man with the high colour on the cheeks, the circle of colour on his chin, the eyes like a clown. I remember making such a figure for *Semana Santa* of 1922. Long before I knew the *señorita* or the *patron*. That Señor Rivera noticed my work, all those years ago, was enough for me.

In the murals of the *patron*, our whole lives sway before us. In the Courtyard of the Fiestas, we teeter on the top of doorways, we surge across stairwells, there are so many of us that we seem to have taken over the building. We are all shapes and sizes and shadings. And we are beautiful.

The landscapes of Mexico, the sea, the mountains, the plateau. The dryness and the fertility. The ways we have been robbed of our land. The promise of a future in which the land becomes ours. The promise of a future. The lessons of our history, our destiny, on those walls.

In the palm of a hand, we also see history. The same promises and destructions. The false turns. The foolishnesses. And as I sit here this day behind my stall, I am led back to the colour and the movement of those walls. And I think again of the famous man that day in my house, Señor Trotsky, the man with the *señorita*. The things I saw in his palm. What could I have told him about his history that he didn't already know? That he was a man of destiny? That his left palm was rapidly losing its lines because his end was coming. That the whole of his future and his past was dissolving, the etchings of them moving through his bloodstream from the left palm to the right, something that science cannot explain. Should I have told him then that his potential was almost exhausted? His palm full?

JORDI MARR
REPUBLICAN SPAIN
3 MAY 1937

For weeks something had been building, the way the atmosphere tightens before an electrical storm, the rising humidity, the difficulty in breathing. The irritability of it. Everyone felt it that year in Barcelona as spring eased into summer. The workers who ran the trains, the trams and the bus services. Everyone felt it, this unease.

In the months before, all of it like a newsreel, speeded up. The trams full of comrades, shouting, victorious. Red-and-black flags at right-angles. The bullet holes in the walls, sandbags in the streets, the curfews. The euphoria. For the Anarchists now controlled Barcelona. Jordi wished that his father had lived long enough to see it.

This glorious experiment.

Most industries in Catalonia were now collectivised. And despite the problems: the shortage of markets and raw materials, the drop in industrial output, Catalan workers felt that their experiment was a noble one, a just one, something to be proud of. Another way of being.

But the Left was fractured, bitterly divided. Stalin was pleased. And in the distance, Franco's planes circled overhead. The atmosphere tightening, something beneath the surface about to erupt.

Jordi Marr remembers standing, drinking coffee, at a wooden bench in a bar in Barcelona. Behind him, the American and English voices. The clatter of tables overturned: the smell of spilt coffee as everyone pushed through the swing doors and out into the street. And as he pushed out with them, he wondered about these comrades. Just who they were, where they were from. How they came to be here.

And in all this confusion, who was a comrade and who was not, in this brief span of the historical present, when the people who once worked everything now controlled everything?

Who indeed?

And who was he, testing himself, trying to prove himself, the coffee bitter on his tongue with the truth of it?

The shots came from the direction of the Telecommunications Exchange.

Glass exploded on to the streets below.

Everyone listened closely. Jordi Marr heard those shots and immediately reached for his rifle. All over the city, men did the same thing. An instinct, a reflex. For the shots signalled the beginning and the end of something as beautiful and ephemeral as fireworks.

Years later, people outside the conflict would marvel at the internecine warfare, the ideological battles. For wasn't there only one enemy? General Franco, wasn't he the enemy?

Jordi Marr would live to have these conversations. Words were never enough. He felt that if you had been there you could not fail to understand. For the future then seemed within reach, worth dying and arguing for. They were fighting on many fronts. *It was about Franco and it was about more than Franco* . . . He would hear his voice grow more insistent as the years passed . . . *It was about Stalin, Mussolini, Hitler* . . . *It was a dress rehearsal for what happened after: the rise of Fascism, of Stalinism and the Second World War* . . .

In that street battle in Barcelona, Jordi fought with the POUM, the anti-Stalinist Left. Everyone was running in the direction of the Telefonicá. Young boys pushed sandbags into position. For everyone had a position and for three days a battle blazed amongst the Left behind sandbags and crossfire. And Franco laughed from his exile in Tangiers, pleased at what his agents had achieved, crowing that the Left was a desperate confused animal that had run blind into a trap.

And Stalin laughed alone in his Kremlin apartments, pleased at what his agents had achieved. The annihilation of any Left opposition. For the Left, he said, was like a desperate confused animal that had run blind into a trap.

Jordi had run to the edge of the city. Had seen the Stalinists, the PCE, strechering their wounded into the Hotel Plaza. He crouched in a doorway with his rifle as two PCE colonels were levered through the revolving doors. He took aim but did not fire. One of the colonels tilted his head and saw Jordi's shadow crouched in the doorway opposite. The man was bearded and filthy. His eyes flamed, seeing Jordi, the enemy.

After the May days in Barcelona, Jordi was on the run. The Anarchists, the handful of Trotsky supporters and all members of the POUM were on the run, everyone on the non-Stalinist Left. From Stalin's GPU. From Franco.

The Anarchists no longer controlled Barcelona.

Jordi escaped by foot. Taking the reverse route by which he and so many other volunteers had entered Spain, walking for days and nights over the Pyrenees into France, his boots around his neck, the rope-soled *alpargatas* on his feet gripping every stone and crevice.

From France, his feet bandaged and bleeding, a slow boat to Mexico.

I ARRIVED IN Mexico at the beginning of 1938. Mexico, the one country to welcome political refugees from the Spanish War. Trotsky and Natalia were living at the Casa Azul. I went to visit them as many activists did then. And very quickly, I became a part of their entourage, filled a vacancy created when one of the bodyguards left. For I had my uses, at the time. I had honed my skills in Spain. I was discreet, a good organiser, I could handle a gun.

At this time, Frida still came to visit, and I realised that something had passed between Trotsky and Frida. The air vibrated with it.

In the beginning, that time at the Casa Azul seemed like a respite for Trotsky and his wife Natalia. And for myself, after Spain – something much needed. But I was unprepared for what I found. The walls around them, the bricking-up of loss:

The death of the youngest daughter. The death of the eldest daughter when they were in Prinkipo. The death of the youngest son when they were in Norway. The death of the eldest son when they were in Coyoacán. The death of friends and comrades, and of comrades who had once been friends, the way life turned, the horror of it.

How memory becomes an ossuary.

After this massing of loss, how I had hoped, I admit it now, to step into the breach. For I was ready for it, young and eager to do it, to see the mutual need acknowledged, and it never came, however indispensable I made myself, in those three years, it never came, that warm embrace from the Old Man, the hand on my shoulder and the words filling my soul: 'You are like a son to me.'

And my feelings over the years became tangled. Frida complicated my feelings for the Old Man. Exposed my contradictions, one could say. What it was I was searching for.

It is only now, here in Mexico, fourteen years after the death of the Old Man, some days after the death of Frida, it is only now that my journeyings seem to make sense, to form a pattern.

How the mind searches for a pattern in the maze of a life.

I could not have imagined then that my search would lead me away from the Old Man. *To be outside of the Revolution means to be in emigration.* Trotsky had said that more than once. To question what was meant by *revolution, emigration*, seemed impossible at the time. The courage of those questions came later, when he was no longer around to answer.

I stare again at the newsprint in front of me. Frida is gone. The Old Man died years ago.

And I am in transition, from participant to witness.

RAMÓN MERCADER
MEXICO CITY
JANUARY 1940

R AMÓN MERCADER STANDS in front of a store selling mountain equipment and guns on the Avenida Lopez. In his back pocket he carries a .45 calibre star automatic pistol with eight bullets in the magazine and one in the firing chamber. The weight of it feels good. He is in training and there are two hours he must fill before the gallery opening and so he finds himself in this sector of the city, looking at firearms and crampons. Next week he is to start training on Popocatepetl. On the lower slopes first, for he is slightly out of form, hasn't done much climbing since the end of the Spanish War. He still feels bitter about the Spanish War. How could it be called a civil war, when it was not civil, was not in the least, with Mussolini and Hitler arming Franco and the rest of the world idling by, how could it be called an internal matter? The only one who had aided his countrymen had been Stalin, for that he was grateful. More than grateful. The only one who had the courage to stand by his convictions was Stalin.

He had heard the stories from the POUM and the Trotskyites. He had heard the charge that Moscow had demanded payment for their support for the Republicans, that barges full of Spanish gold lay unemptied in the port of Leningrad. As if Comrade Stalin would put money over ideological considerations! It was unthinkable. More evidence, if such were needed, of the utter bankruptcy of the Trotskyites. Of course something had to be done. Slanders such as these could only weaken the Soviet Union. Hitler was on the move, although the pact between Ribbentrop and Molotov still held. Unity was needed. Trotsky and his Opposition critics weakened the Soviet Union and destroyed unity.

Ramón Mercader checked the inside pocket of his grey suit for his new identification papers. He was travelling as a Belgian, escaping the threat of war on a French-Canadian passport. The GPU had obtained the papers for him in Spain, from a dead volunteer in the International Brigades. He was now Frank Jacson, businessman. French was supposed to be his native tongue. His French was almost there, he thought, only a few Catalan inflections remained. But here, in Mexico City, it was good enough to get by. To speak French and English with a slight accent suited his purposes. He deliberately limited his Spanish to a few essentials.

He tapped out another cigarette from the packet and inhaled deeply as he looked in the store window. He held the cigarette in his left hand. He had a scar on his right forearm sustained during combat in Barcelona. He looked up at the sky. He never wore a watch. He could feel time to within a minute of accuracy. He had learnt this out in the mountains, climbing. Had learnt to read the sky, the sun passing across it, had tested himself without a watch. Had stubbed a lit cigarette out on his skin if he got it wrong. He was rarely wrong. His perceptions were inordinately tuned and honed. All the GPU doctors remarked on it. Inside the shop he walked over to a table with guns laid out. He shut his eyes and passed his hands over the guns. Feeling which shape and make they were. Testing himself. A Remington. A Colt. With his eye he measured the distance between the tray of guns and the door and walked out with his eyes shut. Testing himself. It was important that he could follow a chosen path in the dark. Walk a straight line with his eyes shut for six yards. For when the moment came. He could recognise complex objects in the dark by touch. Take them apart and put them back together again. In his hotel room in Central Mexico, to pass the time he would blindfold himself and take a Mauser rifle apart and put it back together in three minutes and forty-six seconds. He was extraordinarily skilful. The GPU doctors had rarely seen anything like it. His mother Caridad had told him so.

He had the lean tensed body of a trained athlete. He was highly observant, could imitate anyone. Even as a child he astounded his mother by the roles he could play. In charades, he *became* the character. *He was perfectly equipped for espionage and murder, the GPU doctors had said.* His mother loved that about him.

The only rifles he didn't trust were Remingtons. How could you trust a typewriter company to make guns? Such diversification unnerved him. If you were going to do something well, you had to specialise. There was something effete and nauseating about a man using a gun with the name of a typewriter. And Remington reminded him of Trotsky, tapping away in exile. Still alive.

It is almost six o'clock. He can smell it. As he approaches the Galería de Arte Mexicano, the first private art gallery in Mexico City, he hopes that there will be a large crowd inside in which he can lose himself. It is the opening of the International Surrealist Exhibition. Frida Kahlo is exhibiting. He wants to see her work.

There is an excited hum emanating from the room. Enough people are present to allow him to slip through easily. When he walks in, the faces are familiar to him. He checks them off. Breton, handsome in a dark, dissolute, early-jowelled sort of way. Rivera, rounded, gargantuan, next to him. Frida in one corner, looking slightly worn. She had separated from Rivera at the end of the previous year. The divorce had just come through. Frida kept looking over at Rivera when she wasn't surrounded by people. Frida – she was not really his type. He preferred small rounded fair-haired women. But Frida was arresting. So plumaged. He found it hard not to look at her, rings on every finger of her right hand. Every finger slashing the air silver as she spoke. He enjoyed the drama of her. He had come close to her once before at the Mexique Exhibition in Paris. He had admired her earrings. Had tried to steer her on to the subject of Trotsky. But Frida was clever. She dismissed him. He did not believe that she would recognise him now. He looked so different. A respectable businessman in a suit. Clean-shaven.

He moves through the crowd at the Surrealist Exhibition. Thinking it through. Was surrealism a form of bourgeois decadence? The last gasp of the nonsensicality of the bourgeois world? Was Kahlo a surrealist? Should he therefore feel guilty for liking her work? Surrealism. *A lion in a wardrobe when you expect shirts*. He had read that once. It struck him as ridiculous.

He stops before a Breton collage. Although he is not fond of Breton's writing, or his political support for Trotsky, he nonetheless finds this small work intriguing. A black-and-white cutout of a fairground horse, a gold butterfly superimposed on its back, a red pot with purple hyacinths protruding from the genitals. It amuses him. The fairground horse is rearing up. Along the bottom of the collage, in a newspaper typeface, is the legend: *Le Déclin de la société bourgeoise*. It makes him smile.

Frida's work was different from all the others on show. They may claim her as a surrealist, he thinks, but she never cuts loose completely from her moorings. It was only that her Mexican reality seemed surreal to European eyes. After coming to Mexico he appreciates this. This Mexican surreality of every day – the grue-some crucifixes in the ornate churches; the pink walls in a grey *barrio*. Children dressed as skeleton figures, tumbling out of school on the Day of the Dead, running to picnic in the graveyards. A long way from a lion in a wardrobe he thinks, but equally surreal.

Frida. He loves the anatomical detail in her work. He shares her fascination for the assemblage of blood and bone and muscle in the human body.

In one corner of the gallery, he sees his mother talking to the muralist David Siqueiros. He recognises Siqueiros from his time in Spain. They had both led PCE battalions. They had slit the throats of Anarchists and Trotskyites on the streets of Barcelona. He turns away. He registers that they have also seen him.

His mother had also led a PCE battalion in Barcelona. Was renowned in GPU circles for her marksmanship.

Later, his mother will say to him, 'You look so thin, after two years, I almost didn't recognise you. You look like another man in that suit.'

He feels thinner, has noticed it himself. He feels as if he is inside a parachute. Inside someone else's clothes. But he has been wearing someone else's clothes for so long that now it comes easily. He enjoys the disguises, the subterfuge, the escape from himself. He catches sight of his reflection in the glass frame of a painting.

He adjusts his face and straightens his tie. He is Frank Jacson. Businessman. He must never forget it. He feels that he will be Frank Jacson for a long time to come.

Although he is interested in art, the exhibition bores him. He is only there to see his mother and Siqueiros. And Frida Kahlo.

He wanders around. Looking. The juxtaposition of images and events. Reality and imagination. The conscious and the unconscious. He regards all of this from a distance. From a Marxist standpoint. He has read Breton, knows his emphasis on automatism. The erotic. Woman . . . He stops. A large canvas stops him, bars further thought or movement. His path blocked by a canvas depicting two women, really one woman. He has never seen such a large self-portrait of the artist: *The Two Fridas*. He has never seen anything like it.

He suddenly feels exposed by the painting, standing there in his too-large suit.

The Two Fridas. They follow him around like a *trompe-l'oeil*. The eyes seem to glitter strangely, from strange angles. And he approaches the painting from all angles. He steps up to it and then away again. He confronts the painting. He looks closely, studying its markings. He is stirred by it.

The double. The *doppelgänger*. The shadow. The mirror image of the self that is always asymmetrical. She captures the asymmetricality of the human body. One eye slightly elongated; the left plane of the nose slightly different from the right plane. He admires this.

In the course of a week he comes back every day to the exhibition. To stand before this painting. The gallery attendant notices the businessman in the large suit. He notices the sharp nose, the large eyes behind horn-rimmed glasses. He motions to the businessman on the fourth visit. 'Señor, why do you like this painting so much?'

'Because it makes sense.'

The gallery attendant shakes his head. Nothing at this exhibition makes sense to him.

In the painting, the two Fridas sit side by side on a bench with hands clasped. They are wearing different outfits. The Frida on the right wears a Tehuana costume. The Frida on the left wears a high-necked Victorian dress with lace collar and cuffs. Both of them sit with legs apart. Human hearts precisely drawn are hung like badges on their clothing. The hearts are linked by blood vessels which ribbon between them. The Victorian Frida holds a doctor's clamp around a vein which slowly drips blood.

Blood. Ramón Mercader is entranced. That's another thing he likes about Kahlo. She does not flinch from blood.

He is interested in the human body. The way Kahlo serves her own body up for examination. He is interested in lineaments and ligatures. The effect of a blow to the lineaments and ligatures. He remembers, suddenly, the face of the Trotskyite he killed in Barcelona. How he had befriended him, taken him out for a meal. Driven him to the port, and down behind the container ships had cut his throat. He had inspected the gash exposing the oesophagus. Had witnessed the last pumping and breathing. Had seen the blood start to congeal. The limbs start to stiffen.

When he was out climbing there was only his breathing, only the muscles moving under his skin to focus on, the knotting and blueing under the skin. First one hand, one leg and then the other. Everything lean and taut and ready. The human body was a miracle.

He was interested in different effects on the human body. The altitude in Mexico City, for example, the cramps at the back of his knees that first week of his arrival, the heaviness at the top of his chest, the extra work for his heart and lungs.

In a Frida Kahlo painting he always met an anatomical precision and the effect of extra work on the heart and lungs. Emotional or physical work. She showed it as it was felt. The painful exertions of the heart, the lungs, the internal organs, as life pressed in.

He longed for Frida to anatomise a skull. He had been interested in skulls from a young age. Had observed the skulls of animals dried and pale in the fields near Barcelona. He was interested also in contusions and bruising. How easily a skull could crack. Like a block of ice under a *piolet*. He was skilled with a *piolet*. Could crack a block of ice at high altitude with one blow.

On his second visit to the exhibition, he notes that the heart is cross-sectioned, exposed on the body of the Frida in Victorian dress. He notes that the Tehuana Frida holds a small locket with a portrait of Diego Rivera as a child. The locket is linked to a blood vein which vines around her arm, through her clothing, across her collar bone, merging with a full red heart, closed and pumping intricately. The vein winds across the disturbed background to encircle the neck and into the exposed heart of the Frida in Victorian dress. There is a rent, bloodied quality to the paler-skinned Victorian Frida. The heart rends her clothes, the aorta pale with effort. Part of a breast, slightly darker than the face, is revealed.

Every time he stands before the painting, he notices something different. The duality and exposure of it.

After his first visit to the exhibition, he walks out away from the gallery. He walks past the Palacio de Bellas Artes and along Lazaro Cardenas. He looks up at the dome of the Palacio, azure and gold in the sunlight. He turns left into 15 de Mayo. Past yellow *taquerías* and a man grinding an organ accompanied by a chained monkey, a tin cup in its hand. He comes to a blue-tiled building. Two floors of blue-and-white tiles. The building gleams. He stands opposite, taps out a cigarette and bends down to light it, looking left and right as he does so. He takes his time. Walks across the street, loose-limbed, relaxed. Stands directly outside the bronzed-edged doors, lace curtains in small windows. He notices that the tiles are hand-hewn, uneven, each pattern similar but not exactly the same. Blue-and-white fleurs-de-lis, blue-and-white circles, blue-and-white squares. It is one of his favourite cafés. He pushes through the heavy doors. Customers sit in red-leather booths. Waitresses in pale-pink uniforms with pink ribbons crowning their hair move between the booths. Sun filters through the curtains.

He walks towards a booth in which a tall, beautiful, sculpted woman with long brown hair sits in conversation with a dark small man. Mercader sits in the booth next to them. After he has ordered his *café solo* and a glass of water, he turns around to the couple and asks for a light. He looks into his mother's eyes as she proffers the match. Her eyes green in the flame. The man opposite her engages Mercader in conversation. They speak of the Surrealist Exhibition. Mercader is enthusiastic about Kahlo's work. His mother Caridad thinks Kahlo is a bourgeois individualist painting a myopic reality.

The dark man, Siqueiros, praises Kahlo's technique, but deplores her subject matter and her even more deplorable choice of husband, now ex-husband. 'She is well rid of that Rivera,' he says. 'Her painting will improve without that *chingado*.' Siqueiros spits this out. Mercader smiles to himself. Detecting a certain envy in Siqueiros's voice. He thinks to himself: that's the problem with artists. Even Communist artists. They always lack a certain objectivity. Eventually he joins their table in the manner of an acquaintance.

Operation Utka, says Siqueiros. The time has come.

One evening, five months later, Mercader finds himself walking down the Avenida Viena in Coyoacán in full police uniform, flanked by eighteen men, most of them miners from Jalisco and Communist Party members. The night of the May attack is unaccountably cloudy. There is no moon. The uniform is new and stiff. Siqueiros strides slightly ahead of him. Outside the villa, there is only one policeman on guard. The other policemen are two streets away at a party given by some women, GPU operatives, who have easily seduced the men away from their posts. Mercader cuts the alarm wire that runs along the outside of the house. Siqueiros commands the sleepy guard on duty to open the gate by flashing his police badge. They all surge through, easily overpowering the guard. The men take up positions. Mercader runs across the garden to where the bodyguards lie sleeping and barricades their door. He shouts *Almazán por Presidente* several times. He stands there pouring machine-gun fire across the courtyard. Siqueiros shouts orders. Machine-gun fire jumps and flares. Inside, Trotsky and Natalia in one room and their grandson in another fall to the floor, crouching behind their beds. A man called Alberto stands outside their door and fires off into the bedrooms and into the mattresses. It is so dark; no one can see a thing. Then it is over quickly. There is silence. Some miners leap over the wall, tearing the police uniforms as they do so. Leaving scraps of blue material behind them. Others run back through the front gate. Where there were flares and smoke and confusion and the shouting of election slogans now there is only silence and the weak moaning of the grandson for his grandparents.

Later, Trotsky and Natalia will marvel at their good fortune. It is amazing for the three of them to have survived the attack. Great holes gape from the walls above their beds. The mattresses are shot through. The grandson is the only one injured; a graze mark where a bullet glanced his foot. They are alive.

The whole thing energises Trotsky. He runs out into the garden with his pistol, shooting at silhouettes. He is transported by the adrenalin of survival. Thirty minutes later the telephone rings. Trotsky answers. At the sound of Trotsky's voice Siqueiros, on the other end of the line, shakes his head in disbelief. How could the Old Man have survived the attack? He looks around helplessly at Mercader and his mother. He doesn't say a word. He listens to Trotsky, jubilant and taunting. He clicks the receiver, cutting Trotsky in mid-sentence. He turns to Mercader and his mother. 'The *chingado* is still alive!'

He looks at Caridad Mercader. 'You know what this means,' he says, inclining his head towards the son. 'You tell him.' He puts his head in his hands. He is full of disgust, at himself, at them all, for their failure. He wonders what Moscow will make of it.

'We will talk tomorrow,' she tells her son. 'Go back and get some rest.'

The next day, Caridad Mercader swings her long legs out of bed and feels remarkably cheerful, considering the failure of the night before. She is not fearful of the *Khozyain*, the boss, and the reaction in Moscow. She feels above reproach. Siqueiros will have to deal with that. She is happy now because the next time they cannot fail, because the next time she is in control. She is a strategist and a woman of action. She will direct a simple operation, involving only her son. It will not be a grandiose plan like one of Siqueiros's canvases nor as clumsily executed. It will involve attention to detail, a smaller canvas, finer brushstrokes. It cannot fail. She combs her long brown hair until it gleams in the slightly bent mirror in her hotel bedroom. She opens the orange curtains. It is a beautiful day. Next time, they will not fail.

As she walks along the Avenida Madero and into Isabella Catolica to meet her son, she reflects on how her whole life has crystallised around this moment. Everything she has endured, everything she has trained him for. Her son will be a hero. She will be the mother of a hero. Already, she sees the Order of Lenin medals on his collar. It will be the fulfilment of ambition and longing. Stalin would see what she had made of herself. Would see how magnificent her son was. How well they had served the Motherland. That would be their reward.

Men whistle as Caridad moves down the street. She is effortlessly athletic and feline. She is still a relatively young woman. Late forties. Still slim and handsome. She passes for at least ten years younger. She waits for her son in the foyer of the Hotel Reina, sitting in a red-leather armchair, staring up at a large portrait of La Reina Isabella and at a coat of arms carved in brown leather. Next to the portrait a moose head protrudes from the wall with an intensity that makes it seem alive. She gazes up at the glass brick tiles of the first floor above her. She can see the shadows of people moving over the floor.

A group of American journalists clatter down the stairs, with cameras and press passes around their necks, in Mexico for the elections. She can hear them discussing the attack on the Trotsky villa the night before.

Her son comes down the stairs after them, a crumpled look about him. She can see that he has slept badly. They clasp hands, nod *Buenos dias* to the doorman and walk out of the hotel. One block on they turn left into Café Bianca, a large noisy place on Republica Uruguay.

Her son orders *huevos de la revolución mexicana*. Caridad orders *café con leche*. Her son listens while she outlines the next phase, and more importantly, their role, his role, in the next phase. Mercader grows pale. Stops chewing. Pushes his plate away. Loses his appetite. He sees a *piolet* cracking a block of ice in one motion. He substitutes this with a human skull. In his mind he sees it split, an uneven fissure across the head. One swift easy motion – he sees the contents of the brain spilling on to the floor. He feels nothing. A simple isolated action, a blow to the head. His mother looks at him, worried at his silence.

'Of course,' he says, pushing the eggs around on his plate. 'It must be done.'

He goes back to his hotel room to lie down. After the attack the night before he did not sleep well. Wondering what would happen next and what his role would be, if any. He has a huge double room in La Reina. Walls of salmon and green. Gold curtains. A wrought-iron balcony and french doors which do not open, for the balcony is unsafe. The room is stifling. He has complained twice about the bathroom. Water seeps from the sink on to the floor. The hotel is a maze, it is crazy, nothing functions as it should. But he likes the faded grandeur of the place. It amuses him. All broken chandeliers and dusty stairwells. He throws himself on the bed and starts smoking. He feels depleted. He needs to rest. He thinks about his mother's dreams for him. He has no doubt about his abilities, but when he eventually rises to go to the bathroom, sees himself in the sepia-tinted mirror, his pallor seems green and he does not feel well. Images of *The Two Fridas* rotate in his mind. The two figures. The same circulatory system. The two selves. The split. The unity in the split. He lies back down and eases himself into a guarded sleep.

When he wakes, there is a question, insistent in his head: *What does he really think of Trotsky?* He wanted to get this clear for himself. His few encounters with the man had confirmed his suspicions that Trotsky was an egoist of the highest order. That the revolutionary movement would be better off without him.

For the past six months, Mercader had been romancing Sylvia, one of Trotsky's secretaries, with a view to getting close to her boss. He had been successful so far. He had seen it as information-gathering. Now it was something different. Sylvia told him stories. How the Old Man would make her type and re-type something because one of the margins was slightly crooked, a page of some-thing relatively unimportant, minutes of a house meeting, something only for the files. How he would rage and stamp if the new dictaphone cartridge was not delivered on time. How he seemed to have a short fuse for minor things.

Of the two of them, Trotsky and the wife Natalia, he was more wary of Natalia. Trotsky was so full of his own lustre, so certain of his influence on those who entered his orbit, it marred his judgement. It was his weakness, the weakness to exploit. But Natalia was not so susceptible to an audience. She was not so interested in winning people to the Idea. She sat back, she listened, she poured tea with tiny strong hands, she spoke deliberately and insightfully. She missed nothing. She made you comfortable and she waited for you to reveal yourself.

This is what Sylvia had told him.

B ACK IN HER hut, Rosita Moreno, the best Judas-maker in all Mexico, sits frowning. She is not pleased with her work. Had not wanted to make a Judas-figure of the *señorita's* famous friend, although she knows that the man is no longer friendly with the *señorita* and the *patron*. Alberto has told her this. But was he really such an enemy, this Trotsky? Was he as bad as the corrupt judges and policemen and all the others she created as Judas-figures and took the name Judas? She did not trust Alberto on this, but he had forced her to construct the figure, telling her that the Party would pay her much money if she did it, and *Madonna santa*, they needed the money.

And so she had worked from her memory. From the times she had seen him. Had put him in a black suit with a red tie and white shirt. Blue eyes behind the glasses. Goatee beard. It was a big commission. She constructed the figure with his palms upturned and a look of surprise on his face. Alberto had been very pleased. Six men had carried the figure over their shoulders, piled it into a truck and driven to the *zócalo* in Mexico City. The wires were packed so tightly she knew that when it exploded it would leave no trace. Exactly as the Party, through Alberto, had requested.

Her Alberto hated Trotsky. Ever since he had gone to work in the mines at Jalisco, had joined the union there, come into contact with the Communists. He now called himself a Communist. He now worshipped Comrade Stalin and he hated Trotsky.

Shortly after his joining the Party, Rosita had questioned him hard. She questioned his motivations. And Alberto had driven her into Mexico City, saying, 'I want to show you something.' He had taken her to the Ministry of Education building. He took her hand and they walked straight to the east wall in the Court of Labour. They stopped in front of the frescos of the mineworkers. At the time of the first visit with Frida she had not stopped long in front of these paintings. At that time it was the dyers that had claimed her attention. But now she looked closely at *Entry into the Mine* and *Exit from the Mine*. They stood in front of the paintings. In the first fresco, the miners with shovels and pickaxes over their shoulders, heads bowed, begin a descent from the light into the dark. The lead figure carries a lantern which illuminates a gaping hole. Each figure is solitary. The pit is an unknown. In the second fresco, a dark-skinned man in white stands on a platform, having come up from the mine. His arms are outstretched. His feet together as if bound. He is searched – for weapons, for valuables, for something stolen – by a mine official, fair-skinned, in a uniform. There is abandonment in this stance of the miner. Beneath the miner with his arms outstretched is another miner, climbing out of the pit, and yet another man on the wooden ladder behind him. There is a look of suffering on the man's face as he reaches for the light. The light is a deliverance – but from what? To what? The ascent and the descent. Alberto turned to face her. 'This is the mine. This is the life when I am away from you. This is why I am a Communist.'

She felt, in those minutes in front of the fresco, looking up at the dark life her Alberto led when he was away from her, that it was all understandable: his silences, his drinking, his passion about politics. It was all contained there. In the sad frescos of the *patron*.

They had walked up into the north-wall stairwell and stopped in front of *The Burial of the Revolutionary*. Alberto pointed to the red flags coiled around poles. To the indigenous angels in the heavens, to the darkness surrounding the burial. Rosita had a flash of the future then, tried to stop the image forming in her head. 'That is not your end, Alberto,' she said. But Alberto's face glowed. He was silent. She saw herself as one of the weeping women in the painting, heads covered by their serapes, faces hidden.

She could never argue with Alberto because she did not have the arguments. She tried to tell him that they had seen enough bloodshed in Mexico to last ten lifetimes. One million killed in the Revolution of 1910. She did not want another revolution. But the Communists had taught Alberto to read. He was becoming an educated man. 'An educated drunk,' she would correct him. He felt he owed them his life. He had been a religious man when they first met, a believer, like herself. Now he was an atheist. She had observed this switch on other occasions. With Alberto's friends. For she was observant, intelligent, understood people; saw their lives in their faces and their palms. And this she understood: a great passion can transfer to another great passion. Commitment to one thing can turn into its opposite. So it was with Alberto.

Sometimes she longed for the devout Alberto of her youth. How he had lovingly fixed the mantilla over her hair. How they used to go together on Sundays, arm in arm, to receive the Blessed Sacrament. Afterwards, circling inside the church, making signs of the cross on their foreheads and their lips. Bowing their heads, blessing themselves with a finger dipped in holy water. How they had offered up prayers for themselves, for their families, for their country and for their life together. But that time had gone and he was gone from her, away to the mines, which was a necessity, she knew. He sent money back every few months. And each time he returned he was different. And she stayed on in Coyoacán with her fruit stall and her Judas-figures and the children, always the children.

Señora Rosita had not seen Frida for some months. Frida had been in North America and then Paris for an exhibition. The *patron* had also been away. The last time had been when Frida attended the funeral of Inocencio, Rosita's youngest child. It would be the last baby, Rosita was certain of it. The *señorita* had arrived at the hut with a tall man, dark hair curling, very handsome. They had sat and eaten *vegetales con mole*. *Quesadillas con pollo*. The doorway to

47

the hut was decorated with coloured-paper cutouts, tiny, butterfly-patterned. Señora Rosita had sat her dead child up in his accustomed place, a crown on his head of gold paper. Her other children had offered the child some candied sugars shaped like watermelon. The tall companion of Frida, the good-looking young man, did not say much, seemed very uncomfortable, to see the dead child propped up at the table like that. Frida, of course, was accustomed to such things. 'Inocencio,' she addressed the child, adjusting the pink *rebozo* over her shoulder. 'Some fruits?' And she passed the bowl to the top of the table, to be placed in front of him.

Rosita's other children were talking and singing to the child, lifting up its grey arms and playing with it. Above the head of the dead Inocencio, tacked on to the adobe walls, was a small tin painting of the Dolorosa. Rosita saw the man looking at the painting. '*Si*,' she said, with her mouth full of *mole*, 'the mother always weeps for the lost son.' Later, Frida placed a bunch of marigolds in the hands of the dead Inocencio. Frida put the orange flowers in the frozen fingers of the child. The man turned away.

Frida explained to the man about the *angelitos*, the little angels, as dead children were called. How they were free from sin, because they were so young. Death, therefore, was a celebration of the *angelitos'* assured speedy path to heaven. There was a tradition of mortuary portraits, she said, begun in colonial times. The wealthy would employ someone to paint their child. These days they employed photographers. But Frida wanted to paint the dead child. She had taken out her sketchbook in the middle of the meal at Rosita's and while one of the other children combed the baby's hair, Frida made rapid sketches. She later painted the child with his eyes half open, his feet bare and the marigolds blazing against his chest.

The children drummed on cooking pots. A neighbour came by with a guitar. Someone sang for the dead child. Everyone clapped. Later, much later, after everyone had gone, Señora Rosita wept like the Dolorosa, her tears like white drops painted on tin. She was happy for Inocencio's sweet path to God. How he was destined for a special paradise. But she would miss her last baby. The last one. She was sure of it. And she prayed to her God to spare her other children and give them good lives; lives very different from her own.

COYOACÁN
EASTER, MARCH 1940

L EV DAVIDOVICH HAD long been known by the name of his
Siberian jailer. The name hastily inscribed in his false
passport at the age of twenty-three. It was the name that
came to him on escape from that first exile: *Trotsky*. For almost forty
years the name had been his. These days his entourage, he knew,
referred to him as the Old Man. Lenin had also been called the Old
Man. This pleased him, this continuity.

Handcuffed by history to the name of his Siberian jailer, sitting in
the sunshine of exile in Mexico, in the courtyard of the house on
the Avenida Viena, one block away from the Casa Azul, Trotsky
leaned back in his chair and closed his eyes.

Outside the walls he could hear the explosions of Judas-figures
in the streets and church bells calling the faithful. He opened his
eyes and looked around the garden.

He thought of how the flowering cacti in this garden always
made him return to that other garden, that other house, the
memories of that other time.

'*Piochita*.' Trotsky's wife Natalia hears laughter and murmurings
from the next room in English and Spanish, neither a language she
understands. They have been at the Casa Azul for some months
now. Most days, Frida and Diego come to visit. This day Natalia
walks in with a bowl of ripe pomegranates to see Frida smoking and
staring at Lev Davidovich with her eyes half closed. Frida is blowing
smoke rings, teasing Lev Davidovich who is vehemently opposed
to women smoking. Frida sits on the edge of a deep-green settee,
swinging her good foot, her bad foot tucked underneath her.

'Come on, Old Man, stop me!' and Frida continues to blow deep smoke rings into Trotsky's face and Natalia sees his hair and goatee framed blue-white and he is laughing hard, waving away the smoke with his hands and admonishing the young woman. His tone is gentle. Frida's deep throaty laugh makes even Natalia smile for an instant, but she stops herself. 'I'm sorry,' she says to her husband, placing the fruit bowl down in front of him, 'I did not know you had company.'

'My dear.' Trotsky turns to his wife, extends long fingers, eyes shining like a small boy's. 'I was just telling our hostess how unbecoming it is for young women to smoke.'

Frida leans back defiantly, her long neck displayed and her breasts thrust forward through the gold-embroidered camisole. Closing her eyes, she blows another smoke ring. She is almost too beautiful. Natalia looks on, fascinated and chilled.

Frida gets up to leave the room and Trotsky hands her a small book: *The National Question*, attributed to Stalin, and actually written by Lenin, he tells her. Frida thanks him and tells him that she will study it carefully with reference to *the Mexican Situation*. She emphasises this heavily and looks him straight in the eye. Her fingers brush his and she says goodbye in Spanish to Natalia, and to Trotsky in English she adds, 'All my love.' She flounces out of the room without a backward glance, underskirts of crimson and pink rustling along floorboards, the book under her arm, the note from Lev Davidovich concealed in its pages.

Natalia has wary eyes in a clear, intelligent face. With her head slightly tilted, she poses for a group portrait of the exiles in Mexico. She positions herself next to the Mexican painter with the bird's-wing eyebrows and intensity of gaze. Natalia's slight form angled between the young woman and her husband. She does not smile. She never smiles in photographs. Europe is burning. Fellow comrades are dead. Her sons taken from her. She is full of foreboding.

In her journal she writes: *We wander around the garden of Coyoacán surrounded by ghosts with gaping foreheads.*

In the portrait, Natalia stands stiffly, wan and fragile, smaller than

Frida, one foot in front of the other, elegant in the black cloche hat with the white flowers, the black jacket and skirt, the two-tone shoes with the ankle strap. Like her husband, she is always well groomed. Before the shutter clicks she looks over at Lev Davidovich, who is smoothing his white hair, his beard, and is reminded of something Vladimir Ilyich Lenin once said, in the days when they were young and full of hope. 'If L.D. were ever in front of a firing squad,' Lenin had joked, 'his last request would be for a comb.'

She allows herself a small smile at her husband's expense, and then the smile fades, as she feels the heat off the young woman's body, as Frida leans towards her, momentarily touching, elbow to elbow, leaning towards the camera, like a plant to the light.

The shutter clicks and Natalia senses a risk more dangerous than an assassin's bullet.

Sometimes at night, Natalia wakes in the middle of a dream in which she loses everything that she has sacrificed in life with the great and temperamental Lev Davidovich. She dreams that the Georgian, *the man of steel*, has finally tracked them down, after all the houses, the countries, the loss of her beloved sons and most of their close comrades. She is accustomed to these dreams ending in tears and blood. They are talismanic, she believes. These dreams curtained her days. *Not a materialist position*, she admitted, and so she kept them to herself. What would Lev Davidovich say if he knew that she invoked dreams to ward off reality?

The dreams prepared her so that she could almost cope, she told herself, when the days of tears and blood arrived.

JORDI MARR
COYOACÁN
EASTER, MARCH 1940

S O HE HAD been wandering all this time. Had given everything over, not that there had been much to give over. And he had been happy with all that. More than happy. He sits in the garden. A rifle slung across his knees. He listens to the sounds of children beyond the walls and the rocketing of Judas-figures. He sees shreds of papier mâché floating, smoking in the sky as the figures explode.

He leans back against the lime-washed walls of the guardhouse and feels more alone than ever. His thoughts have cordoned him off from other people. Since his affair with Frida he sees everything differently. Most distressingly, he cannot look at the Old Man with the same eyes. Everything is changed.

He thinks about what it means to be happy. The times in his life when he has been conscious of it. In 1936 in a tiny village outside Barcelona, when he had walked into a small church hall and been astounded to see rows and rows of men with white sheets covering their torsos and men with brilliantined hair, clipping and shaving and singing. He had stood in the doorway. Men shorn in rows, dark clumps of hair spattering their fronts like blood clots. All the barbers in town had joined together to form a co-operative. The Durrutti Co-operative. He had sat down, and was moved and made hopeful by the talk, the laughter, the sipping of coffee, the scraps of *El Machete* and sawdust on the floor, the copies of *La República*. There was a camaraderie in that room which would remain with him all his life. The Durrutti Co-operative. The village barbers. He had felt happy with the sawdust over his feet and the men talking politics in his ear and he having his first shave in months as he stared at his reflection in a mirror edged with tin.

Happiness. That line from the American Declaration of Independence about the pursuit of happiness. He thought it both facile and dangerous. He thought that this one line could be held responsible for all the unhappiness and hypocrisy of the Western world. As if happiness were a quarry, as if you could stalk it, pin it down, corner it. But happiness wasn't like that. It came over you, descended; sometimes slowly, sometimes quickly. It was as intangible as mist. Something numinous. And then it was gone. It was half a dozen men with scissors in their hands, working together.

Above all when he thought of happiness, he thought of Frida. The last time he had been truly, unaccountably happy had been with Frida in the Avenida Madero in Mexico City. Frida had been shopping for cakes for her niece and nephew. They walked into a pastry shop. He remembered the fluorescent lights, the confection smells, the wedding cakes tiering over him. Meringues in all shapes. Ice-cream cakes of flags, footballs, cars, faces. He felt overwhelmed by the choices. Frida swam into this world of choice and colour as if it were her birthright. She thought it was everyone's birthright. Frida rustling, bending forward, pointing. Frida, charming samples from the sales girls, tasting, offering him sweet pieces with her violet-coloured fingertips. He tasted the honey cake she offered him. He felt happy.

After that there had been the visit to Rosita Moreno, the Judasmaker. The funeral of the *angelito*, the dead child. He had turned away, embarrassed, full of grief and sorrow. Death: Frida and her people laughed and sang, drank and danced with it. Jordi thought the feeding of the dead the most macabre thing he had ever witnessed. Yes, he felt very uncomfortable. He had seen corpses. He had smelt death. He was not prepared to indulge it and entertain it so intimately. That day had marked a difference in their relationship. Frida had looked at him and he had not measured up, he knew that now. Too imprisoned by background, his asceticism, how he felt he should be, the political self. Unable to bring the emotional private self to the surface. The self that longed to light candles and give thanks. He felt ashamed.

Frida had looked at him with changed eyes. The way he now looked at the Old Man.

Suddenly he feels angry. Wants to go beyond the confines of these walls. Feels that he is being kept from life. He decides to find a pretext to leave the villa that day, to get out into the streets, to stroll the *zócalo* in Mexico City. To see life explode around him, to be part of it. He will tell the Old Man that the provisions have run low. He will be back later. He will take the truck and park near the Alameda.

One hour later, he walks down 16 September towards the *zócalo*. At the edges of the square, he steps over the feet of poor Indians who sit with their backs to the Palacio Nacional. He steps over a worn mahogany cowboy boot which extends from under a sombrero. Another man is slung across this leg. Both men are asleep. He walks the back streets, enjoying the Easter crowds. He wanders past the small Church of Santa Ines. It is ornate and carved and gilded. Everything that he once abhorred about the Church now seduces him back in. The carved doors, the cool dimmed interior. He walks into the church in the middle of a mass. The sermon is about Judas Iscariot, the true meaning of his actions. Was he really a traitor? Why was he the only disciple to be called 'friend' by Jesus? Friend and traitor. *Ioudas Iskarioth. Judas Sicarius. The Sicari – a band of daggermen, Zealots.* Jordi sits down at the back of the church and listens to this account of the life of Judas Iscariot, daggerman. He realises that the young priest is saying something quite radical. That far from being a traitor, Judas had been merely a disillusioned soul, and as such, a mirror for our own disillusionment. Judas had taken Jesus at his word, had thought he was truly building the Kingdom of God on earth. Judas, bemused by Jesus's parables, alarmed at the direction in which Jesus was moving. Judas the apostate. He is the axis on which the whole story turns. He brought the fulfilment of God's plans for his son. As such, said the young priest, he deserves our respect and our forgiveness. There is a scraping of feet on the tiled floor, a clearing of throats and low mutterings after the young priest has finished. The congregation is not wholly convinced. Jordi looks around him. At the downcast eyes and disbelieving mouths. The mass ends. Everyone empties on to the streets. Jordi stays quiet and still. He folds to his knees, head bowed, silent.

His knees click as he gets up and walks slowly around the church. He stops in front of the black statue of San Martín de Porres. The saint holds two brooms in his right hand and a large crucifix in his left. Jordi marvels at these symbols of ordinary life. He finds himself kissing the feet of the black saint. On the wall adjacent to the statue are *retablos* – small paintings on tin depicting calamitous events and the intercession of the Virgin. Underneath, handwritten texts explain the event in question: a fire, a flood, a near-death in the family, and offer thanks to the Virgin for her deliverance. He had seen hundreds of these *retablos*, gruesome, brightly coloured, in the stairwell at the Casa Azul. Diego and Frida collected them.

Small *milagros* adorned another wall of the church. Tiny legs, hearts and arms made of tin and silver, pinned to a felt board with coloured ribbon. He notices a child's white sock pinned to the noticeboard. He sees photos of people who are missing and prayers underneath from their families. Overwhelmed, Jordi dips a thumb in the font of holy water. He crosses himself at the forehead, at the lips, at the heart. He steps outside. He stands in front of a church stall selling *milagros* and *retablos* and buys a small tin heart with a pale-blue ribbon. He goes back inside the church and he pins his *milagro* to the red felt board, closes his eyes and prays for his heart to be whole, for confusion to disappear; for love in his life.

Later, back at the Avenida Viena, he feels calm. He feels almost happy. Trotsky, eager for details from the outside world, asks him for news of the city, about the Easter celebrations, about what he has seen. Jordi feels depleted by the Old Man's questions, his needs and demands.

'Everyone was in church or going to church,' he reports.

'Church,' Trotsky says contemptuously. 'Our greatest rival. The greatest illusion.'

'For some, the greatest comfort,' says Jordi sharply, knowing where such comments will lead.

'Such comfort is an illusion.'

'It is still a comfort.'

The Old Man looks at him as if he has become a stranger.

Jordi returns to the truck to unpack the goods he has brought back from the city. He knows all the arguments. Knows them intimately. But the rational arguments no longer suffice. There is a hollow in him. These past years of movement, of exile in Mexico, of agitation, of belief in the Kingdom of Man on earth, have not filled this emptiness at the core of him. He feels an irrational desire for his heart to be swept clean by a black saint, barefoot. A saint carrying two brooms in one hand and a crucifix in another.

Jordi lies on his bed in the house on Avenida Viena, smoking and thinking of his time in Spain. What had stayed with him?

Trotsky had once said, *Ideas that enter the mind under fire stay there securely and for ever.*

At the International Brigades school in Albacete he had learnt many things: how to handle a Maxim gun, the heavy water-cooled guns sent by the Russians; how to use urine to cool the gun if he was far from a water supply. He could dismantle the lock blindfold. He had learnt, in the artillery section, how to ensure a steady stream of crossfire by first taking the measure of the range, the angle of movement, and ensuring that the other guns overlapped with that movement. He could operate well under fire; he could focus on the job at hand; he enjoyed the discipline and the responsibility of it.

He had learnt, most importantly, that if you can't hear gunfire in battle then it is already too late, the bullets have reached you. The bullets have entered your bloodstream.

On guard at the Avenida Viena, in the unnatural silence of the night, he often wondered if it were already too late, if the bullets were lodged in their bloodstreams, turning their bodies into corpses.

What had stayed with him? The smell of dead men, of dead mules, rotting in the fields; bodies, heads blown off, limbs distorted. Men in pieces with wooden boards across their chests, signifying name and battalion, if known.

For months, before the May days in Barcelona, he had worked as a messenger between the different volunteer battalions of the International Brigades. He remembers that job as the worst of his time in Spain. Always inadvertently getting lost, attracting fire, failing sometimes to get the message through at all. Once a shell had exploded so close that he had been knocked off his feet, unconscious. Afterwards he had lost the power of speech for three days. He remembered seeing peasants after a bombing raid, doubled over, running towards a river and plucking the fish that had been stunned or killed in the bombing, then racing back across the fields, heads bent and hands silver with fish.

War taught him to rely on his instincts, to live in the present, because that was the only moment that counted.

The abiding thing was this: in war there are no abstractions. Every detail becomes your own. With shells skimming the sky, it is *your* sky that is split. It is *your* trench that is shelled. It is *your* war. As personal as the shape of the bruise on your shoulder, the mark left behind by the recoil of a rifle. Everyone's bruise assumed a different shape and colour. Everyone's war was his own.

On the run from Stalin's GPU after the May days in Barcelona, he had rubbed arnica into his shoulder to rid himself of a bruise that would have betrayed him as a member of a POUM brigade.

Now in Mexico, finding himself in Trotsky's entourage, he rubs his shoulder at the memory. Here the war was a silent one. Trotsky shelled the world with words. Stalin moved silently closer to them. The silence made Jordi uneasy. For there were those who had gone before him.

There was a roll call: André Nin, head of the POUM and former secretary to Trotsky, had disappeared in Barcelona, presumed dead. Erwin Wolf, half-Czech, half-German, former secretary to Trotsky, kidnapped in Barcelona, had disappeared, presumed dead. Rudolf Klement, French former secretary to Trotsky, had been found in a cloth bag in the Seine with his throat slit.

But he believed that he could face any threat when the time came.

Lately, it was his hostile feelings for the Old Man that disturbed him and not the threat from the tentacles of Stalin's GPU.

He had the darkest feelings sometimes, when the Old Man was irascible and demanding. When he took unnecessary risks. On the question of screening visitors, for example. Just recently Trotsky had rejected his proposal that all visitors to the house undergo a weapons search.

Trotsky's episode with Frida had been an unnecessary risk. Now the break with Diego and Frida made life more difficult for all of them. Away from Diego's magnanimity, life was a lot harder. Emotionally, financially. For himself, there was the loss of the freedom Frida had provided.

At Trotsky's insistence, Jordi wrote letters of appeal to all the European and American sections. The Americans accused Jordi of extravagance with the household budget in Coyoacán, urged cuts in the wages of all household staff. Trotsky agreed. Jordi looked at the Old Man with his regal bearing and his refusal to carry money, or to deal with finances. How many countries had the Old Man travelled through, where he would not have recognised the colour of the money? This was always someone else's business. At that moment, with Trotsky railing about expenditure, Jordi looked at him and remembered something he had once read about Karl Marx, a comment attributed to Marx's mother. 'If only Karl had made capital,' she is reported to have said, 'instead of writing about it.'

Jordi looked down at his one pair of good trousers, brown corduroy, frayed at the edges. He had one good suit, which had belonged to his father. He calculated the months, the years, he had worked, they had all worked, for no money, for the cause of the Opposition. Even the small retainer he received was tithed to the Party – the Mexican section of the Fourth International.

Wages? he wrote back, with a loaded pen. *We do this for love.*

The enemy of my friend is my enemy. Trotsky operated a strict code of conduct. And how quickly a friend could be transformed into an enemy. Through Trotsky he had found Frida. Because of Trotsky he had lost her love and friendship. He had been forced into a decision. At the beginning of 1939, after Trotsky's break with Diego, they had moved from the Casa Azul to a draughty house in need of renovation, two blocks away on the Avenida Viena. Nothing was simple any more.

In Spain he had worn the corduroy trousers, the khaki jacket, the rough blanket around the shoulders: the uniform of the International Brigades. Here in Coyoacán Trotsky's bodyguards and secretaries were dressed in almost identical outfits. The thought was oddly comforting. Information from his time in Spain came back to him. It helped in preparations against an attack on the house, an attack which they all were forever anticipating. That day, at a drill in the yard, Jordi had explained what to do in the event of a gas attack. In the absence of masks, he advised pissing on a handkerchief and placing it over the mouth. He outlined this measure to the other bodyguards, the two secretaries, the chauffeur, the typists and the cook. Natalia had looked at him with laughter in her eyes. *Easier for men than for women*, was all she had said.

In Spain, at night, they had learnt to camouflage anything that shone. A belt buckle, a ring. The lid of a tin can.

Here in Mexico the most valuable possession in the house, Trotsky, shone with a force that was out of all keeping with his influence. In isolation, in exile, with a handful of supporters, the man still shone.

Maybe that was the story of the Old Man's life. Even in exile, far from the centre of events, too isolated to influence the flow of things directly, he shone. From exile in Istanbul, Norway, France and Mexico he shone. Like the reflection from a dead star.

Impossible to conceal.

RAMÓN MERCADER
MEXICO CITY
EASTER, MARCH 1940

R AMÓN MERCADER JUMPS in his hotel room as thousands of Judas-figures detonate across the city. The figures are packed with explosives and firecrackers; like muscle and tendon beneath the colours of the papier mâché. His girlfriend Sylvia sleeps on beside him. She is a heavy sleeper. He is fond of her in a way. Although he thinks her naïve and ridiculously attached to that egoist Trotsky. He dresses quickly and climbs out on to the fire escape and up on to the roof of La Reina. From here, he looks out on to the *zócalo*. The *zócalo* is full. Strung across on wire – rows of Judas-figures – in the form of policemen, judges and politicians – shatter one after the other. The noise is extraordinary. Minutes after, the paper carcasses hang limply from the wire. He is not a religious man. But he enjoys the cheerful destruction of these Judas-figures, for the Mexicans believe that the Judas, the traitor, will find release only in suicide, in death. He sees a group of Communist miners walking across the square. They are shouldering an outsize figure of a man in a suit with a goatee beard and spectacles. It is propped on the wire fence near the cathedral. It exceeds Mercader's expectations, this figure of Trotsky. It explodes on this Easter morning and there is nothing left, no scraps of papier mâché, no trace of colour. Every part of the figure is blown clean away. Mercader observes this with satisfaction.

Beriya walks up the steps to the third floor of the Lubyanka; his mind focuses on the step above. The steps are worn, sagging on the right and the left, each one a double layer of concrete pressed together by a multitude of feet. How many feet? Beriya tries to calculate, the numbers multiplying in his head, then loses count. All he knows is that the numbers will continue to multiply.

For this is what vigilance demands.

The stairs are so uneven, he feels he is walking on waves of concrete, or on lips slightly parted. The thought makes him smile. Makes him remember the girl from yesterday, and the girl from the day before. In the recesses either side of his feet, it is easier to see the human imprint on the steps. Beriya imagines a head on these steps, the mouth slightly parted into an agony of O as his boot sinks into the side of the skull. It is a specific head, a specific agony he imagines as he breathes heavily into the final curve of the stair. The joy of seeing that agony on the face of Lev Davidovich Bronstein, Trotsky, that betrayer of the Revolution, that *Yudushka*.

Yudushka: Little Judas. A far-off phrase once used by Lenin and the Bolsheviks to characterise Trotsky. It had applied to the pre-revolutionary past, to the days when Trotsky was still a Menshevik, the days before he had gone over to the Bolsheviks.

It still applied.

Beriya reaches the third floor and pauses for breath before entering the largest of the Operations rooms. These rooms and the files they contain, the rooms where men sit hunched over maps, barking communiqués down international phone lines, span three floors of the Lubyanka prison. Three floors are devoted to the elimination of one man. Three floors and three continents, Beriya thinks to himself with satisfaction. Indeed the whole edifice of the Lubyanka, every stone of it, bears the imprint of Trotsky, every *zek*, every Jew, every *kulak* is in part connected to the man in Mexico.

For it is a fact – every event loops back to Trotsky. From 1936 on, Trotsky's pernicious influence has become more and more apparent. From his study in Mexico, Leon Trotsky directs the poor harvests, the consequent hunger, the unrest. All of it. He is on record as an opponent of the Soviet Government. In a recent *Opposition Bulletin*, Trotsky had written:

The twelfth congress of the Bolshevik Party is its last. No normal constitutional paths for the removal of the governing clique remain. The only way to compel the bureaucracy is to hand over power to the proletarian vanguard by force.

He is an enemy of the state. And an enemy of the state is a personal enemy. Splitting and wrecking is the man's stock-in-trade. The whole country knows it to be true.

For there must be someone to blame.

Beriya moves to a filing cabinet and pulls out a blue folder marked *Operation Utka*. Inside the folder are lists of names. Beriya consults these lists regularly. Organisation, rigour, discipline; the measure of a comrade was in his attention to detail. The lists were the proof of this. He looks out of the window across Moscow at the fine grey mist covering the south of the city. It gives him such pleasure to see the names on the lists and later to see those names reduced to a smoke haze.

For not everyone could be shot.

From the window he sees a bread van sweeping towards the Don Monastery. How satisfying it would be to see Trotsky, that *Yudushka*, amongst those in the bread vans. He imagines the muffled sounds and faces contorting as the engine fumes start to pump – the bodies upright, entwined: gassed. The bodies are poured from the vans as one body, multi-limbed, to be burnt and interred at the Don Monastery. The bread van as gas chamber. Really, it is marvellous. What is the word? *Ingenious*.

The bodies gassed and burning. The bodies cremated with the ease of lit paper curling in an ashtray. It is that simple. And the time is coming for the man at the top of the list. Preparations are in order.

Fine grey smoke pushes up softly into the air outside the Don Monastery and caresses the cheeks, legs and arms of passers-by like a cashmere garment. After some days, the soft greyness settles in throats, children playing in the streets come inside, mothers wipe clean cloths over the children's faces and still the greyness settles in pores and on eyelashes, like a memory.

Political prisoners are often sent with picks and shovels to the Don Monastery. They are set to work digging ditches, into which they will later fall, bullet-holed by guards high on vodka. Afterwards, the guards enjoy the throwing of quicklime and the satisfying dissolution of flesh.

Slowly, slowly, the men in the Operations room at the Lubyanka pursue the trail of Trotsky's former allies, family members, and acquaintances. They work through the lists. They pursue those who protest that they are neither allies nor acquaintances. The trials of the Old Bolsheviks: how easily the accused collapse into appeals and denunciations. Soon Bukharin will be tried. They will show the man in Mexico that there is no one left for him and nowhere left to go. They are closing in. They have wiped his past. They will wipe his future. They are certain of it.

I N BERLIN, A small man clips at his moustache after seeing a
film starring Charlie Chaplin. He clips at his moustache until
it fits even more snugly under his nose; a small rectangular
block. This will become his defining feature. From the newsreels,
Stalin very much admires Hitler's moustache, copied from an
American comedian. He is tempted to create an identical one for
himself. But something stops him. Across many borders two men
face the mirror and contemplate what is right under their noses.
Stalin believes that the pact between them will hold, that Russia
will consolidate herself, annexing Poland, protected. He believes
that the German had the right idea, purging his High Command
of homosexuals; for they are not to be trusted. Stalin will not
imitate the moustache, although he clips it shorter as a sign of
confederacy. At night, he stands in front of the mirror, worrying
at his moustache. He has recently purged his own Red General
High Command. Hitler will see how serious he is. How much
room there is for common ground. And for expansion. He knows
that this has met with opposition. He must root out the opposition.

He clips away at the moustache. Feeling that he is getting closer.
First the Red Generals. Then Bukharin. Then Trotsky. Soon it
will be Trotsky. He puts down his scissors and moves into the
dining room to re-light the lamp under Lenin's portrait. He checks
the oil-level. He remembers his wife, how this was always her task.
He thinks of her betrayal. A man can only tolerate so much
betrayal. He puts through a call to Beriya. It is 2 a.m. He gives
further instructions for the Mexican plan. After the failure of the

May attack, the next time there must be no mistake. *Operation Utka*, he says loudly into the mouthpiece, smoothing his moustache: *by whatever means necessary.*

THE DIARY OF
LEON TROTSKY IN EXILE
COYOACÁN
MARCH 1940

E VERY DAY, I write about my enemy. At this desk, within these walls, the enemy is arrowed in my sights. Surrounded by old photographs and documents and reports to Party Congresses. This enemy who is both real and an abstraction to me. My motivation is not revenge. It is, rather, the fact of what he represents.

. . . Our paths have diverged so far and so long ago and he is for me a tool of such inimical and hostile historical forces, that my personal feelings towards him hardly differ from my feelings for Hitler or the Japanese Mikado. I therefore think I have the right to say that I have never raised Stalin in my mind to a feeling of hatred for him.

The enemy of the world revolution is a hydra. I fight it on many fronts. Iosif Vissarionovich Stalin is one such enemy. But he is not a noble adversary. It troubles me to fight him. And this conflict, let me make it clear, is not about two men, one in Moscow pursuing his enemy like a Khevsur with a dagger, the other in Coyoacán, anticipating blows.

No. It is about men with different approaches to world revolution.

Permanent revolution versus *Socialism in one country*. I trust in the revolutionary zeal of the masses, their unerring class instincts. The Revolution in Russia cannot stand alone. It is our duty to support others in struggle, beyond our immediate borders, beyond our immediate self-interest. But Stalin places his trust in the inertia of the mass, the old slumbering sentiments of Great Russians, the chauvinism of the steppe.

It was Stalin first made me a Jew. This I can never forget.

He armed the Spanish Republicans only on receipt of Spanish gold.

The mendacity of it. It shakes me still.

Stalin never journeyed beyond Russia. He was never in foreign exile from the Tsar's police. He never walked a Parisian boulevard, never sampled the delights and horrors of the bourgeois world. The greatest journey of his life took him from Gori to Moscow. He remains the boy from Georgia, in thrall to the first city lights he saw.

I try to understand Iosif Stalin. Where he has come from. The rote-learning of the seminary in Tiflis, how it stayed with him. How he learnt his catechism, knew his Lenin by heart, his lips moving over the passages in the Kremlin. Night after night I can picture him, by a low lamp in his apartment, a slow-moving finger stamping the lines to memory. This rote-memory was impressive. But the inflexibility of it. The manner of it – the crushing of opponents with a sentence from the text. The deficiency of imagination.

This is Stalin's greatest defect, this absence of imagination, his fear of anything different. His peasant distrust of the new.

I sit here, assembling documents, thinking about my enemy. I have some old newspaper photographs. One of the young Stalin with his black hair and pocked skin, his bad arm hidden beneath his coat. Photographs of his family also. Of his wife shortly before her death, walking through a snowdrift in a Moscow street, her collar pulled high, one hand clutching the collar, her eyes focused in front, trying to keep balance. The snowdrift seems to press in upon her. Walls of snow like concrete.

They say she died at her own hand. Some even say he pulled the trigger.

There is so much to understand. So much that we will never know from photographs or documents.

★   ★   ★

I sit here writing this book that does not engage me fully. It does not uplift or inspire me. I write about my enemy, the enemy of the working class, but at this period in my life, I would rather write of friendship and collaboration. The book that I wish to write, the book that draws me, is about friendship. The depth and charge of it. Friendships of two days or two hours. What it means in a life to say those words: *this is my friend*. I read the letters of the young Engels to Marx. Every friendship begins as a variant on a love affair. Entranced by the person and the idea of the person. You want to know more, you must. Then this deepens and spreads. Even though the object of affection may be absent, the thought remains of the person, and the thought of the friend sustains you.

At this point in my life, I have few friends left. Even my enemies have gone before me. I read the letters of the young Engels, struggling with his devout merchant father, sending numbered letters to Marx, devising codes between them, sending manuscripts in wax-sealed envelopes via booksellers in Germany, Brussels, Paris. A passionate friendship. Engels first met Marx over ten days in the August of 1844, and an enduring friendship was born. Engels, early on, helping Marx with his finances, the pattern of his life. I imagine Karl Marx immured in debt, his trouser-legs filthy, struggling with his writing, in permanent exile. Marx, covered in boils from his cheeks to his penis, lacerating his skin with a razor blade, unable to sit or to stand with the pain of it, joking to Engels that the bourgeoisie *would have reason to remember his carbuncles*. And the words of those early letters from Engels, the pattern of them unchanging, the reassurance of them, the great friendship, the great idea, the great work sustained in that friendship, and I feel a longing when I read those letters:

> *Well, goodbye dear Karl and do write soon. I have not been again in so happy and humane a mood as I was during the ten days I spent with you.*

I turn to the correspondence of Marx and Engels for the sheer joy of it. The energy contained there. Engels urging Marx not to allow his moods to overtake him. To finish his manuscripts, alternately cajoling and encouraging him to set himself deadlines, and to honour them. Engels, fundraising for Marx upon his expulsion from Brussels. Giving him the advance on the royalties from his own marvellous *History of the English Working Class*. Engels' belief in Marx's talent and his vision. Together, they could take on the bourgeois world and win. Engels, the second man. Engels happy in this role.

And I wonder, if Vladimir Ilyich Lenin had lived, how the course of our friendship, always fiery, not always conciliatory, but always respectful, would have run. Whether together, we could have fulfilled the ambitions of Marx and Engels, and felt proud. Vladimir Ilyich did not live long enough for our friendship to develop in this way. And I was not content to be the second man. And perhaps the nature of such a political friendship is the willingness for one partner to accept this secondary role. And now I see that perhaps such a deep and passionate friendship was not in our natures. Neither of us could yield enough. And sometimes I feel that lack. Vladimir Ilyich, the respect and grandeur of him. The friend lost to me now. A stroke is a cruel thing. Lenin. At the end as I am now. As we all are at the end.

The aloneness of it.

It is almost spring. I do not feel the joy of spring. I feel older in myself than I ever have. Every day I grapple with the life story of an avowed political enemy. Every day this forces me to look at my life, in relation to the enemy. In knowing my enemy I sharpen myself. The intimacy of enmity. How deep it is.

I am that which my enemy is not.

It is almost spring. It seems that we can inhabit a long winter of the soul and yet with the prospect of lightness – the dark winter of the soul cuts deeper. I have read that there are more suicides in the spring than in any other season. Here in Coyoacán, after the deaths of everyone close to me, I think of these things.

I remember once sitting in a café in Paris, near the banks of the Seine. It was around the time of meeting Natalia, 1901, maybe 1902. At the next table sat an *emigré* sea captain, a Russian. A Menshevik, as it turned out. Later a White Russian, completely against the Revolution. At the time, a pleasant enough fellow, sitting at the next table. He had once ploughed a tanker through the Baltic. He had travelled the world. The sea was his home. Now, in exile from the Tsar's *Okhrana*, as we were, he captained a cruise ship up the Seine. He was not unhappy with his life, *because he was still near water*, he said. *But the ocean*, he said, *how I miss the ocean! The quiet expanse of it.* I remember his gaze. Eyes that were accustomed to a horizon. *Not a day goes past*, he confided, *without the memory of the ocean. I carry it always, in here.* And he tapped his forehead between the eyebrows, the mind's eye.

I understood this sea captain. I watched him walk down the tiny steps into the barge, his feet too big for the steps. The clatter of tourists around him. He wore a uniform of navy with brass buttons. A naval cap with gold trim. He seemed bigger than the Seine.

Sometimes I think of this sea captain with the horizon in his eyes and the ocean in his mind. And I think of myself. Landlocked. My great wide journeys all behind me. But I can still think and write and dream. I am, in the words of the captain, still near the water. But I move through narrower straits. And it occurs to me now, how we become accustomed to these economies of scale. One moment, I am leading an army. The next, I am fumbling with a new pen nib in a strange city. I have learnt to adjust. No longer roaming the ocean, I find myself now in a Mexican backwater and, somehow, still afloat. And most times, as for the former sea captain, that is enough.

Spring. Suicide.

Natalia and I used to sit up late into the evening, after the day's work, and listen to music on the radio. She listened. I let the music soothe me and I watched her listen, how she sat absolutely still. Every nerve strained in concentration, her small fingers in her lap, her eyes closed in total absorption. My thoughts wandered, always. I have no ear for music, I confess. But I enjoyed the lilt and sway, and watching my wife's response to it.

Together we listened to Shostakovich, to that first broadcast of 'Lady Macbeth of Mtensk', performed on radio in New York City in 1936. Natalia was entranced. I admit it seemed a cacophony to me. Natalia jokingly called me a philistine. A few weeks later, the

77

copy of *Pravda* crossed my desk and there was the editorial, with the mark of Stalin's hand, condemning the work: *Muddle Instead of Music*. I laughed at the headline. For once, Stalin and I appeared to be in agreement. But I could also read the signs; I knew what such condemnation meant.

That Shostakovich should watch his back, I said to Natalia.

For eighteen months now, since the death of our eldest son Lyova, we have not listened to music. We have sat in silence in the darkness of our room. Listening to our breathing, exhaling our lives. Sometimes we hold hands. Our whole life together contained in our fingertips, the gentle pressure there.

We have contemplated suicide. More than once.

In 1911, the deaths of Paul and Laura Lafargue, Marx's daughter and son-in-law. They were aged seventy. They were tired. Too tired for struggle. Felt the burden of themselves.

A revolution is for the young. We all knew that. We all enlisted on that understanding.

And now I am an old man. I feel this acutely. The high blood pressure. The aching limbs. Old age. It is the most surprising and the most difficult thing for a revolutionary. For a human being. Time at my back and time rushing towards me. I hold up my hands. Nothing can stop this rushing.

Vladimir Ilyich Lenin spoke at the funeral of Paul and Laura Lafargue. Later he confided in his wife: *If one cannot work for the Party any more, one must look oneself in the face and do as the Lafargues.*

All of us supported the Lafargues' decision. We were young. There was no question. We applauded from the vantagepoint of youth. The Lafargues decided that their usefulness had ended. They did the noble thing.

To do as the Lafargues.

Natalia and I have conversations. We reserve the right to do as the Lafargues. It does not mean that I despair, if I take this route. For us, this is not a desperate act. It is a rational act. It is a release.

I remember our later exile in France. For a short time in 1933 we lived in a villa by the sea. We had visitors, as always. The writer André Malraux was one. Malraux and I took a walk along a cliff edge and he said to me, looking down at the looping and eddying of water below, the tide washing up towards us, 'The one thing that Communism will never conquer is death.'

I said to him that when a man has done what he set out to do then death is simple. But to create a society in which every man has a role, every man knows his purpose, *that* is difficult.

For me, death is simple. But if Natalia were to go before me . . . Some thoughts cannot be thought through.

When his wife Jenny died, Karl Marx was too ill with pleurisy to attend the funeral. He was distraught. After everything – all the movings, the death of children, the penury, Jenny pawning the linen and silverware that were her dowry, her beauty leaching from her face – he saw that his life was incomplete without her. For fifteen months after her death, he wandered Europe, subjecting himself to all manner of cures. He endured blistering and tattooing. He ingested large quantities of arsenic and opium. *The cure as punishment.* For all the old eruptions of the skin returned, the skin in turmoil, along with the disordered liver and bronchitis. *The only effective antidote for sorrows of the spirit*, he wrote to Engels, *is in bodily pain*.

These days, pain courses through me. My legs ache, those old wounds from the civil war, my back torments me. I have head-aches. My blood pitches high in my veins.

The self in turmoil.

This is the great puzzle for the revolutionary. We live for the Revolution, for upheaval, for change. For the collective will and spirit. And yet when such a revolution happens to us personally, we feel that we are no longer flowing with the collective, because there is that one individual who has sustained us, who is no longer.

The older I get, the further I move from solutions to these personal puzzles.

In his friend's absence, Engels gave the funeral oration for Jenny Marx. He paid tribute to her and to her role in the life of his friend. He is reported to have said, 'In truth, on this day, Karl died too.'

Stalin also had a wife. They say the death of his second wife – Nadezhda Alliluyeva – altered him, hardened him. I do not know what this revolution in his personal life meant to him. It was after the time of our exile. There were so many events that I could only guess at.

How did people live then, with the famine in the Ukraine? With the building of the Terror? I turn back to old copies of *Pravda*. I read descriptions of a Moscow I no longer recognise. These past years – a frenzy of building and demolition. Metro stations all over the city – walls of onyx and marble – the showpiece of the new Moscow. The construction projects built on forced labour. At what price these dreams of construction? The whole nation run like a barracks. Socialism of the fist and the gun.

And I sit here, looking at these photographs, willing them to speak. My last memories of the time before exile are of Moscow. It was 1927. I had just been expelled from the Party. I gave the funeral oration for our friend and comrade, Adolf Joffe. Stalin's wife Nadezhda Alliluyeva was also at the funeral. Across the heads of mourners I looked over to where she was standing. She was young and pale. Even then, the snow seemed to press in around her.

My friend Joffe died at his own hand.

People were shooting themselves then.

Stalin's wife died before him. I sit here looking at her photograph, trying to understand. I can only imagine the things she saw, the life she led.

The individual. History. The individual in history. The life history of the individual. I break the concepts down. I build them up again. Each component seems indivisible to me. But is it possible that the death of one link can shatter the whole chain?

If my Natalia dies before me . . . The thought that cannot be thought through.

My enemy once faced this thought.

This I fear more than an assassin's bullet.

2

THE LOGIC OF POETS

NADEZHDA ALLILUYEVA
MOSCOW
1932

PEOPLE WERE SHOOTING themselves then.

Moscow and Leningrad shook to these small nightly explosions through frontal lobes. Old Bolsheviks walked with one hand curled as if pulling an imaginary trigger: both hands heavy with the knowledge of it. At dawn, black cars transported the dead; bloodied sheets flapping from side doors, so quickly were the bodies disposed of.

Later, when those who had not shot themselves were on trial, Beriya would pronounce with a flourish: *Send the mad dogs down*.

I loathed Beriya on sight. His roundedness. Everything about him circular as if there were no entry point. Chins, pince-nez, bellies. Fat fingers drawing circles in the air. Iosif could not understand my loathing. He thought it further evidence of the maternal curse.

Comrade Nadezhda, Comrade Stalin. Beriya would glide into a room, so low that his forehead almost touched the carpets. For a heavy man, he moved lightly. In the voice something hollow. He loathed me. I could peel him back to himself with a stare.

To my husband, I said, *He is not to be trusted. I will not have that man in the house.*

It was the time of great vigilance, of enemies everywhere. Beriya, the second most powerful man, now head of the NKVD, kept us vigilant. Trotsky was in exile, but the Opposition still existed. The Opposition was clever. Vigilance was needed. Even my children's diaries were read. In the loops and curves of a childish hand, terror hid. Their childhood friends – scrutinised. Beriya's corpulent circlings tightened around shadows of dissent. At night his car cruised Moscow, procuring women. Mothers urged daughters to stay off the streets. Husbands urged wives to stay at home. Beriya squeezed Moscow like a python.

For a time, I escaped the python's circling.

But such knowledge is a dangerous thing.

At the Industrial Academy, for a long time no one knew the name of my husband.

I had my pride.

My father, Sergei Alliluyev, first hid Vladimir Ilyich and later Iosif Vissarionovich. My father worked for the Electric Light Company in St Petersburg and was respected as a mechanic of the first order. He knew a lot about light. He knew about the darkness also. His grandmother was a gypsy and it was from his family that I inherited my dark looks. My father had a special place in the hearts of Old Bolsheviks. When they were in the mood for reminiscing, my father would pour vodka and point proudly to the large wooden cupboard under the stair. I knew the story well. Vladimir Ilyich had crouched on a shelf in that cupboard during the police raids of July 1917. 'I was worried that Lenin's head would shine through the slats,' my father would say. 'And so I gave him my cap.' Afterwards, when the danger was passed, my father gave it to him as a memento. Vladimir Ilyich demurred, knowing that we were poor workers, knowing that it was my father's only winter cap. But my father insisted.

Three years later, on May Day 1920, along with thousands of others, my father, my mother and I stood in procession at the edge of Red Square. I remember as Lenin passed us, he lifted the fur cap from his head, extending his hand in our direction. By now the cap was threadbare in places. *The special cap*, he called to my father, laughing, arms outstretched. *Almost as bald as myself!* The motorcade slowed for a moment and Vladimir Ilyich leaned from the car and grasped my father's hand. My father turned to me with tears in his eyes: his cap had a place in history.

Iosif Vissarionovich was a man of almost forty when my father hid him. They had known each other from the early days in Baku;

from the time when my father set up the illegal printing presses and Iosif, then known as Koba, had set up bank raids all over the Caucasus. My father thought him direct in the Georgian way. He seemed very strong and sure to me. My mother paid little attention to him, the reasons for which only later became apparent. He spoke of prison. Of exile in Siberia; hunting and fishing. He spoke of growing up in Georgia, in the village of Gori, in the shadow of the Kazbek Mountains. He spoke of how he had finally chosen his Party name: Stalin – *the steel one*. He too hid in the wooden cupboard below the stair. But with Stalin's dark hair and pockmarked skin my father was not worried that he would be seen. 'The man of steel is accustomed to the shadows,' he said.

Iosif was as steely as a shadow.

Of course this came to me much later as such knowledge does. If I knew then . . . but what does a schoolgirl really know?

I was a daughter of revolutionaries. My childhood memories are of muted voices, of men with inky hands and of pamphlets bundled in cupboards, of the adults in my life appearing, disappearing. Of standing outside the Tsar's prisons, the snow around my knees as if I were planted there, waiting for my father to be released. I knew no other life. By the time we moved to Petersburg, carrying our belongings under a flat dark sky from one apartment to the other, the children on the lookout for the Tsar's secret police, the system of hand signals we evolved, that level of alertness, seemed as natural as breath.

In 1917, during the July days, I watched Iosif Vissarionovich, my future husband, shave off Lenin's beard and moustache in our Petersburg kitchen. The care he took, his hand steady. Copies of *Pravda* curling under the chair, an ancient towel fraying around Lenin's neck, the bristles foaming wiry against the blade. Vladimir Ilyich emerging shiny and new, his child-skin concealing the man. Iosif Vissarionovich Stalin, *the man of steel*, stepping back, admiring his handiwork. As if the whole of his revolutionary career until this point – the brutal robberies of banks in Tiflis, the relative calm of exile in Siberia, the concealments and transformations – had led up to this overwhelming moment.

I fell in love with Lenin's barber, that was the truth of it. In my own way, I love him still.

My father suggested that Stalin should also shave his facial hair. But Stalin said that he was not in immediate danger, and in any case, 'With my moustache, I am everyman. I am safe.' And at the time it was true enough. With a flat cap on his head he looked like any other worker on the Petersburg streets. Even then, Iosif had the ability to merge with a crowd and to wait until the opportune moment to step forward. He was remarkable in his ordinariness.

In 1917, his enemies characterised him as a *grey blur*. That was their first mistake. To underestimate the remarkable ordinariness of Iosif Vissarionovich Stalin.

I was sixteen years old when I worked as Lenin's secretary. Seventeen when I married Iosif Vissarionovich. I believe that Iosif loved me in his way. He called me his gypsy queen: I reminded him of a girl he had once seen on a circus trapeze in Georgia. *So slim and dark and twirling high above me.* Iosif always loved spectacle and illusion. In later years he was in thrall to the cinema. He wanted me to walk on the trapeze for ever. But I was not content with air and light. He was much older, steeled in shadows. As his wife, I, too, became much older than I ever intended.

'Your notebooks are precise and clear, Nadezhda Alliluyeva.' My instructors at the Industrial Academy praised my work from the beginning, even before they knew the name of my husband. These days, although my technical sketches are fluid, sometimes I distort the arrangement of polymer chains on the page.

Just to test them.

'Nadezhda Alliluyeva will be our finest chemist,' they say, although I feel more and more convinced that my work is no longer judged clearly. The hands of my professors shake as they turn the pages. In recent examinations, in a question on amino plastics, I intentionally substituted an oxygen atom for a sulphur one.

Still I am awarded top marks. I protest.

You are mistaken. Your work was 100 per cent correct in all details, says the Professor.

Such duplicity depresses me.

There are rumours at the Academy. Since the time of the comrades' return from the Ukraine, several of my favourite professors and fellow students no longer come to class. People avert their eyes when I walk by. There is another Moscow that pulses at the edges of my vision. Another Moscow that I long to see clearly. Another country that I want my husband to see. I have these longings, but I am now as cloistered as a Tsarina.

And so I plunge into this New World of plastics and artificial fibres. On my desk at home, I keep a lump of Baltic amber, which reminds me of my mother's amber bracelet. Amber is a natural plastic. Malleable. I pick up the amber and turn it to the light and marvel at a honey colour so perfectly formed and moulded by the compression of heat and earth. There is a tiny insect trace caught inside the amber. I'm reminded of clear days in the Crimea, Iosif in a white suit with a broad-brimmed hat. The children churning up the sand. The pale thin white legs of the Politburo members caught up in a clear amber wave. I keep an old tortoiseshell hairclip on my dresser, from my great-grandmother, in the days before women wore their hair so short. My daughter sometimes plays with it. Tortoiseshell is also a natural plastic, a malleable material. I compare these natural plastics with the materials we create in the laboratory. In the new plastics I see the future. I want to reproduce these natural plastics because we are now in an age in which we can triumph over nature. In the reproduction of nature we can triumph over need and want. *This* will be my contribution.

My husband does not understand my affinity with these materials. Does not understand my pleasure in something that is lighter than metal, something that can be moulded into any shape, capable of mass production, a material for our age which is not dependent upon the caprices of heat and earth. He thinks that it is not a fit subject for a woman. And when I think of him, try to understand him, I compare him to the materials I work with. He has the fixity of a thermoset plastic. And I see that his is a Bakelite nature; once moulded into shape, it remains in that form. At very high temperatures, however, it can break down irreversibly.

Sometimes, Iosif lies down on the sofa, his hands to his face. I have seen the cracks.

It is said that, in the West, along with the new plastics, new fabrics are in production. Artificial fabrics more beautiful than viscose. An artificial silk is not far off, they say. I await these discoveries.

I am as cloistered as a Tsarina, I long to see things clearly, the other Moscow, beyond these Kremlin walls.

I long to wear a fabric to which memory will not adhere.

THE METRO. THERE is always the Metro. A serpentine maw. In the mornings, Mikhail Kosarev nods to his boss, the Moscow Party Second Secretary, now overseeing construction, as they feel their way along dank tunnels and up into the opal light of the streets. As one of the team leaders, as chief mining engineer, he is directly answerable to the Second Secretary, Nikita Khrushchev. Mikhail drags his charcoal heart along shafts half built, away from the heaviness of the apartment. He seeks the engulfment of the tunnels. On this underground morning, as he makes his way to work, assessing the work of the day before, close to the earth's core, he feels as if he is dowsing for love, vibrating over the earth, trying to find its source.

Underground, everything seems solid, although he knows it is not. Out on the streets, in his small apartment, he feels as if he is walking on something as fragile as cloth. In the apartment, the relationships are sedimented like sand, continually shifting and changing. He is exhausted. He sometimes feels that if he cannot escape then he will go under, as others have gone under, that not even his footprints will remain.

He feels alone, dowsing for love down there in the tunnels, the salvation of another fourteen-hour day ahead of him. Once he would have found a measure of escape from aloneness in the camaraderie of the Metro, in the adrenalin of days without sleep in the construction of something beautiful, something that would outlast them all.

The Metro is to be the centrepiece of the New Moscow, a

symbol of *Socialist Reconstruction*. They have seen the blueprints, those inky pointers to the future. They have seen the artists' models: the chandeliers flickering, the rippling bronze of proletarian statues, the twenty different kinds of marble sheening the walls.

In all this they have had a glimpse of tomorrow.

Since the news of his friend, however, a glimpse of tomorrow has not been enough to sustain him. There has been only the repetition of days. The tunnels in-between. In the evenings, he watches himself emerge from the deep shaft near his apartment, watches himself in a small crowded bar with the other comrades, watches himself laughing and ordering drinks that taste like fire, cajoling his team, remonstrating with them. Exuding energy. He is a good man. A good leader.

Not all of the comrades are as enthusiastic as he. With over seventy thousand workers, most of them illiterate *muzhiks* from Kazakhstan and beyond, that would be impossible. It is far easier to construct a section of railway, even underground, Mikhail thinks, than it is to construct new attitudes. He has only to look at his mother and sister.

Certainly, underground they have other problems to confront: many of the workers are also *zeks*: political prisoners, Trotskyites, former camp inmates, not to be trusted. The work is aimed at rehabilitating them, involving them in the process of Socialist Reconstruction. From the dull eyes and set faces scrabbling in the soil, however, Mikhail sometimes wonders whether full rehabilitation is possible.

There had been some successes, of course. His childhood friend Oskar – rehabilitated and released – had been transferred to the Metro project because of his expertise as a mining engineer. Oskar had spent two years at a camp outside Moscow as punishment for leading a strike in the Donbass. They never spoke of it. But still those two years clouded his days. Oskar's children held hands tightly on the way to school, walking carefully in the spaces marked out for them. Everything marked out for them.

Somehow Mikhail could never reconcile the fact that his friend had been a *zek*. The fact that, privately, he had never regarded his friend as an enemy of the state, the fact that Mikhail himself was an esteemed Party worker with an unblemished record meant that he had to be careful in resuming a friendship with Oskar. Khrushchev himself had warned Mikhail of associating too closely with this former political prisoner. Vigilance was needed. Even though he had not seen Oskar since their youth, since before his friend had left to work in the Donbass. But one could not be too careful. At work he was mindful not to appear too familiar with Oskar. After work, in the bar, it always seemed by chance that they might find themselves enjoying a casual exchange, while making their way across the room for a drink. But for weeks after, he would ensure that this would *not* happen, conscious of *not* making eye contact with his friend across a crowded room. The space around Oskar had to be carefully managed. Strategically negotiated. Mikhail was always conscious, as a group of them burst drunkenly from the bar out into the night, that he would *not* be found singing with his arms around Oskar's shoulders. He hoped that Oskar would forgive him for this. For Oskar was a good man, a diligent worker, a fine comrade. But he was tainted – *a former Oppositionist*. Mikhail was forced to acknowledge that.

Now, in the evenings sometimes, now that there is no Oskar, when his comrades eventually rise, unsteadily, to leave the bar, Mikhail remains at the stool by the window, watching them return to children and wives and another life beyond the Metro shafts. A cramped life, but a life nonetheless. Every *Metrostroyevets* jokes about it: 'One day, we're moving the family down here.' Indeed, whole sections of the underground shafts are larger than the fifteen square feet of the average apartment. It is not only the Metro workers who covet such space. After months of construction, the workers and the rats in the tunnels are joined by other vermin – *kulaks*, escapees from political exile and petty criminals. Mikhail senses their presence, smells the fear off them, feels their pupils dilate in the darkness, even when he does not see them. For Moscow is full. Moscow now expels its refuse down Metro shafts. Recently, the foundations of a whole section caved in, flooded by one of the underground streams. After dredging the area, twenty bodies were found, bloating like air bubbles on the muddy floor.

None of them *Metrostroyevets*. Police now keep vigil over tunnel entrances.

Mikhail ponders a life underground as he watches his comrades depart. To him, they are more than family. The relationship transcends blood ties. They are united in a glorious enterprise. It brings them closer than brothers. He empties his glass. He watches the *bonhomie* depart. Joylessness settles in his bones. He prepares to face his mother and sister in the mausoleum of their apartment. It has been three months. This mixture of relief and guilt. He cannot now remember a time before joy leached from every pore.

He has wide palms, wide as spades. He is a big man. There is a big space inside him. We are our work, he says to himself. How can we be more than the sum of our work? And yet. The hunger for love, for space, for camaraderie persists. Sometimes that hunger is not assuaged by work, even by a project as audacious as the Metro. In the three months since the news of Oskar, he has been unnaturally preoccupied with such questions.

He inserts the key into the lock. The familiar ritual of pushing his bulk twice against the door, until the rusty lock gives way and permits him entry. It is 11 p.m. as he pushes through the door of their *kommunalka*, a communal apartment formerly a bourgeois residence near Ulitsa Gor'kogo. The first section of the Metro tunnel is scheduled to open nearby. His family has occupied this apartment for some years. They are the fortunate ones. Along with twenty other families in the mass appropriations of 1920, Mikhail's family staked their claim. Twenty families now inhabit the space that once housed a merchant and his six children.

He knows it is 11 p.m. because in rooms off the main entrance, the bells of the Kremlin's Spasskaya Tower crackle and toll in unison from old radiograms fashioned from spare parts. The voice, *Govorit Moskva!* assails him with an authoritative familiarity. On the news bulletin, he hears First Moscow Secretary Kaganovich rasping about the bold new construction projects. He hears Kaganovich declare: *The Metro is one of the fronts of the great war we have been waging . . . for beautiful new things and a new man . . .*

He walks along the ground-floor corridor. Nightsoil pans are placed outside rooms. Grey laundry stiffens on string cast across the exposed roof beams. There is coughing and wheezing and the cries of small children. At the end of the corridor the tap drips, rotting the floorboards underneath where twenty families queue daily to splash themselves with cold water and fill their samovars.

His apartment is separated from the communal kitchen by a heavy curtain. The kitchen consists of several primus wood burners and a few tables. In the evenings women huddle around these burners providing for their individual families. The inefficiency of it exasperates him. But he has become resigned to these vestiges of bourgeois morality in the communal kitchen. He separates the curtain, takes a deep breath and booms: *Govorit Moskva!* His mother and sister start up from their chairs, as if jerked on a pulley, and then back down again. Two pairs of eyes beam accusation and remorse at him from lamplit corners. They mutter at him, do not understand the irony in his tone. He strides through to the edge of the room, to his space, and the women shrink, pinkly soap-scented, into the opposite corner. Today is Friday and his mother and sister have been for their weekly hot tub at the public baths. He peels back a thin bedsheet, his curtain, and throws himself on a worn mattress, the length and breadth of a coffin, his boots still on, and stares up, his hands crossed under his head, trying to make sense of his life in the damp patches on the ceiling.

He is not responsible. Oskar's death was not his responsibility.

Everything in the small apartment is loud and damp although no one is talking. His sister fertilises the mushrooms on the windowsill with nightsoil. Her back now turned from him. The odour is intense. Even the odours are loud and damp. His mother opens the door of a rabbit hutch in the corner of the room. Four tiny grey shapes tumble out. His mother inspects them and then pushes them back, with difficulty, towards the large shape maternally hulking in the corner of the hutch. 'They will be ready soon,' she pronounces.

His sister turns from the windowsill: 'When?'

'Soon, I said.'

'How soon?' his sister asks hungrily.

'When God wills it.'

His sister turns back to the mushrooms; her mother's brusqueness slaps against her shoulder-blades.

'Why wait for God's will?' He hears himself, baiting them, from behind the curtain.

His sister, in frenzy, throws back the sheet. 'Because we starve, waiting for your Party!'

He laughs, which enrages her even more.

'Stop it. *Stop it*!' His mother puts her hands to her ears. It is all so familiar. Every night a variation on this exchange. He behind the curtain. The rustling sounds of rabbits and the fetidness of nightsoil.

With the rabbits and the mushrooms, they will see it through until next winter. His mother is convinced of it, heeding Comrade Khrushchev's exhortations. The only exhortations she ever heeds concern food and shelter. Everything else is screened out: intellect subordinate to instinct. He watches her in the communal kitchen sometimes, weaving around the other women, barely pausing to acknowledge their existence, stepping over the salivations of thin children to carry steaming plates back into her *own* apartment, to her *own* children, to her *own* table behind the curtain. He has never once seen his mother share anything: not an onion, not a kitchen utensil. He does not understand it. Cannot now remember if she was always like this, and if she was, how his father had ever survived it.

It is 1932 and there is hunger in Moscow. The city is changing: new buildings, factories, the Moscow-Volga canal, the underground. But there is nowhere to live. Nothing to eat. They are the lucky ones. It has now become a revolutionary duty to grow mushrooms and keep rabbits to ease the food shortage. Although there has been no drought, no natural catastrophe, the grain is no longer reaching the cities and rumours abound of skeletal remains carted around the Ukraine. The Red Army is called in to harvest the sugarbeet. The *kulaks*, intransigent, watch them move gracelessly over their fields. They slaughter half the country's cattle rather than surrender it to the state. Millions are deported. These are the rumours. The sugarbeet harvest, and the wheat harvest in the Ukraine, is lost.

These are the rumours.

Even on the outskirts of Moscow, filthy *kulaks*, refugees from collectivisation, hands outstretched, are moved on, because they do not carry the *propiska*, the labour permits required of all Moscow citizens. Homeless juveniles and adults are ferried in trucks at night, forty or fifty miles outside Moscow, and then spilt, oozing like waste material, on to the road. Mikhail has no sympathy for them. With their pathetic holding on to small, inefficient patches of land, with their circumvention of the state farms through the black market. With their wilful slaughter of cattle. They have brought it all on themselves. *Most of them are not even Russian*. These escapees from the countryside are putting pressure on the cities. Holding them hostage. Moscow is full. And every windowsill stinks of mushroom and every other corner of rabbit droppings.

And behind it all, Trotsky and the Opposition, directing, disrupting, even now from the comfort of exile.

He has explained the disruptions of the Opposition to his mother and sister so many times. They were in agreement on the pernicious influence of Leon Trotsky. For different reasons. And yet, beyond Trotsky, his mother and his sister seem to blame him for this situation. But he is not responsible. He has told them time and again. But as a member of the Party they hold him accountable.

As a non-believer they held him accountable.

Hadn't he been there in 1931, cheering alongside the League for Militant Atheists as the Cathedral of Christ the Redeemer crashed to the ground? Cheering as explosions split ceilings and doors and icons hurtled through the air?

Hadn't he known that no good would come of it? His friend Oskar, recently released, drunkenly cheering, had also been present. God would eventually express his displeasure, Mikhail's mother had warned him. Anticipating the form of this displeasure had coiled around her years. His mother waited, stoically, for some horror to befall them.

His mother and sister could not forgive him for this.

But hadn't he also retrieved a small golden fragment, a relic for his mother, pressed it into his pocket, as four hundred pounds of gold leaf were carefully prised from the cupolas? He had moved in close, watching the workmen dismantle the fourteen bells, a dissonant tolling as the marble and granite tumbled from the walls, and the heavy crucifixes thudded to the earth. The whole procedure had fascinated him. Yes, he had cheered them on, up until the work became too onerous by hand and the orders came to dynamite the building. After two attempts, the large dome and supporting columns still remained. The Moscow skyline shook. He did not cheer. A small gathering of the faithful, including his mother and sister, offered up prayers, claimed a miracle that God had intervened to save their church. But the OGPU foremen were unimpressed. A third detonation destroyed the church completely. He felt badly shaken. He remembers the dusty air and the gold-leafed cassocks of priests and the moaning of the faithful.

He remembers the three explosions.

He saw priests prostrate in the dirt. He saw them dragged away. The League of Militant Atheists cheered. The sound stuck in his throat. He had always believed in the scientific method. In the construction of the new. In the relegation of superstition to the past: the lessons his father had taught him. But there was something in the dragging of cassocks through dust that held his attention, that disturbed him. More than that, it shamed him. He could not face his mother and sister. It was whispered, much later, that five of the priests who had protested at the removal of holy relics had been arrested and shot that same evening.

Since then, construction on the site had been constantly impeded. *The site was cursed*, his mother said. And now, after two years, he feels that perhaps his presence there that day, and the demolition of the cathedral itself, had been a mistake. Superstition was not so easily exploded. But he could not admit it to himself. To admit would be to cede power in the shifting sands of familial relations.

Now the Palace of Soviets was to fill that space left by the church. It was to be taller than the Empire State Building in New York, topped by a hundred-metre statue of Lenin which would fracture the clouds. Now, every time he walked past the din of cranes and tractors still shifting the rubble, the image of blood-filled soutanes soaked his mind.

The whole of Moscow had become a huge construction site.

Destruction, his mother said.

Construction, he insisted.

His sister hissed at him from the corner.

His mother kept the gold-leaf fragment he had collected that day in a layer of tissue paper. She occasionally took it out and fingered it and then looked at him, and then away again, coldly folding the tissue into tight precise corners, like a fine envelope. She placed the tissue with the gold leaf underneath the portrait of the Madonna near the rabbit hutch, above the red oil lamp that never burnt down. Next to the Madonna was a portrait on cloth of Lenin in profile. As a young Komsomol member, Mikhail had stuck it next to the framed icon, nailing the cloth into the wall. Now, after a decade, one corner of the portrait was torn. A section of Lenin's index finger fraying into infinity.

Three months earlier, Khrushchev had enthused about Comrade Stalin's eye for detail. 'More public toilets! The *Khozyain* worries that Moscow needs more public toilets.'

It was true, Mikhail conceded that evening, flat on his back, ignoring the rustling silence in the room, public toilets had been scarce. Up until three months ago, where could a man shit in Moscow outside his own home? And what was the point of constructing Socialism if a comrade couldn't piss any time he wanted?

To find space in one's own home, stumbling over nightsoil buckets, was difficult enough.

Priorities.

A week after Khrushchev's enthusings in the underground, public toilets had proliferated like mushrooms in nightsoil, faster, even. Mikhail watched as public conveniences were erected more quickly than the tunnels of the Metro, more quickly even than the *baraki* – the shoddy wooden bunkers on Moscow's periphery.

More public toilets. He shook his head.

Priorities.

His sister and his mother turned a cold eye on all these new developments. They deplored the trains loaded with wood, metal and equipment which steamed into Moscow. They preferred the cobblestones, the unpaved roads and the horse-drawn carts of Moscow as it was, as it had always been. They were suspicious of his tunnels. He could not discuss any aspect of his work with them or even any aspects of his thinking. And the one person with whom he felt he could discuss things was now gone.

There was the silence and the space between the silence. As a leading cadre, he had been assured of his own small apartment in the spring. That was a year past. It was again almost spring. He now felt that the energy of spring was as predictably foreign as another country.

For a single man in a *kommunalka* with his mother and sister and nineteen other families was not a priority – no matter how valuable a comrade, or how desperate.

His sister had a taut look about her, as if hostility were wired too tightly. Day followed day and suddenly she was forty-eight years old with no prospect of marriage. She was becoming an exaggerated shadow of their mother. His sister imbibed everything his mother said, but inside her it transmuted into something even more bitter and vicious. Since their father's death all those years ago in the Civil War this bitterness had become as pronounced as scar tissue.

His sister had first conveyed the news about Oskar, a triumphal note in her voice.

He had felt the urge to beat that triumphalism out of her. Instead he grabbed the cushion she sat on, wrenched it from underneath her. His sister toppled from the chair in surprise, and put out her hand to retrieve the cushion. The cushion, her favourite, red-and-white embroidered, had been brought back from the Ukraine by their father. Her smug appropriation of the cushion, and of their father's memory, antagonised him. They fought over the cushion, tugging at it, the seam of it splitting and a dozen cards shooting over the rug, as if some crazy dealer had thrown in his hand. Ration cards. His sister fell to her knees and scooped them up quickly into her apron. He stared at the cards. At the distinctive red-and-black stamps denoting cards for workers, for non-workers, for the infirm, for the aged and so on. It appalled him. Such hoarding. Even more, he was appalled that he should be wrestling with his sister over a cushion, after the news of the death of his closest comrade. His mother shouted out at them both, moved across the room to separate them as she had done ever since they were children. He pushed his mother away so hard that she pitched into the wall. He struck his sister across the mouth: *Stupid bitch*. His voice was hard and low. *You could have us all arrested.*

For a second, he imagined the satisfaction of reporting his sister to the authorities. There was currently a campaign in the Moscow branch to penalise the hoarding and trafficking of ration cards. He imagined having the apartment to himself. His sister seemed to intuit his thinking and, still on the floor with an apronful of ration cards, her face upturned and twisted: *Did you want us to starve?*

'Be quiet, both of you!' His mother moved to the curtain and drew it more firmly across and stood there, holding the curtain, hoping to blunt some of the noise with her bulk, her head angled to the corridor. She was listening for Andrei Konchovsky's emphysemic step. Konchovsky was the building superintendent. No murmur escaped him. He had a basement room all to himself. Just recently, a new stove had arrived for him after his discovery of the *kulak* down the hall, a cousin of one of the families, being hidden during the day, working illegally at night, without *propiska*. The *kulak* had been duly reported. Konchovsky's new stove had arrived the day after.

All of the families were fearful of Konchovsky.

At that moment, with his sister on the floor and his mother pressed against the curtain, he was aware of a power he hadn't known he possessed and wasn't entirely sure he wanted. He despised his mother and his sister. Their backwardness. Their lack of engagement with anything outside themselves. Their petit-bourgeois emotions. He had presumed that they were merely indifferent to him.

He realised, then, that his mother was not so fearful of Konchovsky wheezing in upon them and discovering the ration cards. No, she was fearful of him, her son, betraying them to Konchovsky.

He was living with two women outside space and time. The great prejudices of Mother Russia slumbered in his apartment night after night. They were True Believers. He had once joked to Oskar that his mother and sister so lacked sophistication that they could not distinguish between *metropoliten* (the Metro) and *mitropolit* (an

Orthodox priest). Change alarmed them. They trusted no one. He had escaped their cloying backwardness, had claimed an education, after the Revolution. But his mother and sister were from a time before the Revolution. Before history. It suited his mother and sister to stumble over cobbled streets, past steaming horse dung. They were in agreement with Comrade Stalin on two things only: the danger of the trolley cars, and the dangerous influence of Leon Trotsky. Like Comrade Stalin, they worried that a double-decker trolley would career uncontrollably around corners. They refused to travel by trolley.

As for Trotsky, his mother desired vengeance. She had never recovered from the Civil War. The loss of her husband, fighting the Whites. The loss of her brother, a sailor at Kronstadt, fighting the Bolshevik government. She despised all government leaders, she said, but above all, she despised that Trotsky, that *Yudushka*. For the news spread quickly that day in 1921, his mother told him: *And we thought: surely this can't be happening, surely the government will listen to the demands of the sailors. For their demands were reasonable. For bread, for democracy. We were tired in the cities. We wanted to sink into some kind of a peace. No one can sacrifice for ever.*

And then news of bodies falling on the ice. Trotsky directing the assault on his own sailors in the Kronstadt garrison. Trotsky naming them traitors.

How her brother never returned from the Kronstadt garrison.

How she never forgave Comrade Trotsky. Laughed when she heard of his expulsion from the Party and subsequent exile. *He's cursed*, she said. *Blood on his hands.*

Mikhail nodded mutely every time Trotsky was mentioned. It was the only subject on which they were in agreement.

The rest of her beliefs completely confounded him.

It amazed him that outside that room history unfurled like a banner, while inside the room time was like a cat coiled in an endless slumber before a fire, too complacent even to stretch itself.

This reactionary somnolence oppressed him. He did not understand how his father, an atheist and a committed Communist, had ever married his mother, or how he himself had ever been born into such a household.

He stayed with his mother and sister because Moscow was

crowded. Moscow was full. In cramped apartments everywhere, enmity wracked the air.

The waiting was difficult. For some, the proximity became intolerable. Some could find no salvation in work. And for comrades with too much past, people like Oskar, there was not even the prospect of waiting for something better.

NADEZHDA'S GAMBLE
MOSCOW
1932

A T HOME I am even harsher with my daughter. I force her to practise French and music so that she will know the joy of her own accomplishments while she can. So that she can know the measure of herself, before others come to judge.

I was too young to know this before I married.

I am alone yet I press myself against the cream Kremlin walls and feel them exhale with me.

I long to introduce disorder into our routines, as I do with my technical sketches at the Industrial Academy. To see if what is underneath the regular is true. High up in the Tsar's old apartments, I no longer know what is regular or true. Iosif now insists that I be driven to my classes at the Academy. I sense another Moscow, another life pulsating faintly beyond the pages of *Pravda* and the sessions of the Politburo which last into the night. I glimpse this other Moscow sometimes as I am driven along. I see a thin man with two rabbits in a cage. I see an elderly woman, a kerchief wound around her head, tending mushrooms in a ditch; I see policemen standing watch over tunnels for the new Metro. I telephone my mother at Zubalovo. She complains of the *kulaks* roaming the forests near the dacha. She fears that they have stolen eggs and bread. She warns me against informing Iosif.

Meanwhile, Iosif is concerned with public amenities in Moscow. He and Beriya foray into the streets at night sometimes, when Beriya has had enough of women and my husband has had enough of everything, and that is how it started, this obsession with public toilets, because one night, while Iosif was out inspecting the tunnels and the projects for the New Moscow, he suddenly found that he had nowhere to urinate.

He felt that, as General Secretary, it would not be seemly to piss in a ditch full of mushrooms. The next afternoon when he awoke, he was still furious about having to do just that.

And that is how the campaign for more public toilets began.

I attend a party for the comrades from the Academy returning from the Ukraine. I had waved them off, those bright eager faces, part of the twenty-four thousand mobilised to restore order in the countryside. I watched them leave. I watched them come back. They have stories to tell me and I try to suspend judgement. For I see that these are not the faces that were sent to the countryside. These eyes have a cast now, the eyes of young people who have seen too much. I stand politely nodding, the glass in my hand refilled, sad eyes encircle me. There is much drinking at this homecoming, but no joy. One by one they approach me and hand me their stories as if they are handing me a badge or a brooch or a medallion – something ornamented and sharp. I close my hand around these stories and my flesh is pierced. They speak of hunger like a virus, multiplying effortlessly across the wheatfields. Of whole families devouring their dead: of an elderly man roasting the tongue of his dead granddaughter over a flame. Of the slaughter of animals. They speak of impossible requisition orders calculated in the new manner from Moscow – 'the biological yield' which counts the wheat only as it stands before harvesting. They tell of peasants flogged and sentenced to death for hoarding an onion. One very young volunteer, no more than eighteen, breaks down as he recounts the raids on filthy hovels, the smashing of wood with crowbars, as every inch of the peasant houses were prised apart in the search for grain. *There is no more wheat in the fields.* The returned volunteers are adamant. *There is no more wheat to harvest.*

I stumble for a response: *But the* kulaks, I say. The kulaks. *Surely they are responsible . . .*

A young comrade interrupts me, puts a steady hand on my arm: *The* kulak *does not exist*, he says. *The* kulak *is a figment of the imagination. A* kulak *is a man who once owned a cow, a man who once* could never imagine eating his brother. *The village is full of* kulaks. *The rich peasant, the middle peasant, the village proletariat – they do not exist. There is only one class in the countryside: the starving.* He pauses. *And we have destroyed the villages. And I am ashamed of what I have seen. Of what I have done.* Inhaling deeply, he whispers: *Man-made famine. Tell that to your husband.* He removes his hand from my arm and I feel the pressure of it for days after.

I lean back against the wall. My glass is refilled. I keep swallowing the stories down. It is just before the time of month when I take to my bed for days with the iron taste on my tongue and a dragging in my womb. It is not the time for me to drink. I keep the needle-edge of their stories pressed into my palm. The lights bulb brightly above me. The mood lightens. We dance. The comrades watch me hopefully.

One of the instructors organises a car for me. I am carried into the Kremlin, singing, arms outstretched. I am a keeper of stories. For once, by virtue of my marriage, I can make a difference. For the first time in many years I have much to tell Iosif. I think to myself: so, this is happiness.

My husband comes in and sees me lying on his wheat-coloured *takhta* – the beloved Georgian sofa sent from his birthplace in Gori. He looks at me for a long time and then walks out of the room.

I wait, while the room turns. I expect something to happen.

He returns after some time and picks me up in his arms, his weak elbow behind my head.

'And now to bed, Nadusshka.' He is so tender with me. As he was in the first months of our marriage. My arms feel heavy and limp. I cannot move them. I feel paralysed by the alcohol and the responsibility of telling him that something must be done.

I look up at him, at his heavy face: *Iosif, the comrades returning from the Ukraine . . . the things they have seen . . . the hunger there . . .*

He seems shaken. Looks at me. 'Who tells you such things? If they poison my wife with vodka and fables, perhaps they also will poison her against me?'

'No, Iosif, no one poisoned me. They gave me their stories. I need to give them to you.'

'You're cursed.'

He carries me to bed and walks quickly out of the room. I remember weeping.

The day after the party at the Academy, my head hurt. The bleeding started. I looked out on to the Alexandrovsky garden and the first snow bending the trees.

I knew I had ruined everything. I had kept control for so many years. Now to have the whole thing unravel like a ball of artificial silk.

The deliberate introduction of disorder.

Iosif's suspicion of me would grow. Beriya would rub his hands.

I lie in my bed. I sleep and I wake with the pain of it. The latest copy of *Pravda* lies near my pillow. At 5 a.m., my abdomen aching, I turn the pages of *Pravda* and look at the banner headlines: *THE COUNTRY NEEDS TO KNOW ITS HEROES.* The new Party campaign is underway. The current heroes of Socialist labour are there. Thirty-two photographs of engineers, work-brigade leaders and aviators. My husband pictured alongside them.

I find that I have no interest in these heroes of Socialist labour.

Two days later, my fellow students, those comrades who went to the Ukraine, who gave me their stories, do not come to class. I do not see them again. I confront Iosif, who says he knows nothing of the habits of students who are too lazy to attend class. That he cannot supervise every detail. It is a branch matter. In the Party branch at the Academy, I raise their names with the Secretariat. They seem embarrassed by my request. Weeks later, my list of the disappeared also disappears from my work folder.

I again raise the issue with the Party branch at the Academy. They tell me that the young comrades have been dispatched once more to the Ukraine. Entrusted with a special mission. *Too important even to be discussed*.

I commit their names to memory. I recite them to myself. So that in the naming they will not be forgotten. I store these things away. I resolve to leave Moscow.

I take the children with me to Leningrad for three months. I leave late one night and Iosif does not know I have gone until the following afternoon. For three months he rings me daily. He sends letters and flowers. He woos me back. The Party members in

Leningrad treat me coldly. They know my husband. Cannot understand why I am away from him. I tell no one my real feelings. My family side with Iosif: *He is a good husband. Better than most. What more can you expect?* When the train arrives in Moscow, I step off the platform as if my knees have been broken. I hobble back into my old life. Iosif covers the children with kisses. The night of my return, after I have filled the lamps with oil, Iosif comes in to see me. His arm branches in an angry shadow across the wall and the force of it knocks me to the ground. *Don't ever do that again*, he says in a low voice.

I am a keeper of stories too dangerous to tell. My life is like a long chain of repeating molecules, under pressure.

THE OTHER MOSCOW:
MIKHAIL'S STORY 2
1932

MIKHAIL HAD PIECED it together in the months since his sister had delivered the news. The facts were that an inebriated Oskar bled to death in a public toilet in Central Moscow. Behind the death, though, behind the death? Mikhail still grappled with it. It was agreed that Oskar drank, although no more than most and it had never interfered with his work. Home was a mattress on a floor in a *baraki*, one of the draughty wooden buildings on the outskirts of Moscow. There were fifty comrades to a room, two square metres per comrade. They slept in shifts. He shared this floor-space with his brother, his sister-in law, the children and his wife. He rarely saw his wife. Working all day, working off his past, on days off attending meetings, he was fully absorbed by the Metro, the centrepiece of the new Moscow. Only by establishing himself at work, by showing himself to be an exemplary comrade, could he hope to move. This was his ambition. To move his family away from the squalor of the mattresses, the fights over the primus stoves in the corners, the smell of shit, the ooze of it coming through the ceiling slats after the top floor had been transformed into a toilet. All sorts of diseases ravaged their mattressed existence. He had admitted his error in leading strike action against the state. It was established that he had no connection at all to the Trotskyite Opposition. He had been granted a second chance. He did not want to squander it.

His plans were disrupted by something wholly personal. During his time in prison, he had suspected his wife of having an affair with his brother. Had whispered as much to Mikhail one day down in the tunnels. On the night he died, Oskar came home late after a day underground to find his wife in a tangled embrace with his brother. He stood in the doorway, gazing at them for a long time before they noticed him. The children and his sister-in law were asleep. He was drunk. His wife started up on one elbow, but before she could utter a word, he had kicked her back to prone, imprinted his boot on his brother's ribs, and then calmly stepped over them both, treading on her long fair hair as he did so. Then downstairs into the night, past a ditch full of mushrooms, oyster-coloured, down into Central Moscow.

Just that day, Oskar had been elaborating a scheme to deliver his family from the squalor of the *baraki*. He had stumbled across a disused coal shed, not far from the tunnel they were working on at Ulitsa Gor'kogo. He planned to transform it into living quarters for himself and his family, over two nights, by stealth, moving them in. Such appropriations of vacant space were happening all over Moscow. Broom cupboards and backstairs were being pressed into service. It was a good plan. He had invited Mikhail to join him.

That much was known.

Oskar stumbles into one of the new public toilets. A descent from the street. Past the still-gleaming urinal. He puts his left fist inside his sleeve and punches once, twice, at the new mirrors over the wash-basins. With a thin-edged mirror strip he shreds his wrist veins lengthways and slumps down to wait, slumping into a difficult darkness where he at last has room to think and to be. He is no longer a former *zek*, to be despised and pitied and shied away from. He has his own room, vacuum-sealed, the walls pressing against his chest. In his mind his wife returns to him. But as the pressing starts, Oskar tries to struggle up, remembering too late his father's gun and the ease of a trigger.

I T WAS 14 April 1930. For me, from that date, the pages of
Pravda started to signal dread. Under the old calendar, it was
April the 1st. I could even tell you the time: ten o'clock in the
morning. High up in the Tsar's old apartments, I shuddered as I
stirred my tea, watching the jam slowly dissolve, a pink eddying
around my teacup. My chest hurt, I felt unable to breathe. In the
streets, rumours gathered force, like drumbeats.

The next day, I opened *Pravda* and read about strikes by textile
workers in Bradford; strikes by railway workers in India; plans for
the Metro; plans for the reconstruction of Moscow. The growing
of soya beans and maize and the importance of these in the
national diet. On page five there was a small article about the
death of the poet Mayakovsky who had shot himself the day
before. The obituary stated that the suicide was motivated by
purely personal concerns. *The poet's social and literary life were not
factors in the suicide.*

People were shooting themselves then.

And this particular shooting reverberated in my chest.

After Mayakovsky shot himself through the heart, at 10 a.m. on
April the 14th, April the 1st under the old calendar, my life was
never the same.

Pushkin, Lermontov – these literary deaths I could understand.
They were from a different time. Before hope and the new order.
But Esenin, now Mayakovsky?

I had first seen the poet in March 1930, at Meyerhold's theatre,
for the Moscow première of *The Bathhouse*. Iosif had refused to

accompany me and so, as usual, I went with Polina Zhemzuchina, my good friend Molotov's wife.

I said, 'Polina, the man in the green overcoat – I am sure it is Mayakovsky!' My bodyguards turned to stare. People followed our gaze. Mayakovsky seemed thinner and taller than his photographs, his eyes carved out like a dolorous icon. I smiled at him and he looked at me for what seemed an embarrassment of time and then away again.

I did not understand why he could not return my smile.

I did not look closely enough at his right hand; fingers curled like an Old Bolshevik waiting to take aim.

Mayakovsky had decorated the stage and theatre with banners, provocatively positioned. In my line of vision was a large yellow banner with black writing:

Bureaucrats
Are helped along by the pens
Of critics.
Critics like Yermilov.

I could see the back of Yermilov's head, angrily twitching in the second row. It was Mayakovsky's revenge for Yermilov's damning critique of the Leningrad première.

After the first act, the audience remained silent. Some hissed and booed. There were murmurs of *Incomprehensible!* I alone was transfixed by Mayakovsky's dissection of bureaucracy. I clapped. The sound hollowed out around the walls. There was no echo. People filed out silently. Beriya stood in the foyer, coiled around a drink, speaking to Yermilov with hushed intensity. Polina Zhemzuchina condemned the play as petit-bourgeois, a disgrace. *Where were the ordinary Communists in the story?*

Mayakovsky left before the second act. His overcoat a green trace in the stalls.

Yermilov complained. Mayakovsky was forced by the Revolutionary Association of Proletarian Writers to take the banners down. In his suicide note, Mayakovsky said that he regretted the removal of the banner with Yermilov's name.

I went home and waited up for Iosif.

I saw the poet Mayakovsky tonight, in the crowd.

My husband's back stiffened. *Mayakovsky? Vladimir Ilyich never liked Mayakovsky.*

But, Iosif, I protested. *In 1917, the sailors sang Mayakovsky all the way to the Winter Palace.*

Iosif stared at me: *We do not ask where a man has come from but we do question where he is going.*

I knew then that the subject was closed and I would never see Mayakovsky with his hand raised in salutation. I knew then the meaning of his lonely green trace against the theatre curtains.

One month later, as the snow thawed and spring began, the poet frowned bullets at me from the pages of *Pravda*.

I, VLADIMIR MAYAKOVSKY
14 APRIL 1930

In this life, there's nothing new in dying; nothing new, of course, in living either.

Sergei Esenin, suicide note, 1925

Yes, the poet left a note. And at the time it was the despair of Esenin's last lines . . . I was preoccupied for months with how to neutralise their force. I laboured. I was fascinated, I admit that now, to have Esenin go before me. I longed to ask him – was it painful? Was it more painful than living? Later, in a poem dedicated to his memory, I turned Esenin's last words inside out:

> *Dying*
> *In this life*
> *Is not so hard*
> *Building life*
> *Is harder*
> *I dare say*

Three years have passed since then. Three years. And, as I look back on what I have written, I find that building this life was harder than I ever imagined. The times have turned me inside out.

Yes, Esenin went before me. What to say when one poet inserts himself into the lines of another? Esenin. Always looking for the clods of earth in the proletarian revolution. Clawing back in his memory for the peasant paradise of his childhood. A place that never existed, but which dogged his urban days. He could be as foul as any *muzhik* beating his wife. He beat Isadora until the circles pooled purple under her eyes – the same colour as her hair dye. For a lyricist, his imagery could be as coarse as unwashed teeth. That was his gift. But it was the Revolution that gave the *muzhik* a toothbrush. *The Revolution.* Esenin never understood that. The Revolution was never about the peasant. Was never intended to be. His country lyricism eventually shattered by the dissonance of the city, and Lenin's definition of Socialism: *Soviets plus electricity*, ringing like tinnitus in his ears.

That was the difference between us. When Esenin moaned:

> *The new road's asphalt fingers twine*
> *The village's soft throat about*

I laughed at him.

Progress, I sang.

I was always so certain.

Esenin was a poet who drank himself to death. But in his final note he blamed it on the Hotel Angleterre, for not providing enough ink. He was forced to use his own blood, he said. He was found swinging from a wall bracket in that hotel room, blood everywhere.

And yet now, after all my debates with him from beyond the Necropolis, after years of trying to counter his despair, I find that Esenin's last thoughts twine about my own. All that time refuting Esenin only to find that we shared a melancholy deeper than our differences.

What to say, when one poet inserts himself into the lines of another?

I left enough clues. I left enough traces. This is hardly unexpected.

Esenin's blue-eyed drunken rusticism. It comes back to me now, in this room, at this desk, with this gun.

Things happened to me. Or I happened to them. I'm not sure which.

Two women – first Lili, then Tatyana – happened to me.

The Revolution happened to me.
I happened to the Revolution.
It's all the same thing.

In early life I was famous for my clothing as much as for my verse. My mother sewed me the finest yellow shirt in all Petersburg. Single-shirtedly I became the emblem of the Russian Futurists. A declamatory revolution in gold. Even as a child I was bigger than I was. No one ever addressed me as a child. Women came to my large bed early. I was the tallest man in Petersburg. All my life I've been conspicuous, and now at the end of my life, I've seen two revolutions, and still I feel the loneliness of the clouds, and I'm still asking myself: *Where's someone like me to dock?*

I wrote that in 1916. And now it's the same old question posed anew. The dialectic of love and art and revolution. How I find myself longing for the negation of negation, for a new spiral to begin.

Tatyana was tall enough for me. When we kissed, our eyebrows touched. The deep groove between my eyebrows left a runnel on her forehead. Two Titans. We were a fit. But of course she lived in Paris. Together we would have dwarfed Moscow – I told her this and I was rewarded for my hubris.

In Paris, she married someone half my size, and half hers.

If I had brought Tatyana back to Moscow, if I had succeeded in satisfying Lili, would my life have been different? Would I have been able to tell the critic Yermilov, and everyone else, to go away, to leave me be?

I finally joined the Revolutionary Association of Proletarian Writers, an association I despised, because I was desperate to moor myself. Why could I never moor myself? They said of me:

Mayakovsky . . . has demonstrated his affinity with the proletariat. This does not mean, though, that Mayakovsky is being admitted with all his theoretical background. He will be admitted according to the extent to which he rids himself of that background. We shall help him in this.

The anchor of revolution began to drift. There was no place for me. I couldn't squeeze myself into their spaces. *What did they want me to say?*

Of course, first there was Lenin. People say: *no love between them.* I am the man who failed Vladimir Ilyich. In 1917, during the October Days, I watched him at work in the Smolny Institute. That huge forehead domed my future. I longed to capture the moment. *Comrade Lenin, could I paint your forehead red?* He looked at me as if confronting a madman. And yes, I was a madman. Intoxicated by the insanity of the times. Unlike poor Esenin, who was merely intoxicated. I ran around all Petersburg, erecting signs and banners, proclaiming the new order, proclaiming the new dawn. We held a meeting at the Smolny. The plaster cracking around us. Six of us. To pledge our artistic support for the Revolution. You see. I was there from the start.

It is true that Vladimir Ilyich never understood me. I admit that. It is true that he condemned one of my poems as 'absurd, monstrously stupid, and full of pretence'. But I had my supporters: Trotsky, for example. Trotsky once leapt to my defence. And to the defence of old Esenin. *Poputchiki*, he called us. *The fellow travellers* of the Revolution. The best damn poets in all of Russia were the *Poputchiki*. Trotsky understood that better than anyone. In 1923 he wrote:

> *We are well aware of the political limitations, instability and unreliability of the* Poputchiki. *But if we discard Pilnyak . . . Mayakovsky . . . Esenin – then what will really be left, apart from as yet unpaid promissory notes for a future proletarian literature . . .?*

How strange then, that Trotsky understood me. But Lenin never did. I understood them all, their revolutionary artistry. I also understood Comrade Stalin.

Too well.

Unpaid promissory notes for a future proletarian literature . . .

Do you know what a burden it is to understand too well? To love too well?

But I
mastered
myself
stepping
on the throat
of my own song

Love has many faces. Ideals and love can drive you to distraction.

It's true that the desire to slap the face of public taste never left me. The faces changed, that's all.

For this, the critics accuse me of satire that would be better directed elsewhere. Where else, I ask you? In my plays I fired a warning shot. There were toadies crawling all over. Men out to make themselves at the expense of other men. It had begun with the New Economic Policy and had never gone away. We were creating the antithesis of the Communist Man.

I believed in the creation of the New Man. I believed in my own attempts.

I feel that all I have done is work. What other poet can say that the Red sailors sang his couplets all the way to the Winter Palace? As I load the bullets, I hum a little, and tears burn behind my eyes at the memory of the singing: the beauty and the power of that day.

Here I am, alone in this room, with my memories of Esenin and Lenin and failure, the barrel of a gun against my chest. It is April Fool's Day under the old calendar. And I find I can no longer fool myself.

God, who never made me, left me stranded with a bulk that was meant to be stormed through. For two days now, I have sat here alone. The words have been rioting through me. Ricocheting off walls. I proclaim myself:

God failed me. I failed God.

Love failed me. I failed Love.

Taxman, let me tell you about poetry . . .

My sight-gun for words, all this time grafting rhymes from the gutter.

Surely, this merits me some concessions?

When I speak, time is circular. But words on the page are different. I find their permanence now chills me. I write for a tomorrow I can no longer envisage. Time on the page is like a necktie facing down, arrow-ended. I now find myself left with Esenin's cold bleatings: *The stern October has deceived me.*

But what could a *muzhik* know about deception?

If I can keep speaking, keep the words in the air, like the black-white throwings of dice on a table . . . I've always been a gambler . . . If I can keep the words floating like cards, like a deck spliced quickly between fingers, then time also floats and the good moments will come past again . . .

Lili's pale ovalness smiling at me after I had won at cards. Presenting her with a fox-trimmed shawl. Myself, not the fox so much as the puppy. I carried the shawl in my teeth.

I was the drummer of the Revolution. Esenin was the flute. I drummed away from myself and into myself and beyond myself. I drummed at the boundaries of myself. But still the boundaries held. I drummed for years against my own walls. I drummed up posters and epigrams. I kept the country informed during the Civil War. I knew my poetic-revolutionary duty. I slept with a log under my head in the offices of ROSTA, the Russian Telegraphic Agency. And if you look closely, under my hairline, there is a red imprint from those years of sleeping with such an unrelenting pillow. The times were unrelenting.

Some people, you know, want all art to be curvaceous harmony. But the times demanded the toppling of symmetry. The dissonance of the multitude; the screech of brakes; the caterwauling of factory sirens; the pulsations of electricity.

We excuse poor Esenin because he never understood all this.

And what is my excuse?

How can one be alone in a multitude?

Art makes life; it doesn't reproduce or reflect it.

I am not a mirror.

I am a distortion.

Esenin was a great smasher of mirrors and windows. Esenin, turning on me one night: 'Russia is mine, you understand, all mine!'

Esenin, scissoring through his own reflection.

'Take Russia!' I said. 'Take her, please. Butter your bread with her!'

Esenin, with his arm around Lili, looking to share the muse. 'Take Russia,' I shouted. 'But you can never take Lili!'

But Lili, like the pure impetus of revolution, like the dreams of something better, drifted from me.

I can see young Esenin, peering from under the folds of Isadora's skin.

Trotsky once said of me, 'In order to uplift man, he raises him to the level of Mayakovsky.' The critics can speak of *Mayakamorphism*. Let them.

Let them try to twist such a large frame into such a small space. I straddled the individual and the collective, embraced the seeming contradictions. These days, it seems, there is only individualism in ascendance. A more virulent strain.

Did I tell you all the places I visited?

Myself, tall as a skyscraper in Manhattan.

Paris, Berlin?

My non-stop speaking tours of fifty-two Soviet towns?

My tiredness? My bleeding throat?

Yes, the people's poet bleeds from the throat.

Esenin! Come bleed with me along *the sunken syphilitic streets*. But no. That was before the Revolution. Should I say it again?

I am the poet whose neck bears the revolutionary welt of late nights and endless agitation. Hold me.

I was the man who loved Lili.

I was the man whom Tatyana could not love.

I was the man who loved the Revolution.

I was the man whom Vladimir Ilyich could not love.

And now I find that love is the arrow of a time-server's necktie.

In my desk there are two thousand roubles – pay my taxes.

Lili, love me.

A T NIGHT I sit up in my room reading Mayakovsky. I cling to the last copy in Moscow as if it is a raft. I am still reading when Iosif comes in at 3 a.m. I push the book quickly underneath the covers. Iosif enters my bedroom in a fury. He throws a small newspaper on to the bed. I look at this newspaper. *BULLETIN OF THE OPPOSITION*. On the first page is an editorial, written by Leon Trotsky in exile:

WHAT IS STALIN?
This is the most outstanding mediocrity in our Party . . . His political horizon is extremely narrow, his theoretical level is equally primitive . . . he has the mentality of a dogged empiricist, devoid of creative imagination. His attitude to facts, to people, is distinguished by an exceptional disregard . . . Stalinism is above all the automatic work of an organisation.

Action is required, says Iosif. *The Trotskyist menace. Something must be done.*

I turn my face to the wall and close my eyes. *The Trotskyist menace*. I remember the last time I saw Trotsky. It was in 1927, at the funeral of my good friend Joffe. Joffe had long admired Trotsky. Had spent time with him on the train during the Civil War. I loved Joffe as a friend and comrade. He was the one person who had always shown kindness since my arrival in the Kremlin. I look at these connections. The meanings of them. Through my link with

Joffe, does this mean that I, too, am a Trotskyite? Does this mean that I, too, am a menace? These days, these times, confuse me. I must closely guard my own thinking. Far easier for me to sink back into the past.

It is November 1927. Trotsky and Zinoviev have recently been expelled from the Party. I walk behind the funeral car of my friend the Soviet diplomat, Adolf Joffe, famous for negotiating the treaty of Brest-Litovsk. He was the most elegant and careful of all comrades. We walk in silence. It is rumoured that Joffe shot himself because he could not bear the expulsion of these Old Bolsheviks, could not understand what was happening to his Party. I stand at the front of the crowd.

After the official address by a member of the Central Committee, Trotsky, Kamenev and Zinoviev speak. Trotsky seems subdued, the aura of arrogance dimmed. He speaks quietly and earnestly of the need for Party unity. He does not mention my husband. But one of his supporters in the crowd, an elderly Bolshevik, is angry. He interjects and catalogues the faults of my husband and the misrepresentation of the Opposition to the Party membership. I shift uncomfortably. Trotsky moves over to the interlocutor and puts a restraining hand on his shoulder and nods in my direction. Trotsky shrugs at me apologetically. I move closer to the coffin, I reach out to touch the brass handles, to say goodbye.

Outside the gates of the Novodechi Monastery, a military unit stands ready to fire a salute to Joffe. Outside, the elderly supporter of Trotsky runs in front of the unit and exhorts them to applaud the brave Comrade Trotsky, former leader of the Red Army. *Defender of the Revolution*. But the Army unit is full of cadets, freshly scrubbed and barely out of their teens. My breath stills, waiting to see what will happen. Trotsky, Zinoviev and Kamenev pause. Trotsky looks around defiantly, waiting for the applause that has accompanied him everywhere in his brilliant career. I, too, wait for the applause. Instead there is silence, and Trotsky looks up with awful eyes, moves through the cordon of men as still as trees, and bows his head into a waiting car. Kamenev and Zinoviev are shaking with disbelief.

When the car moves off, the young recruits gather round,

smoking and laughing. They are a new generation. They joke and laugh because they have a future without a past. They have not served in the Civil War. They know the name of Trotsky only as an Oppositionist.

'Trotsky?' I hear one of the young recruits say, shaking his head. 'On that train in the Civil War?'

Another jokes, 'And a train driver expects applause?'

I remember turning away.

And it seemed to me then that Trotsky was something magnificent, but spent, like the last of a species. It seems to me now that if Iosif had seen Trotsky that day as I did, the spectre of Trotsky, a man diminished, waiting for applause that never came, perhaps things would have been different.

The Trotskyist menace? I turn back to Iosif from my reverie. I look at him with incomprehension. I say, *It was spent in 1927. It was buried along with Joffe.*

Iosif does not care for my tone of voice. *Get up*, he says. *Refill the lamp oil, Nadezhda.*

This is my job. To keep the flame alight. I sigh. Slowly I swing my legs out of the bed covers. I move into our living room, past the space on the side table on which there is a pale circle of dust, showing that Iosif has been out of town and taken the bust of Lenin with him. The bust of Lenin always travels with him. I trace my finger idly through this space leaving a snail trail through the dust and move towards the large portrait of Lenin which dominates the room. Underneath is a small red votive lamp, which Iosif demands be kept alight at all times. I refill the lamp oil and walk slowly back to bed. Iosif walks behind me with the bust of Lenin under his arm and places it on the side table. He walks up to where the red lamp glows. As I turn round I see him with his head bowed.

Back in my room, I take off all my clothes and slide beneath the sheets. Again I take up my copy of Mayakovsky.

Iosif comes into the room and sees me reading. I put the book down, quickly, but not quickly enough.

He moves over to the bed. 'What are you reading, so late at night that you must hide it from your husband?'

'Nothing.'

He tries to pull the covers from me. I hold on tightly. Iosif's tongue pushes against my clenched teeth. He forces open my mouth, hand under the jaw. He inhales me, the scents of menstruation. He is tantalised and disgusted in equal measure. He recoils, accusing me: *You are bleeding.*

I nod.

For many years, my husband has not seen my naked body. Not since the arrival of his son. His second. His sons are nothing but a disappointment to him.

And I, too, am nothing but a disappointment to him.

My bleeding nakedness is my defence. The metallic taste on my tongue. Iosif drops the blankets, but puts his face close to mine. 'Tell me,' he says, 'is my wife a mad dog?' I struggle to push him from me. 'It would not surprise me if she were a mad dog, considering the mother.'

'My mother?' I look up at him, holding the blankets tightly. 'Why do you mention my mother?'

'Your mother claims she once walked through the end of a rainbow. Let me tell you, the end of a rainbow, that's not all the whore found!'

I, too, knew this story from my childhood, how my mother once walked out into a field and found herself glistening with colour. The golden rainbow feeling that had never left her. I protest: 'But, Iosif. She really *did* walk through the end of a rainbow.'

'Only when I was fucking her.'

I turn on him coldly. 'You're lying.'

'Ask her. You're either mine or Alliluyev's. Either way. You've got the curse of that old whore.' He walks out of the room.

Is he lying?

I find my hands shaking as I pull the colours of Mayakovsky out from the blankets.

> *But I mastered*
> *myself, stepping*
> *on the throat*
> *of my own song*

Iosif never liked Mayakovsky. He always preferred the simple rhymed poetry of Georgian folk-songs. And now the new words to old songs – the *noviny*. I hear him humming a *noviny* in the next room as he soothes our daughter back to sleep:

> *The Five-Year Plan*
> *Is not a twig*
> *It must not broken be*
> *For the Five-Year Plan*
> *Both little and big*
> *Are ready to fight, you see!*

My daughter is clapping her hands softly, sleepily, to the rhythm of a song that is now popular all over the country. I pull the pillow over my head and wait for the clapping to stop.

You are safe now. I speak to the poet as if he is here with me. I slide the book between my underclothes in the second drawer. Underneath the woollen stockings and above the small Walther pistol, wrapped in a velvet pouch: a present from my brother, bought in Berlin.

Stepping on the throat of my own song.

When Mayakovsky shot himself, were the walls red with words?

I wake up from a terrible sleep.

My mother. I must ask my mother.

It was from my beautiful, fanciful mother that I first developed my scientific interests. My mother would disappear, for weeks at a time. I would see her skirt run past the window, her hands in a hasty sign of the cross, and she would be gone. My father would lift me on to his knees and comfort me. 'Your mother,' he would say. 'Your mother is special. It would be wrong to stop her.' One time I was in the Petersburg streets holding my father's hand and I thought I saw a woman, short and beautifully proportioned like my mother, striding quickly along on the arm of a very young Red Army officer. 'Mama,' I called and tugged his hand. 'Mama!' My father looked over and the woman looked at us with my mother's large grey eyes and away again. 'That is not your mother,' he said gently. 'It is someone who looks like her.'

When my mother was away I was allowed to play with the things in her special drawer. My father gave me permission. She had a beautiful mirror made from shellac. It was ochre-coloured and very light, a perfect oval like my mother's face. What is shellac? I asked my father. I thought that if only I looked into the mirror long enough, understood its properties, perhaps my mother would see me and return.

From the Railwayman's Library he brought me a book, which showed natural and man-made materials. I spent many hours with this book. It was my companion when my mother was away. From this book I learnt that my mother's mirror was made from the secretions of the lac beetle which lived in certain trees in exotic, warm places, far from Petersburg. Since ancient times, shellac had been used to make wonderful things. It could be moulded and compressed. It could be mixed with slate dust or wood flour and pressed into heated decorative moulds. This was the beginning of my love affair with plastics.

I told my father what I had learnt. He called me his little scientist.

When my mother returned, I searched her pockets. 'Lac beetles?' My mother scooped me up. 'Such an imagination!'

She shook her head and smiled. And passed me to my father. He smiled and kissed her and we were all happy, because at that time we all believed that my mother, wherever she had been, always brought the magic back.

My father was always mending things and putting things to-gether. People. Objects. His marriage, also. He understood his wife's absences. When I was old enough to understand, he explained: 'Your mother was a free spirit, a follower of Alexandra Kollontai. For her, monogamy was bourgeois. I can understand the thinking behind it.' For Papa, that was always the most important aspect – to understand the thinking behind an action, to put it into some sort of ideological framework. 'I've been with your mother since she was fourteen and I was twenty. When you have known a person for that long, you know them and forgive them anything.'

In old age, of course, he felt differently. Everything was different.

My mother was religious and a revolutionary and saw no contradiction in her faiths. She was emotional and gregarious and deft and quick. The youngest child of a German Protestant family in Georgia, she was oddly unrestrained, as if she had been unleashed on the world prematurely and was always trying to grow into it, pushing it hard. I was very different from her. I was emotional, romantic, even, but more restrained. I could not express things so well.

My mother wore amber beads around her left wrist. Sometimes around her left ankle. She could make a new dress out of three old ones. She was special. She was a free spirit.

By the time of my visit, my mother the free spirit and my father the mender of things lived at opposite ends of our dacha at Zubalovo. By this stage of their lives, they were quite estranged. Over time my father complained of always waiting for her. Of feeling neglected. 'I was a Communist in my head, but unfortunately, my heart was another matter,' he once confided. 'It took me years to realise this. But believe me, I tried. It was a problem for all of us in those days. You see, I could agree with her intellectually, but in my heart, I wanted her to be mine. To be with me only. For a long time I tried to hide my real feelings.'

The years corroded my parents, the bond between them. But it was never completely severed.

On the day I visit she is sitting cross-legged on the floor, cutting a dress pattern for my daughter, full of complaints about the mismanagement of the household. 'There are so many people here, the dacha full of people. We don't know any of them. We don't trust them. But they seem to trust us even less.' She sniffs. 'Tell *that* to your husband.'

She looks up from her scissors, appraising me carefully. 'But this is an unexpected visit.'

'Yes,' I say. 'There's something I need to ask you.'

'Well then.' She puts her head down and resumes cutting. 'Ask.'

I feel my heart grow small and then large again. That constriction. 'Mama,' I say casually, 'how long have you known Iosif?'

'Too long.' She sighs. 'A long time. As long as your father . . . many years. I remember once, when you were two years old, you almost drowned in a river in Baku and Iosif rescued you . . . So, a long time. Yes . . .' Her grey eyes hold mine. She smooths the tissue-pattern with her fingers.

'Iosif says that you slept with him.'

My mother closes her eyes and leans back on her elbows. She steadies herself.

'It is true that I preferred Southern men.'

'Were you intimate with Iosif?'

I see her swallow hard. I am still unprepared for her answer.

'Yes,' she says simply.

'When?'

'Before you were born. I was with your father also. I was easily infatuated.'

'Is Iosif my father?'

'Don't be ridiculous. You don't look anything like him.'

'But you're not sure?'

She puts the scissors down and in one movement has positioned herself at the window, tying back the sash and letting air circulate around us. Busying herself. 'You look nothing like him,' she says. She lifts her wrist to the window to inspect the dark amber beads and does not turn round as I leave the room.

I feel cursed. From that moment. I run out of the house and down the path to the waiting car, choking, while my still-beautiful mother inspects her amber beads.

'A gun?' In 1930, Iosif had looked disbelievingly at Pavel, my brother. 'Why would you buy your sister a gun?'

'She may need it one day.'

'For what, exactly?'

'For self-defence. These are dangerous times, Iosif, I have heard you say as much. Your young wife needs protection.'

'She has protection. She has bodyguards. They can protect her.'

'It looks like a toy,' I interrupted. I loved the feel of the tiny pistol in my hand. The handgrip inlaid with ivory. 'It is my beautiful toy. Thank you for my beautiful Berlin toy, Pavel!'

Pavel accepted my kisses. Iosif picked up the gun in his large hands and aimed it at my forehead. I stood very still and listened to my breath. 'A woman's gun.' Scornfully he said this as he took aim.

'It can't do much damage.' He handed it to me and then walked out of the room.

Pavel whispered to me about the bullet. *It has one bullet. To be used only for times when roulette is needed.*

It won't be needed, I say. I am well-protected here.

Yes, said Pavel. *I can see that.*

I had not thought consciously of the gun in some time. Now I take it out often and look at the ivory inlay in the handle. It is still beautiful. Most things in my life are no longer so beautiful.

THE OTHER MOSCOW:
MIKHAIL'S STORY 3
1932

F OR MONTHS AFTER, Mikhail wondered about the death of his friend Oskar. He had heard other stories, of other deaths. There were even rumours that Nadezhda Alliluyeva, Stalin's wife, had committed suicide. A darker version had Stalin pulling the trigger. These were difficult times. It was here in the cloying silence of his own apartment that he could understand his friend's decision. Out there, underground, in the real world of Socialist Reconstruction, in the business of building tomorrow, there was no time to think. It was only in his dreams that he could think clearly.

Mikhail wakes sweating, in the middle of the night. He tries to focus on the tasks for tomorrow, away from the undertow of the personal, those visions of Oskar, which threaten to drag him out into strange waters, away from himself.

He has some important proposals to consider. For many months they have been digging shallow open trenches, according to the so-called German system. Treacherous work impeded often by underground springs and saturated earth. Now, a young engineer on the project, a comrade he respects, has spoken to him about changing the plans. But wasn't it impossible to change plans at this point? The young engineer had raised a radical proposal to switch to the deeper, closed-tunnel English system. The English system had the advantage in that they could tunnel right under buildings instead of being confined to the main transport lines. This would solve the problems of the underground springs. Then there was the question of how to transport passengers. Already there were plans, according to the German system, to build elevators. The young engineer, however, favoured escalators, like the ones at Piccadilly Station in Central London. Escalators would entail deep drilling, were more expensive, but in the event of a war, the deeper tunnels could be used as a defence.

The more he thought about it, the more he favoured the closed-tunnel system and the escalators. He hoped that the officials of the *Metrostroi*, the Metro Trust, had been cautious, had signed documents in pencil and not ink. He would speak with Khrushchev tomorrow. If they could convince Khrushchev, they would have a chance with Stalin, the *Khozyain*, the boss.

He starts drifting off to sleep again with these calculations. He wakes some hours later, with the face of his friend Oskar floating through his dreams, covered in gold leaf. He sits up. He slides his boots off his feet, his socks damp and putrid. He looks at a plate of cold mushroom stew that his mother left by his mattress hours ago.

Soon it will be dawn. Spring. Another day. His friend, Oskar, is not in this day. He thinks of all the times he dared not look at Oskar. Sometimes negating the very existence of his friend. Now he does not have to worry. The rationing of his friendship with Oskar is over. Numbly, he wonders why Oskar did not use a gun. He puts the spoon to his mouth and starts eating and chewing. The food has no taste.

He forces himself to think of other things. He speculates, idly, about his prospects for marriage. He dreams of it, but it seems unlikely, given his tunnelled all-male days. There is only the certainty of work and more work. The solid beauty of malachite and porphyry and onyx inlay on the walls, the dream of the mosaics and cupolas of the soon-to-be Metro. There is the romance of this huge construction project that will outlast him. This is his contribution. This is worth everything. What else is there?

He has seen a woman at a branch meeting in Moscow. If she could only wait until the completion of the Metro, maybe they could get an apartment. Priority, after all, was for married couples.

He resolves to shake himself out of this mood that has gripped him since the news of Oskar.

He imagines his sister's face, mouth distorted, hands full of ration cards, in front of a Party tribunal. His mother's face collapsing.

He imagines a room to himself.

The thought pleases him.

THE ANNIVERSARY
NADEZHDA TAKES AIM
NOVEMBER 1932

T
ONIGHT IS THE banquet to celebrate the fifteenth anniversary of the October Revolution. We are to attend a Politburo dinner in honour of my husband. There are many new faces in the Politburo now. There are few old faces.

My husband is in a good mood. He is drinking more than is usual. He looks over at me and says, 'You – why aren't you drinking! You know, gentlemen, that my wife holds her drink like a sieve holds water – ask her comrades at the Academy!'

For some reason, I bite back, in front of all these new and eager faces.

'Iosif,' I say angrily, 'I am still your wife.'

Iosif flinches. No one has spoken to him like that in years.

Beriya whispers something in Molotov's ear. I can feel myself wanting to force disorder.

'Let my wife drink up to the Glorious October.' Iosif sneers this at me and moves to fill my glass.

'No, Iosif, really.' I place my hand over the glass.

Drink, he says.

Drink, he repeats.

I remove my hand. I raise the glass and the vodka slices through me.

Again.

Iosif, please . . .

And then there is a voice: 'It would be my pleasure,' and the air suddenly thickens and Beriya is moving towards me, a bottle in his hand. I feel him circling behind my chair. He leans over, his belly pressing into me. He places one hand in a friendly gesture at the back of my neck. The pressure of his fingers like a noose. With the other hand he pours the clear liquid into the glass. Beriya increases the pressure of his fingers. I have no choice. All eyes at the table turn to me. I raise my glass and drain it. *Again*. Beriya is insistent. The procedure is repeated. He then removes his hand and glides back to his seat. We stare at each other for what seems a long time. I close my eyes and stand up. The alcohol takes hold and everything drops away. I rap the table with my knuckles, draw attention to myself. Beriya's pince-nez gleams like a fat moon.

Everything drops away: 'To the memory of October,' I say. 'We mourn its passing.' The Politburo members are silent.

Their heads hammer in my husband's direction.

Stalin rises. 'Gentlemen, I think my dear wife is confused tonight. This is a *celebration*. Raise your glasses!'

There is relief evident in the stamping of feet, the clapping of hands and the slapping of backs.

I drink another glass of vodka quickly and then another and when I am finished I bring the glass down so heavily that it shatters in my hand. As my friend Polina leads me out of the red-panelled room, I turn round with a bruised voice and say, 'We mourn its passing.'

Stalin does not look at me. He addresses his audience: 'As I said, my comrade wife holds her drink like a sieve holds water.'

Polina Zhemzuchina leads me out of the room as the laughter breaks above me.

It is a cold November night. Polina walks me around and around the grounds of the Kremlin until my breathing steadies. My arms feel heavy. Soon it will be the time of the bleeding and this knife-edge anxiety will ease. I feel the vodka flowing cold through my arms. I cannot move them.

Polina puts me to bed. As my husband had done months earlier. *Does he love me?*

I weep on my friend's shoulder.

'He lives for the Revolution.' She says this simply. 'You, too, must learn to live for the Revolution. To love the Revolution. There is no other way.'

The Revolution is a harsh mistress.

Polina is shocked.

To spare her, I say, *Forgive me, Polina. Thank you. Go back now. Apologise for me.*

Polina looks at me with anxious eyes.

Truly. Go now. I will sleep.

'Goodnight, Nadusshka.'

I hear my friend's soft worried footfall where I am accustomed to the heavy step of my husband.

He will not come home tonight.

Tonight, I will slide my hand into the velvet pouch in the second drawer; my fingers will close around the present from my brother. I will feel the cool of the ivory inlay in my palm. I will wait for Mayakovsky's smile to reach me. Together we will spatter the walls red with words.

Iosif Vissarionovich sleeps late and fitfully. His wife's behaviour at the anniversary dinner has deeply unsettled him. It is afternoon when he wakes, drives from the Kuntsevo dacha to the apartment at the Kremlin to find Polina Zhemzuchina and his old house-keeper crying in his living room. He notices that the lamp under the portrait of Lenin is out of oil.

He nods at them. His head is thick with the drinking of the night before.

'Comrade Stalin, we have something to tell you . . .' his house-keeper starts.

Stalin looks at her, without listening. 'Call Nadezhda,' he says. 'Tell her the lamp is out of oil.'

Polina Zhemzuchina steps forward. 'There has been an accident, Iosif . . . that is why I am here.'

Stalin looks at her, eyes pinched with suspicion.

'Accident . . .?'

'Iosif . . . Nadezhda shot herself last night . . .' Polina Zhemzuchina's voice falters and falls.

'And did she succeed?'

Polina Zhemzuchina nods unhappily, tears sliding. The house-keeper sinks to the floor, her hands cover her face.

Stalin turns on them, his mind reels through the list of those who could be held responsible. That such a thing could happen in his house! He fixes on Polina Zhemzuchina: 'But you were the last to see her . . .'

They lead him into Nadezhda's bedroom. A book of Mayakovsky's verse lies open on the dresser; the second drawer is open, a velvet pouch lies empty. The side lamp is still on. The curtains are still drawn. There is a letter addressed to him in his wife's hand. His wife lies elegantly crumpled on the floor, one arm outstretched, a tiny pistol under her fingers, the fingernails crimson, dug into the Georgian carpet, now dark and sticky.

He looks at the prone figure of his wife. He moves to pick up the envelope on the side table. His head hurts as he feels the dehydration of alcohol and loneliness slowly take hold.

Polina Zhemzuchina is not to be trusted. He makes a note to himself.

He turns away. 'Clean it up,' he says.

In his living room, Iosif Vissarionovich Stalin sits very still, staring at the samovar and the letter in his hand. The letter is brief and full of recriminations. She blames him for everything: for not loving her enough, for the famine in the Ukraine. The hunger in Moscow. Even the death of Mayakovsky. He drinks a cup of inky-coloured tea, crumples the letter in his hand and feels the anger of betrayal overcome him.

And so, the chemist thinks she is a poet? Stalin shakes his head, and shreds the letter. To think that for many years he had shared his bed with this Judas! This was the keenest betrayal of his life.

In *Pravda*, his wife's death is reported two days later as a sudden illness. The housekeeper is dismissed, along with the rest of the staff at the Kremlin apartments.

Stalin, the members of the Politburo and members of the family come to view the coffin prior to the memorial service. Stalin walks halfway towards the coffin, then turns on his heel abruptly and leaves. He looks into the large grey eyes of her mother as he passes. He sees a child falling into a grey river in Baku many years before. He sees himself, wading in to help. He does not stop. He does not attend the memorial service. He does not visit her grave at the Novodevchi cemetery.

For weeks he sits alone in his study. He summons her brother to the house and shouts at him through the drink. 'Wasn't I a good husband?' He opens the drawers to his desk and Pavel Alliluyev sees envelopes stuffed with rouble notes. Stalin points to the money. 'I spend nothing. She could have had anything she wanted.' Stalin rips the drawer from the desk and piles of rouble notes flutter to the carpet. 'Wasn't I a good husband?'

'There was nothing more that you could do.' Pavel Alliluyev stares at the rouble notes on the floor.

'She was cursed. It was in the blood.'

'As you say, comrade.'

'Before you leave, I have a present for you.' He hands Pavel Alliluyev the Walther pistol wrapped in a cream towel soaked in blood. 'It needs cleaning,' he says and Pavel Alliluyev walks out of the room cradling the blood-soaked towel.

His last image is of Iosif Vissarionovich Stalin kicking rouble notes around his study as if they were autumn leaves.

THE DIARY OF
LEON TROTSKY IN EXILE
COYOACÁN
JUNE 1940

THIS MORNING I watched Jordi working on the old truck. He was methodical, as always, slipping the spare tyre out from underneath, assembling the tools beside him; the jack, the spanner. I watched him replacing the old hubcaps, kicking them into position with his boot. For the first time in many months, there was an ease between us, and we spoke of our love for all things mechanical, his visits to his father's workshops as a child in Massachusetts, how he played with the spanners and loved the smell of gasoline, the revving of engines. And I tell him of my own childhood memories of a very different machine shop on the farm at Yanovka; of horses and carts, of the beginnings of electricity; from a time before time.

In the mechanic's hut, there was laughing and shouting. After the day's work was finished, it was a magnet for all the labourers on the farm. I was young, the young Lyova, and I loved the camaraderie and the acrid smell of vodka steaming out of tired pores. The mechanic, Nikolai Pavlovich, showed me how to turn a lathe, how to dance, how to swear and roll up my sleeves. He showed me how to cut the threads off nuts and bolts, how to fashion a screw. He even allowed me to grind up the material for paint, rolling it with a round flat stone particled with many colours, like a hen's egg. Nikolai Pavlovich watched me closely at the grinding, stroked his red beard, and then afterwards, lifted me down from the bench to stir the thick white mixture with a stick, as if I were the family cook.

I loved the machine shop. The different world. The ease. I wanted to understand it. For I sensed that that place, full of nuts and bolts and tools, was the template of the future.

The machine shop was full of wonderful things. There were jars of marbles and butterflies pinned under glass. Buckets full of nails and tacks. Hacksaws and hammers. Coloured sand in small cylinders. Objects bright and strange which Nikolai Pavlovich had salvaged and collected. That machine shop contained the world. It was so different from the world of my parents.

I would spend hours climbing the split wooden crates, the backs of chairs and wheel spokes piled high in one corner. I fashioned boats and cabins to take me to imaginary lands. From a young age my dreaming took me to other places.

But the most beautiful thing, I tell Jordi, was a block of limestone which stood in one corner. Nikolai Pavlovich had inherited the limestone from his uncle, a lithographer. He loved that stone. He would lift me up on to the workbench in the corner to look at it. Together we would marvel at the stone's memory. For it was soft and porous and absorbed ink. An impression of each drawing penetrated beneath the surface of the stone. After each impression the limestone was rubbed down to remove the drawing, in preparation for the next one. But portions of a drawing sometimes seeped up again to the surface after the stone had been rubbed down. 'Underneath is what is important,' Nikolai Pavlovich said to me. 'Not everyone is lucky enough to have a memory-stone.'

And we would look at the memory-stone and fashion stories from the patterns there. The fragments of drawings pushing up through other drawings.

When my parents were busy supervising in the fields or bargaining with *muzhiks* over the price of grain in the mill, I spent most of my days following the red beard of Nikolai Pavlovich, who loved me and could remember the night of my birth. When he wasn't working at his tools, the mechanic was often at this block of limestone, inking his own drawings of machine parts, of wheels, of farm implements on to the stone and then later rubbing the impression he had made, looking for a revelation underneath.

Years later, crossing the country by armoured train, I looked out on to the steppe of Kherson, running beneath the wheel tracks. I felt parts of myself seeping to the surface, like old ink on limestone. And it was the machine shop: the paint grinding, the sawdust on the floor, the cobwebs strung like nets across the ceiling, the lithographic stone and all its memories that came back to me.

I remember a night in which there was no dancing or laughing. The time of the night-blindness and the start of my political education. I remember walking into the mechanic's hut and in the corner of the hut three men turning eyes dry as grain upon me. They blinked rapidly. In the glow of the lamplight, they could hardly see my neat outline – the blue shirt, the carefully combed dark hair. The three men were in various stages of blindness. They cursed David Bronstein, my father, for spending less on the food of his reapers during harvest than any other farmer on the Kherson steppe.

I listened in astonishment. Although I had also thrown this accusation at my father, I had been uncertain. Now I felt torn. Wanted to protect my father. *No*, I said to a young man with eyes foamy and opaque, eyes like milk rushing from a cow's udder. *My father is a fair man. He gives what the other farmers give.*

The third man, older, had risen shakily to his feet. His eyes were too terrible to look at. An egg-white membrane remained where once there was blue. He turned to me. 'Three years ago, we came here to work for your father. For four months we moved with our scythes for him, for twelve, maybe thirteen hours a day. He gave us grain to eat. Your horses ate better. After some months, the light faded behind the eyes. We pleaded with him. Some red potato. Some cabbage. Some fruits or a small portion of meat. Then the night came into day. We three sit here in darkness. It is true that your father feeds his labourers no worse than any other farmer in the district. But also no better. And the result, over these years, is that we are all slowly reaping into darkness. Feeling our way, with the edge of our scythes, like animals of habit.'

I looked into the faces of the men. I was still fighting the charge that somehow my father had caused all this suffering. I argued, with passion, that this was the way things were. I tried to echo my father's views. *My father must run the farm carefully – or next year there will be no work.* My friend the mechanic silently turned away from me lifting the jar full of marbles to the light overhead, turning it slowly. There were three pairs of eyes upon me; their retinas melting and milky with accusation. I looked at them and felt that I could no longer defend my father's name. I turned to them. Ashamed.

The oldest of the three spoke. 'We must show your father that this cannot go on. Tomorrow we will not work. We will wake the other reapers before dawn and sit outside our huts until we get better food. Food that will enable us to see in the dark. Food that will help us to continue.'

The pressure of the eyes upon me and the pressure in my head grew too great. I jumped up and ran outside.

And Nikolai Pavlovich told me later that the men feared that I would tell my father. They feared that none of them would work ever again.

But Nikolai Pavlovich reassured them. 'No,' said the mechanic, who knew me better than anyone. 'He understands now. He will go to his bed, he will think about what we have said. He will say nothing.'

I had dreams that night of eyeless men and scythes that transformed themselves into animal shapes. In the morning, I rose with the cockerel. My father was already awake. I remember ribbons of light in the sky and a hard silence everywhere. Outside, rows and rows of men, their bare cracked feet upturned, sitting with their rusty scythes across their knees. 'Get to work,' my father was shouting. 'I have a farm to run.'

'We need more food. And better food.' I recognised the old man with the egg-white eyes from the night before.

My father stood still. He could not understand such defiance. He wanted to stand there forever until they all starved. But he had to harvest the grain. He had plans to rent more land. He wanted to expand even in the face of the Tsar's *ukaz*, which said that no Jew could purchase land any more, even in the steppe. Two hundred pairs of eyes, blind in the night, were upon him. And the blue angry eyes of his son.

'I am not a rich man.' He pleaded with them. His hands cut the air and he looked over at the wheatstalks bending under pressure of dawn.

He turned and walked back in the direction of the house. He returned with my mother carrying bags of dried fish and huge watermelons and potatoes red as the sun. The reapers stood up, formed rows, and my father quietly distributed the dried fish and the watermelon and, from a large pot, my mother ladled vegetable soup with a little bacon. No one spoke and the men with the egg-white eyes and cracked yellow feet filled their bellies and returned to work, humming to themselves in the early morning air.

This scene was repeated every morning for the duration of the harvest.

A week later the fat *zemstvo* inspector from Odessa rode up to our door. Alarmed by what had happened on our farm. *The blindness was caused by not enough fat in the diet,* he challenged.

He left later that day, his pockets a few roubles heavier. In his report for his superiors he wrote: *The labourers on the Bronstein estate suffered night-blindness owing to excessive vodka consumption.*

My father felt relief to his fingertips.

It was the beginning of my political education.

I felt anger hum through me as I looked out into a morning scythed with rust.

3

THE MEMORY STONE

DAVID LEONTEVICH BRONSTEIN
CIVIL WAR: THE ROAD TO ODESSA
1920

'YOUR SON HAS a big heart.'
 Another old man who has lost everything walks next to the large farmer from the Kherson steppe. 'His heart does not extend to his family.'

David Leontevich Bronstein has a long march ahead of him. He does not wish to talk about his famous son, for whom he sacrificed all and received nothing. It is the folly of parents, he thinks, to believe that the sacrifices for their children will be rewarded.

My son.

I named the boy after my own father, Leon, who had left the town of Polatva to settle on the steppe. One of a handful of Jews, splintering the steppe with their hard work. The urban Jews felt superior to him. They called him *Am Haaretz* – a man of the land. *Yes, I am a man of the land!* I remember my father's voice, booming around the town on the day we left. The curtains of the village watching us go. My father ignored the real meaning of *Am Haaretz* – lacking culture, boorish, a man unacquainted with the Scriptures. It meant nothing to him.

 It meant nothing to me. I built myself up and surpassed my father, surprising even him with how hard I could work. With hard work and Anna at my side, we were happy. The child inherited our hard work and stubbornness. But no one could sneer at him as *Am Haaretz*. No, my son became a man of the city. He turned away from the land, turned back to the places his grandfather had left.

My son leapt from his mother's womb, dark and perfectly formed, on the 26th of October 1879. I was there. I saw the way the child hurled himself out, head first, his hands flailing, grasping for air, his mouth open. Thirty-eight years later, to the day, I hear news of my son in Petrograd, hands flailing, mouth open and millions of people flying on his words. The night he was born was a full moon. The cows walked in circles. The chickens laid eggs. The older labourers cried out, and walked over to their scythes, cutting the ground in their sleep. Everyone was affected. My wife recited words from the Scriptures: *bone of my bones, flesh of my flesh*, over and over, the words easing the pain. After he was born, I walked outside to look at my land, the white beam of the moon across it; the small stables, the millhouse, the hut where the young mechanic Nikolai Pavlovich worked and lived. I heard my son squalling into the still night and felt proud.

I went to wake Nikolai Pavlovich, but when I arrived at the hut, he was already awake, buttoning his shirt, smiling at me. *Yes*, he said, as he opened the door, and embraced me, although I had not said a word. *Your boy will make the moon run backwards*.

That morning, Nikolai Pavlovich had almost cut off his thumb while cutting millstones. I remember the thumb attached to a few tendons dangling in front of him.

Nikolai, who knew all about nuts and bolts, who could rebuild engines and re-string the spinet, who was fascinated by all things mechanical, knew little of nature and the body's regrowth. For me, it was the opposite. I knew little of machines and more of nature from years of working with animals and men on the farm. And so I bound the finger for him in cloth, and called the doctor to attend him and I could hear him questioning the doctor.

'Do you think? Really, the finger will grow back?'

In later years, Nikolai Pavlovich liked to confuse the two events. 'At the moment of your birth,' he would tell Lyova, 'I cut off my thumb. And when you came crying into the world my thumb grew back.'

No wonder my son thought he was special.

The child was bright and strong. He could have had the land. He could have become an engineer and been of use. Now the land belongs to the state. But who is the State? What does it know of the land? What are its intentions?

I think of my tall handsome son home from Odessa for school holidays. His head full of books, full of the city. The changes in him.

I remember the summer when Lyova changed. Then there was no stopping him. He came home from school in Odessa. He was wearing glasses. I said to him, 'There is no need for eyeglasses. There is no one on the farm that wears eyeglasses.' I was dismayed by my son who, overnight, adopted all the softness of city people.

'Papa,' he said. 'I am nearsighted.'

'From the books. So you need these glasses only with the books. Now come to the mill and help me argue with those *muzhiks*.'

Lyova was furious and followed me to the mill with his new glasses in his pocket. When it came time to weigh the grain and do the calculations as he had done every summer since he was small, I saw the glint from his pocket as the eyeglasses were brought out and balanced on his nose and he suddenly looked older, my son, and I felt him move away from me.

He weighed the grain and calculated the labourers' wages. And for the first time, with those glasses on his nose making his eyes larger and smaller at once, he calculated too high.

'We cannot afford it,' I said. 'Do you want me to lose everything?'

The things he called me! *Papa*, he said. *The labourers have nothing. You have money enough.*

As if I had never held a scythe in my hand! As if I didn't spend from dawn to night working. I always saw to it that they had enough. But it was not enough for Lyova.

With those glasses, he saw us all differently. That was the beginning. But one time stands out from the others: the time of the night-blindness.

Lyova, home for the school holidays, stood outside watching as the reapers filed past, thin as stalks, swaying like wheat in the twilight, arms outstretched, touching the shoulder of the man in front, some with eyes open, some with eyes shut, and all of them blind.

'It will pass,' I said to him.

My son, back from the city, turned on me with eyes of the accuser. In Russian he said to me, 'Do something.'

'I don't understand you,' I said.

He spoke slowly for me, in a mix of Ukrainian and Russian, as if to a child, as if I were an idiot. Full of anger. 'They work for you all day and you repay them with oats. Now they cannot find the way back to their beds!'

I spoke slowly back to him. Mixing the Russian with my language, like the chaff with the grain. 'I am no better and I tell you no worse than any other farmer in Yanovka. If I fattened them with meats and breads and the finest fruits, would there be money left for your education? Would my son come back from Odessa, speaking in a language better than his father? Would my son have glasses on his nose from too many books?'

My son spat on the ground in front of me and ran to the mechanic's hut. Sometimes, I envied Nikolai Pavlovich. Lyova felt closer to him than to me, his own father. I sat down, calmly, and Anna warmed the samovar and I watched the reapers, single file, making their way to the huts, stumbling like the sleepwalkers on the night of my son's birth, and I thought to myself: if there is a God, in his eyes, I have done nothing wrong. I have provided for my family. I have provided my son with a good education.

I was not guilty. Why, then, did my brilliant son, who with four eyes could calculate as fast as a comet, try to heap guilt upon me? There was a natural order and flow to life. There were those who had more and those who had less. For working hard, for having more, I became suddenly a criminal. Later they would call me a *kulak*.

After we sent him away to the school he lost his feel for the rhythms of the seasons and the land. He became attuned to the rhythms of page-turning and timetables and traffic through dirty streets and the white pulse of electric light. A different pace of things. On the steppe, I moved to the rhythm of sowing and reaping and turning indoors towards the fire in winter. Everything went on as it had before. The *muzhik* put his head on the dirt of his pillow, entered his wife night after night, and woke in the morning, still a *muzhik*, with an extra mouth to feed.

That was the way of things.

Lyova understood these things as a child. But after we sent him away, he grew too clever. I blame Anna with her low whispering over the Bible, night after night in the winter, Lyova listening to her whispers and watching her long fingers underlining the words as she went. Now he knows – how many words does my son know?

But does he know the meaning of a season with no grain? Does he know the meaning of no food in the belly? Does he know the meaning of losing everything you have worked to build?

Now everyone is lost and on the road.

Now we all have nothing. We share misfortune. Some call this Communism.

There is an order to everything. It is not ours to disrupt the order. Lyova came back one summer, even angrier than the summer of the night-blindness. He had fallen in with a bad crowd. Trouble-makers. In the village that summer he saw a *muzhik* beating his son, blood running over the son's eyes. The son was being beaten for an offence that the father had committed. Lyova was repelled by this violence. It did not seem right to him. But I told him that it had been right for these people for centuries. They had their own system of justice. Who was he to interfere?

My son turned away in disgust: 'What kind of a country is this? Tsardom breeds savagery. The Tsar must go. He will go in my lifetime.'

I said to him, 'It will never happen. Not in my lifetime. Not in yours. *Not in three hundred years.*'

Already, I feared for my son.

I T IS ALMOST midday and Trotsky hears the sounds from the street. In the kitchen he hears Natalia, carefully placing pots and kettles for the meal, conscious of not disturbing him. It is Sunday. He consults the flip diary on his desk with the red letters. From beyond the walls, children's shouts echo. Sunday – the meaning of it in Mexico. A day of families and respite from work. A day of children in best clothes and ribbons and clean faces upturned for communion. He had seen Sundays, from the back of the old Chevrolet, himself and Natalia hidden under a blanket. Driving through Coyoacán, he had seen families in cafés and in restaurants, the conviviality of it. The ordinariness of it. Sometimes he wondered and hankered after such ordinariness. But then the very idea of it, to be a father on a Sunday, carving meat, ordering a meal for a family, seemed impossible. He was never destined to be such a father, with his belly pressing against a restaurant table. Full, satisfied. He was never destined to be surrounded by such a family. His breath came shallow at the thought of the life he had led and the lives he would never lead. And he picked up the empty dictaphone cartridge on his desk and looked through it, a black cylinder, and looked around his study through the prism of the cylinder, one eye squinting, like a sailor through a telescope; a photographer through a lens. He put the cylinder to his mouth and blew a sound through it, like a child. He put it up to his ear and listened through it. He played with the cylinder and this playing made him forget himself at this desk in this place. The sounds of children, arguing over the toss of a flattened tin can, filtered through to him and energised him. He felt a desire, insane, he knew, to smash through the leadlight panes of the door throwing diamonds of light on his desk, to run out into the garden, and to keep running.

He idles back in his chair. The black dictaphone cylinder in his hand. He turns around in his seat and looks at the large map behind him, bringing the cartridge again up to his eye. Looking through it. Trying to see things differently. REPUBLICA MEXICANA. The blue of the Gulf of Mexico. The lime colours of the land. He looks at the map with the eye of an explorer. Or the eye of a film director. Eisenstein maybe. He puts the cartridge down and stands up to inspect the map more closely, the way it curves down and away from its northern neighbour. How Eisenstein had loved this map. The visit of the film director came back. It still brought him pleasure. He looked at the places on the map he had visited with Eisenstein that day: the hills around Taxco, the columned cacti, those sentinels of landscape. He remembers dust over his shoulder, carrying enormous cacti like bundles of firewood, dust on his boots. Eisenstein framing him with his hands. Eisenstein wanting to capture them both, scrabbling at the roots of desert plants. It had been a hot clear day. And he felt happy with the memory of it. A moment out of time. The two of them in that moment. History would not record it. There were many whose visits to Coyoacán remained unrecorded – their signatures too dangerous for the visitors' book. But he had the memory of Eisenstein scrabbling in the dust, marvelling at the variety of cacti. He had pointed out his favourite to Eisenstein – an elongated cactus topped with strands of sparse snowy hair – *el viejito* – the little old man. The name speared his heart. It was all in his memory: '*Viejo*,' Frida would say, playfully messing his head of white hair and white beard. The archives of the mind. That unofficial record – Frida, Eisenstein – they were all stored there. Like the hermeticists of old, he built a memory palace in the mind; storing people, places, things. He imagined the illumination of his memory palace. How the light cathedraled across ceilings; all those spires and arches of light. How no corner was dusty.

His friends and family, those left behind in the Soviet Union, had burnt all their archives. A whole generation had cinders for memory. Small bonfires, it was said, could still be seen around Moscow and Leningrad on clear nights. Small inexplicable fires. Photographs from the past. Old letters. Telegrams of congratulations from Trotsky perhaps, or any of the old Bolsheviks. Whatever these small voluntary immolations achieved, the archives of the mind were the most difficult to destroy. As long as he could sift through those, assemble and categorise these images, construct his memory palace, he knew he was alive. He had purpose.

He looked over his rough-hewn table. So many tables. His exile was a record of these working surfaces. The pens and pencils in a jar. The ivory blotter. The gooseneck lamp. The dictaphone. The Colt .38 that he kept oiled and reloaded in the drawer, always, wherever he happened to find himself. Under the desk, he felt for the switch that would trigger the alarm system, newly installed after the May attack. The couch in the corner with the green-striped blanket folded for his daily siestas. How life expanded and contracted then settled on a room with a table and the light coming through.

He puts down the dictaphone cartridge, stands up and stretches. Fortifications are almost complete. He leaves his desk at midday to go out to inspect the digging, the noise. He stands bareheaded in the strong light, inhaling the scent of the eucalypts beyond the wall. Natalia comes up to him and wordlessly hands him his white cotton cap, to shield him from the sun. He holds it in his hand a minute longer than is necessary and a look crosses her face – will he take the cap? – and then he decides to put it on and she smiles at him, one of her rare smiles, a perfect thing, and disappears back into the kitchen.

Since the May attack, the house has become a fortress. Twenty-foot walls are constructed. Double steel doors with electronic switches replace the old wooden entrance, three new bulletproof towers are erected to dominate the garden and give a view of the surrounding neighbourhood. Barbed wire tangles across the top of the walls, broken glass pushes up through cement. The Mexican government triples the guard on duty. The American Teamsters Union also send extra guards.

Trotsky confounds them all. He had earlier vetoed a weapons

search. Now he vetoes Jordi Marr's proposal that he never speak alone with anyone in his study. *This is not a prison*, he says, annoyed at these suggestions. *This is my home. Natalia's home. Either we trust the people we admit, without a search, or we do not admit them.* Some comrades protest at the danger, how it is never really possible to trust everyone, to know everyone. But the Old Man feels confident that an agent from Stalin would be easily won over, easily won away from the pedestrian arguments of Socialism in one country. In the midst of all this activity, on this Sunday, he wanders about the patio, inspecting the changes, suggesting improvements. He paces the paths alone, carrying on conversations in his head with people who can no longer answer him in person.

This small fortress in Coyoacán reminds him of his first prison. The time when his father had come to see him and had seen him caged. The terror in his father's eyes. How long ago it seemed now. And what would his father have made of it all? Here now in a Mexican town, with the sounds of drilling and hammers and Spanish invective. The labyrinth of a life.

He sees Sylvia's boyfriend, Jacson, at the gate, waiting to pick her up, chatting and exchanging cigarettes with one of the guards. He moves over to the gate, greets Jacson, asks him his views on the fortification.

Jacson pauses, looks over Trotsky's shoulder. 'Yes . . . very impressive . . . but do you think it will be enough?'

'More than enough.' Trotsky is adamant. 'If we can survive an attack like the last, we can survive anything.'

'Yes . . .' Jacson sounds unconvinced. 'As you say.' Jacson looks at Trotsky and then down at his feet as he stubs out the cigarette. 'Good luck with it all,' he says quietly, in accented English, and smiles, as Sylvia comes through the gate and kisses him on both cheeks. 'Regards to Señora Natalia,' says Jacson, and walks off towards his car, parked at right-angles to the house, with an adoring Sylvia on his arm. Trotsky watches them leave. Thinking they make a strange couple.

DAVID LEONTEVICH BRONSTEIN
CIVIL WAR: THE ROAD TO ODESSA
1920

'CAN SOMEONE TELL me,' says David Bronstein, rubbing his hands by the fire, 'how we came to this?' He looks about him at the people banking up across the steppe, the way the *muzhiks* once banked up outside his mill for weeks, waiting for their grain.

'Ask your son.'

'Yes – that son of yours – ask him. He has an answer for everything.'

Voices are raised in weariness and indignation. He looks around him. There in the corner is Zaslavsky and his family. Neighbours. Now they, too, have nothing. Fleeing. From the Whites. From the Reds. It is all a politics that none of them understand and even fewer can read about. As for himself, David Leontevich Bronstein is proud of the fact that he can now trace letters with his forefinger and can pronounce the titles of his son's books.

Whether he is proud of his son is a different matter.

His son. He sighs and thinks of his young Lev Davidovich, his Lyova, the famous Trotsky, at that moment on the opposite side of the country, a military cap on his head. His son, urging victory, travelling by armoured train; words shooting out of him like stars.

Meanwhile, he thinks to himself, I am an old man walking to Odessa, seeking refuge. I will tell my son that I am too old to care. I am too old to start again.

*B*eyond the facts, I always looked for laws. These words, dream-fragments, are in my head this morning as I look out of the train window, the tracks pulling away behind us. I am in the editorial compartment, scanning the latest issue of *V Puti*, the daily newspaper produced on the train and distributed to soldiers at the front. The headline demands: *BE MERCILESS*. I am pleased with this headline. For three years we have crossed the country like this, agitating, educating, organising. Dispensing newsprint and support. In three years, with these distances, we have circumnavigated the earth five times. My friend Joffe calculated that for me. For a period he joined us on the train. Along with the librarians, the archivists, the artists, the editorial staff, the mechanics, the cooks, the medics and the detachments of volunteers. We have been mired in mud. We have been attacked by Cossack bands. In my blue compartment a large map covers one wall. Tiny red flags mark the territory . . . Samara, Chelyanbinsk, Vyatka, Petrograd, Kiev, Smolensk . . . We have driven through these placenames, our wheels have run smoothly over the syllables.

In the editorial compartment there is the incessant key tapping and coding and the uneven crackle of the telegraph wire. This room is at the centre of our operations. A wireless fizzes like an insect in one corner. The aerial from this compartment transmits from Moscow, from Petrograd, even from Paris, from the *Tour Eiffel*. It is a very sophisticated operation. *The train*. The mention of it terrifies our opposition. We are a metropolis on wheels. We have a garage. Full of armoured cars, munitions, and spare petrol canisters. At each stop, the volunteers load into the cars and travel from the train, with our newspapers, our supplies, our moral courage. The Red Present Commission dispenses boxes full of gifts for the comrades at each front. One whole compartment is full of these gifts for the soldiers. These are the rewards: scarves, felt boots, cigarettes, razors, watch straps, pencils, pocket torches, binoculars, waterproof cloaks. But the most valuable items, the most covetable, are the leather caps of the train comrades and the red metal stars badged to our shoulders, commissioned specially from the Petrograd mint. These stars are large and gold-tipped. There are never enough of these badges.

Our detachments travel many hundred versts from the train. We always remain connected by telephone and telegraph. Just the knowledge that the train is on its way is enough for the comrades at the front. And at each stop, I appear at the door of my blue carriage. Soldiers mass below me. I exhort, I inspire, and I threaten. I am greeted rapturously. Each performance leaves me exhilarated and exhausted.

On the train we wear full uniforms of black leather, belted at the waist, fashioned by the best tailor in all Moscow. Each week the comrades polish their jackets and trousers until they gleam like metal. All of this is important. The care I take with this train. The appearance of it. The appearance of its occupants. These details send a message to the enemy. It is a message to the comrades also. To the stalwarts and to the waverers. For we come bearing gifts and funeral wreaths. Rewards and punishments in delicate balance. And when the doors slide open, no one really knows what to expect. Even the most loyal comrades tremble. Everything gleams, everything is ready. We will not be defeated.

The train once belonged to the Tsar's Minister of Communications. At my orders the soft lighting and opulent furnishings were removed. I wanted the train spartan but comfortable. The troops sleep on green-leather couchettes, bulbs dangle from the ceiling. I see to it that they are well fed. Men cannot fight on an empty stomach.

The interior of my carriage is the only extravagance. The colour mixed to my specifications. I was insistent. Blue. A deep indigo. A deep soothing blue, to enable me to face the days of blood and greyness. With my mind calm I can impose discipline. I can act decisively. I can enforce the death penalty. For it is impossible to run an army without the death penalty. The train is an avenging machine. Deserters from the train, from our armed detachments, know this. For our life here, sliding along these tracks, is the Soviet Union in microcosm. We can afford no deviations. We risk everything. There are few deserters, but those who run do not run far. A bullet to the head and face-down in the mud. When our enemies come across these former comrades and see their end, they know fear. When they see us slide open the metal doors, a deadly black phalanx, they know that we mean victory. We are proud of our uniforms. Proud of the train, this well-oiled machine: the Soviet Union in microcosm.

Many times our enemies have tried to switch the signal faults, to derail us. We have survived the shells and aerial bombardments. Once, the Whites succeeded. The front carriage overturned and a young sentry was pinned under the wheel. His leg required immediate amputation. I remember the black leather boot, knee-length, left by the side of the track, the stump of his calf still fleshy inside. We were lucky, yes. But we were disciplined also. At the gates of Petrograd I fought alongside the men. I was on horseback. I was wounded in both legs. At night they pain me still. But I always lead from the front, this is what the comrades expect. Our soldiers need this example: our leather uniforms and arms full of newspapers, our rifles and cigarette cases. It is an education for the whole country. The enemy cannot defeat our train. This is a fact. For the ideas we spread are like a fusillade of bullets, lodged in the memory for ever. It is a war of ideas. We can slip back into servitude and ignorance or continue to go forward with our great proletarian experiment, an inspiration to the world.

Forward or backwards, I say. *These are the choices.*

At the end of each day I lie back in my leather suit in the blue compartment. I raise my legs on cushions to ease the pain. I surround myself with literature. I plunge into the Paris of Celine, the world of Jack London. I feel myself to be new. This leather is my new skin. I have cast off Lyova, son of a *kulak*. I have cast off my

Menshevik beginnings; that soft intellectualism, that indecision. I have proved myself a man. A true Bolshevik. No one can take this away from me. In war, men discover themselves. It is an important lesson. In a revolutionary war, you test your limits, you see if they hold.

If not, you find yourself prone and bloodied in the mud. The choices are stark.

Typhus is ravaging the country. We distribute medical supplies; we transport teams of doctors and nurses. I hear news that thousands of displaced comrades, my father among them, are walking to Odessa. In two days we begin the assault on General Wrangel's French fortress in the Crimea. The Crimea is the final front. We whistle 'The Internationale'. And a young comrade who is oiling his rifle turns to me and says quietly, *After Wrangel and the French have been defeated you will prepare for your next battle.* I am surprised. 'Where,' I ask, 'with whom?' The comrade looks at me carefully. *With Comrade Stalin.* I laugh. 'It will be more a minor skirmish than a battle,' I assure him. I admit, during the Civil War, I have made enemies. In war, one makes decisions, one does not make friends. I had complained to Lenin of Stalin's handling of Tsaritsyn. For Stalin was no tactician, I told Lenin as much. Already, I know the rumours; Stalin is using my enemies, whose decisions I have overturned, against me. But I am confident. I am Trotsky, Chairman of the Revolutionary Council, victorious. Impregnable in a black-leather suit and an armoured train. I have circumnavigated the earth five times in three years, I have tested my limits, gone beyond the possible.

There will be no future without me in it.

DAVID LEONTEVICH BRONSTEIN
CIVIL WAR: THE ROAD TO ODESSA
1920

THE FATHER OF the Chairman of the Revolutionary Council sits down by the side of the road. He is wearing odd shoes, both of which are too tight for him, and his feet are swollen from the walking. He still has many versts to travel until Odessa. He wonders what his son would think of him, seeing him in those shoes. His son, from an early age always so meticulous about his appearance.

Next to him, an old man, a man his own age, has also paused to rest. The old man asks him if it is true, if he is really the father of the great Trotsky. He would like to know more about this Trotsky. What kind of man is he? David Bronstein tells him that he cannot speak of the man, he can only speak of the boy he knew. He tells him about the fastidiousness of the boy.

I remember my wife's brother, Moissey Filopovich, coming to visit Yanovka. My son, very young, was even then very conscious of appearance. His shoes had two large holes from which his toes, pink and small, shone through after his bath. He looked up at the man from the city and tried to hide his feet under the chair and would not come to meet him.

'Moissey Filopovich,' I said. 'My boy is sensitive about the state of his shoes. And only five years old!'

My wife's brother laughed and picked up my son, now red-faced. Out on the steppe we never troubled about such things. From birth I worried that my son had a woman's sensibility. I sent him off to live with Moissey and his wife in Odessa. My son was very bright. The best schools were in Odessa. He had many opportunities there, and it was the best day for Lyova when we sent him away to school. It was the saddest day for me.

The second time I saw him blush like a girl was with the scythe.

Whatever my son says, I was never afraid of hard work, and I believed it was my place to set an example. It was the school holidays. My son arrived. It was a wheat-hot day towards the end of summer.

We drove out into the fields on a day when the harvesting was in progress.

My son wore a cream suit, freshly laundered, with a brass belt buckle, new in the sunshine. He wore a white cap with a butter-yellow trim. His shoes were brown leather, softly buffed.

We stopped in front of my chief reaper, Yuri. He looked up at me and then from me to my son. My son in his city clothes. Yuri in his worn trousers, his grey cloth shoes with the grey button. I could see what he was thinking. The amusement on his face. Yuri decided to test my son.

'Can the boy reap?'

'Of course,' I said to Yuri. 'He has been raised on the farm. He may look like a boy from the city – but that is only surfaces.'

Lyova shifted uneasily beside me.

'Get down,' I said to him. 'Show the reapers how it is done.'

'I confess,' David Bronstein says sadly as he looks at the old man next to him. 'I confess, at that time, I wanted to test my son with his new clothes and Russian ways. But why did I do this? To see how far he was moving away? To drive him even further?'

The old man next to him scratches at his arms and shrugs. 'We only know such things later.'

Lyova stepped out of the cart and into the road. His shoes were covered in wheat-dust. He moved towards Yuri and picked up the scythe as I had seen him pick up a pen. I turned away, wanting to help the boy. Knowing that he could only help himself.

Lyova looked desperately from Yuri to myself and back again. His cap bent to the task. Delicately at first and then with increased desperation, trying to winnow the stalks and fend off the reapers' scorn. He cut the grain too high and too little. And then stopped. 'More heel,' I urged him. 'Lightly now, with more heel to it.' I saw his heels dig in, gracelessly, and the boy slowly listing into the earth, like a stillborn calf. He lost balance heeling himself in too deeply. Sweat on his forehead. I can still see him, the look on his face, as he handed the scythe to Yuri who wordlessly handed it to me.

I shouldered the scythe and leant into it with my heels lightly resting on the earth, my toes spread, and I put up my face to the sun and breathed deeply before bending from the knees, and I motioned like a breeze through the wheatstalks, for some time losing myself in the rhythm, and I looked up to see the toothless laughter of Yuri and the blue tears of my son. We hardened against each other that day, my city son and I.

Yuri said, 'The sons have much to learn from the fathers.'

Lyova turned round and walked back towards the cart, tightening his belt buckle and wiping his eyes.'

'That is a story.' The old man next to him is appreciative. He chuckles. 'Young Trotsky, eh?'

David Leontevich Bronstein thinks of his son's eyes. He thinks of the boy who belonged to him in the time before Trotsky. The things a father knows.

'My son has very beautiful eyes.' He finds himself saying this, unexpectedly, to the old man. He thinks to himself: *my son's eyes take on all the meanings of blue. The brilliance of summer, the coolness of winter, the slate colour of snow at twilight.*

'I have another story,' David Bronstein says. 'About his first stay in prison.' The old man next to him nods encouragement. And David Bronstein continues:

I remember his first prison time, when he was relocated from Nikolayev to Odessa prison. After some months I was able to visit him. I travelled by steamer to Odessa. By this time he was twenty and had been in prison for over a year. I walked in to see him. The guards standing behind, like fence posts in a field. I looked to see which shade of blue my son's eyes would be, but I was unprepared for what I saw.

Lyova in a wooden cage. Lyova reaching through the double iron bars to talk to me. I grasped his hand which was filthy and black. My son itched his arms the whole time. There were other men in cages. I could hardly speak. He checked my reaction.

'Papa. I am not in here always. It is only for visitors.'

'Farm animals have more room than this,' I heard myself saying. I could not believe that everything we had given my son had come to this – a life as large as a packing crate.

I could not believe that my son who had grown up roaming the steppe like a horse could be so confined. I felt ashamed at the distance between us and the iron bars in front of him.

'Why so pale,' he asks me with concern, 'are you ill?'

I hung my head. I pushed back the tears. I am a simple man who only wanted for his son to be near him. When he moved away from me, I wanted to teach him a lesson. Now I wanted to hold him.

But the time was past.

I said to him, 'Your mother and sisters worry for you. They send their love. Nikolai Pavlovich has had another child.'

'I am glad to hear it,' he said. 'I send my best wishes.' He extended a thin arm through the bars. He was formal and far away.

Then the time for visiting was over. I wondered when I would see him again. The guard led me out of the room. I turned round one last time to say goodbye. I saw the blue of my son's eyes through the metal bars; the colour of a storm passing on a still day.

I finish my stories and we walk on in silence. It is still many versts to Odessa. Beside me, Sofia, Lyova's old nurse, stretches out a hand covered in black spots, like dark pebbles on sand. She asks me for water. She is hot, she says, although all around her are shivering.

'Typhus, war fever,' someone says. 'The whole country is dying of war fever.'

I close my eyes and hold out my hands to the fire that our group from Yanovka has built. I hope that no one will mention the name of my son.

In the morning, Sofia is feverish. This continues for two weeks.

All around me, people are scratching blood channels into their skin. The old man who asked for stories about my son goes crazy from the scratching. We bury him by the roadside.

After six days Sofia is covered in red welts. Our little group from Yanovka tries to comfort her on the road. At night we see the red welts on her feet come alive in the glow of the fire; Nikolai Pavlovich claims to see the lice dancing bronze over her skin. He, too, is starting to hallucinate. The woman moans in her sleep. She longs for the raven of childhood tales. The raven that provides succour for the hero, who delivers us from death; the black succouring sweep of a wing.

We were many when we started out. Yuri the chief reaper, Tatyana the cook and her husband the steward. Nikolai Pavlovich, his wife and babies. Now, weeks later, as the port city comes into view and we limp towards it, we are few. I am glad that my wife never lived to see us driven from our home. I carry the last of Yanovka with me. I have the mule strength and stubbornness of the *kulak*, as my son would say. It has sustained me. I have some headaches and some confusion, but I have the farmer's strength. I cannot die until I see my son again. I have lost everything but my son.

War fever. Typhus. People scratching, infecting themselves from morning to night. Scratching the faeces of the insect into their skin, burying it deeper and deeper into their bloodstreams, everyone with crimson fingernails, scratching themselves to the grave.

I was the only one from Yanovka to finish that long walk. At the time, my son, who does not believe in miracles, thought it a miracle that I had survived.

LEV DAVIDOVICH BRONSTEIN (TROTSKY)
ODESSA
1898

YOUNG LEV DAVIDOVICH paces around his cell, tapping the walls to see if somewhere in the bowels of the prison there will be an answer. He is aware, for the first time, that he is a long way from the farm at Yanovka.

He is in prison for revolutionary activities. He is waiting for a visit from his father. The last time he had seen his father . . . but when was that last time? When his father had burst into the hut? His father with the smell of manure about him, laughing at the clean young men in their filthy room.

His father had looked around the room where they all slept and lived and ate thin stews and put in a few roubles for drink in the evenings. Over the backs of chairs he saw blue smocks flung and on the backs of doors round straw hats on hooks. Around the walls black canes and the thin boots of factory workers were arranged. In the town he had heard whisperings of his son's involvement with a *secret society*.

'Playing at revolution?' he boomed. 'Running away from your fathers also?' he said to the other young men in the room. His huge farm boots trod over the newspapers and pamphlets; he searched under blankets until he found his son.

'Are you coming back to Yanovka?'

No.

'You stop taking my allowance, you move into this filthy hut and listen to an old gardener who hates the Tsar. Are you mad?'

No.

'What are you doing with your life?'

'I have told you before. Things change slowly. The Tsar will not go. *Not in three hundred years*. And what is so wrong with this Tsar and this time that I could send you to Odessa, that you could go to the university, that you could go so far beyond your father that the smell of grain is now only a memory?'

You know there are many things wrong with this time.

David Leontevich Bronstein sees the hostile young eyes flash up at him from behind the stack of papers and pamphlets. He does not understand anything any more. This is his last attempt to save his son, to bring him back.

'So. I must tell your mother not to warm the samovar for you, not to set a place for you this summer? I must tell her that you are wasting your life?'

Young Lev Davidovich draws his knees up in front of his chest. He looks sullenly down at the ground and does not look up until he hears the heavy boots of his father and the smell of manure leaves the room. He looks around at the others. All of them laughing at the smell of his father's boots, at his father's coarse Ukrainian accent.

The last time he had seen his father.

He had not returned to Yanovka that summer. To a place where no one read, except for his mother, from the Bible, a little in the evenings. To a place where the main preoccupation was the price of grain at market. To his father's obsession with work and money. *I don't like money*, his father once told him, *but it is bad to need money and not have any*. The endless round of the seasons and of toil. The counting of roubles, the weighing of grain, the arguments with *muzhiks*, the half-starved labourers. His mother's hair dusted with the flour from the mill; his mother leaving white puffs in the air when she walked. Lev Davidovich was glad to leave it all behind.

No, he had not returned to the farm at Yanovka that summer. Instead he had helped to form the Southern Russian Workers' Union, distributed anti-Tsarist propaganda and found himself jailed for his efforts. His real life was just beginning.

The Odessa prison library is stocked with bibles and religious literature in many languages. Lev Davidovich reads them all. In

Russian, in Italian, in German, in French. He reads the polemics of Orthodox writers against Voltaire, against Darwin, against atheism. He learns from them the importance of exactitude; of aiming words like arrows. He laughs at their attempts to define paradise, to plot its dimensions: *Exact definitions about the location of paradise are not available.* He repeats this to himself, shaking his head over and over at the absurdity. As he taps the walls of his cell he thinks of the folly of seeking a paradise outside of man. The blood and sweat of workers and peasants could create paradise. Paradise could be arrived at through organisation and discipline. But the location of paradise?

He had seen paradise in his mind. Part of him knew the exact location. It was a solid material place. A place of the future. A place of humanity.

. . . While this planet has gone cycling according to the fixed laws of gravity, from so simple a beginning, endless forms, most beautiful and wonderful, have been, and are being, evolved . . .

After reading Darwin for the first time he knew that his mother's sibilant prayers had been a waste. He knew that there was no god but the god of faith in human progress and humanity. In prison he reads the religious arguments against Darwin. He is drawn to this Darwin, under attack from the theologians.

All organic beings which have ever lived on this earth have descended from some one primordial form, into which life was first breathed . . . These elaborately constructed forms, so different from each other, and dependent on each other in so complex a manner, have all been produced by laws acting around us.

The laws of nature. He was enthralled by Darwin's understanding of the peacock feathers: a vision of purple and green rationality, deftly layered, obeying the laws of nature. From his boyhood he remembers seeing peacocks on the farm of a ruined aristocrat near Yanovka. How he would climb up on to the fence and look over, the turquoise tails swaying out of reach. The beauty of them.

Evolution and revolution.

The mutual interdependence of all living things.

Order in beauty. The laws of nature. The laws of history.

He had much to thank Darwin for. The plumaged prison dreams of Odessa stayed with him for many years.

DAVID LEONTEVICH BRONSTEIN
MOSCOW
1921

TWELVE MONTHS LATER in Moscow and I have a job on the periphery of the city. I am a manager in a small state mill. It is very different from my previous life. There are no sly *muzhiks* haggling for grain. Instead there are blue-capped workers with vodka concealed in their pockets. The Commissar for Food, Tzyurupa, a large friendly fellow, comes by to talk to me about agricultural matters. I know that my son has sent him. He tries to make me feel useful. I tell him about the days on Yanovka, of the *muzhiks* trekking for weeks to have their grain ground in my mill. I tell him of the land I leased from the gentry around me who crumbled into nothing and did not know the value of hard work. I speak of that different world, before the Revolution.

Tzyurupa listens to me as a young person listens to one who is older. Our conversations always finish in the same manner. 'You must feel very proud to be the father of Comrade Trotsky.'

'Yes,' I nod, the wheatfields in my eyes and a young bright Lyova weighing grain in my heart. 'Any father would be proud of such a son.'

But I am not any father and Lyova is not any son.

I make my way on foot to the Kremlin. My son is to receive the Order of the Red Flag for his services during the Civil War. His famous train and all the soldiers on it are decorated also. People come up to me and grasp my arm. All around me people are cheering wildly for my son.

I confess. At that moment I felt proud. My son, who had slipped away from us at Yanovka, who had slipped through the bars of Tsarist prisons, now commanded an army. How the child becomes a man.

There is another name read out. Iosif Vissarionovich Stalin. There is a silence. Behind me I hear low voices. 'But Stalin? The Order of the Red Flag?'

'Tsaritsyn,' somebody whispers back. 'They say he saved Tsaritsyn from the Whites.'

There is whispering all around me. Another man moves to the podium, accepting the award on Comrade Stalin's behalf. I see my son, Comrade Trotsky, look away into the audience, a shiver of a smile on his face.

These things I do not understand.

Afterwards, I move towards my son and we embrace. He smells clean and new and his eyes have seen a great deal. I am moved to warn him. Of what I cannot exactly say. But I fear for him. How quickly things turn, like the seasons.

After, we talk about my work in the mill. My son is full of the victory of the Civil War. His eyes are blazing, the blue of a summer sky. He is happy.

'Remember, Papa,' he laughs. 'You said that this would never happen. Not in three hundred years. Now, look around you . . .'

I say to him, in my slow way, in Ukrainian, 'For now, boy, there is change. Whether or not it is for the good. We shall see.'

I see my son flinch. Whether at the language or my meaning I am not sure.

Civil War, he says. We were surrounded by hostile imperialist forces. We could have lost everything we had struggled for.

The words hammer from him. I feel angry.

'Everything *you* had struggled for.' I remind him of this. 'Everything *I* struggled for was already lost. The Whites burnt down the farm. Before the embers were cold, the Reds came through and took all the grain. Don't give me your big words.'

My son, revolutionary leader, hero of the Civil War, looks at me with the cold hard gaze of an animal caught against a fence: *You had plenty to lose.*

He says this and walks off down the red Kremlin carpet. The shine on his leather boots stays with me.

Out on the steppe, no one has boots that shine.

THE DIARY OF
LEON TROTSKY IN EXILE
COYOACÁN
JULY 1940

Life . . . is not an easy matter . . . you cannot live through it without falling into prostration and cynicism unless you have before you a great idea which raises you above personal misery, above weakness, above all kinds of perfidy and baseness . . .

I wrote these lines in 1934. Before the deaths of all my children and all my old comrades. I return to them often.

Sometimes, I confess, it is difficult to continue. I cannot sleep. The nights stretch out, the only release is chemical, to be found in the yellow bullets of nembutal, the sleeping pills slaking the mind's activity, slowing me enough for a few hours' rest. There is so much to be done and each day is a reprieve and I say as much to Natalia, but her mouth turns down sadly, because it is not over.

War. Nine months have passed since we sat, faces close to the short-wave radio, listening to the first news of the German torpedoes and the sinking of a British submarine. I write it loud, this war, a clarion for the world, the horror of it and the opportunities it presents. In the spring of 1939, I wrote in the *Bulletin of the Opposition:*

Having destroyed the Party and decapitated the Army, Stalin is now openly advancing his candidature as Hitler's chief agent.

How this came to pass. How Stalin bought an uneasy peace with Hitler, a truce which cannot hold. The world proletariat abandoned to Fascism while Soviet Russia protects itself – the logic of Socialism in one country. And I will pay for this prescience, this I know. With Europe at war, will the waiting be over? How long will the Kremlin allow me here, with my pamphlets and accusations speeding to them from across the globe, from a room suffused with light and the shadows of jacaranda?

And it amuses me that the view from my window now, constrained, smaller, still seems to be the view of the sun and the light and the freedom, yes, the freedom of the house before.

The Casa Azul. The house before: the patio, the two courtyards and outbuildings formed a perfect blue rectangle out along the Avenida Londres and the Avenida Berlin. The windows facing the streets blocked in with adobe bricks. The blue rectangle that enclosed me for a time and made me feel safe. The blue embrace.

The time of the house before seems like the last time of my youth and *she* was responsible, blood filling my veins like ichor. For six weeks, at the age of fifty-nine, one last dance with youth.

Selfish, yes.

To throw it all in for a woman who is not your wife, who is half your age, a woman who could make an old man forget the Revolution and everything he had struggled for. A woman so different from anyone before or after.

It stays with me, the memory of her, and the view from that room in her house. At night sometimes, when I cannot sleep, I think of Frida, although two years have passed and we have not spoken, and Natalia, dear, sweet Natalia, keeps watch over me, more vigilant than any bodyguard.

Frida. I would like, sometimes, to catch a glimpse of her again, those colours swirling towards me, her brow arching in amusement, those lips turning upwards and outwards. That generosity of body and movement and personality. I would like to be able to watch her again, the slide of heavy rings on to her fingers, the attachment of flowers to her hair, the threading of ribbon through braids, those hands at work. To watch her preparing for a bath, with her bad foot concealed behind the other one, the skin fuzzed and deeply hued, perfect.

I daydream. I am not without guilt. Wondering if Natalia can see into me or through me. The self I present, as transparent as a glass prison – the glimpse of my other self caged with longing behind it.

Natalia has a way of looking at me, fierce, determined, loyal. In May, during the attack, with rounds of machine-gun fire branding the night, she pushed me to the ground up against the wall behind our bed and shielded me with her body, offering herself up for me. And in that moment I knew that I could never repay such love, felt diminished before it.

And still I fantasise about this other woman, now my enemy.

It is common to be obsessed with the enemy.

I hang my head at such betrayal of Natalia.

After all these years, I can work well through the day only if I know Natalia is near. I hear her opening the sash on the window to let air circulate more freely. She is everything to me. And yet a longing persists, irrationally, at the end of my days. For I know that these days must end.

I wrote to Frida in Paris, telling her of the break with Diego, remonstrating with her. Predicting the moral death of Diego without any affiliation to the Fourth International. The break with Diego. We shall say the break was about politics. Diego declared his support for Almazán, the bourgeois candidate in the elections – a politician backed by American oil interests. How could I condone such a candidate? Diego, always inconsistent. Such an extreme individualist. We fought on this issue. We broke apart, like a vessel too fragile for heat. Was our friendship really so fragile?

We shall say the break was about politics.

Frida, as always in these matters, supported Diego.

She never replied to my letter.

My friend, the enemy. In politics, those who are not with us are against us.

I returned the pen she gave me, inscribed with my name. She sent it back.

I write with it still. I work on my biography of Stalin using that pen, the pen from my enemy, inscribed with my name.

I sit here marking the page with that pen, thinking of the last time I saw her.

★ ★ ★

Frida's skirts sweep the streets in rainbow-coloured arcs of dust. As she walks, the crowds fall back, and on this day, the Day of the Dead, Frida limps graciously towards me along the skulled streets, past the miniature coffins. I look up to see her coloured-swirling towards me, and in that instant, my past falls away: Lenin's domed head, all my hopes for the *International*. For a moment I forget the Georgian with the moustache, *the man of steel*, who dogs my dreams and forces me into exile. In that instant with the young woman limping towards me on a dusty Mexican street, I can pretend that this is all there is and has ever been. And I turn away to adjust my round-rimmed spectacles, to adjust myself to the wonder of her.

'Frida,' I say. 'The sight of you makes an old man forget everything.'

She laughs and pats my hand, takes my arm, and the crowd looks at us: the Russian and the woman in Tehuana costume, the ribbons pink against the dark of her hair, pausing to look at the skulls. We stop at the stall of Señora Rosita, the best Judas-maker in Mexico City. Her stall: pyramids of sugar-skulls, of fruit, of Judas-figures and *piñatas* for children. The stall is all colour and papier mâché and split watermelons. Señora Rosita had once read my palm, had marvelled at the life it contained. On this visit to her stall, Señora Rosita gives me a small tin *milagro* in the shape of a heart.

For your protection, she says.

It is my last trip to the market with Frida.

And on that morning, according to local custom, we had exchanged sugar-coated skulls. Frida's husband Diego, then my benefactor, had rushed into the Casa Azul to give me a present. Diego and Frida, how they looked then – *the elephant and the dove*. Diego flushed and excited, his huge body heaving with exertion like an overstuffed schoolboy. I was not amused. For Diego, laughing, had presented me with a chocolate skull on which was inscribed in pink icing: STALIN.

Every day I write about my enemy. And every day, like buzzards around a corpse in the desert, my enemies hover with accusations and slander. Some say the Terror began much earlier, that the signs were there from the start. Such accusations invariably turn on one episode: *Kronstadt.*

But let me say, quite clearly: *There was no Kronstadt.*

Let me say: *I am that which my enemy is not.*

I never said a revolution could be made without bloodshed. It is not a school for humanitarianism.

In the midst of Civil War we were fighting to stay alive. Fourteen capitalist armies encircled us. White Guards and Socialist Revolutionaries and Anarchists put up their claims. We had two choices — *crush or be crushed.*

So, let me say quite clearly: *There was no Kronstadt. There was no Terror in 1921.*

I appealed to the sailors of the Kronstadt garrison. They had the advantages: a fortress, an arsenal, the Baltic Fleet. Meanwhile, in Petrograd, we had starving workers, striking workers. A descent into chaos.

A revolution is not bolstered through chaos.

SOVIETS WITHOUT BOLSHEVIKS.

Such demands! How quickly they turned, the soldiers and sailors of Kronstadt: *the legalisation of parties; the end of rationing; freedom for small traders; release of all political prisoners.*

Impossible demands at an impossible time. What were they thinking?

I did not hesitate. I appealed to them and they did not listen.

Kronstadt shook me. Undeniably. But from the vantagepoint of years, there is nothing I would change. I would again give the order to fire and attack, sliding across the icy Gulf of Finland before the ice thawed and the fleet could overwhelm us. I would do it all again. For it bought us time and time was what we needed.

That day in 1921 there were two assaults on the Kronstadt garrison. By the second assault, we were not fighting our own men. We were fighting the class enemy masquerading as our own.

In politics he who is not with us stands against us.

That day, *there was no Kronstadt.* There was merely a fight for hope against people who had lost hope. These were political decisions for our own survival.

Let me say quite clearly: *I am that which my enemy is not.*

4

KOBA LEARNS TO RIDE

IOSIF VISSARIONOVICH STALIN
GEORGIA
1889

H IGH UP ON Sergei's shoulders, the world seems different. We run around and around the Byzantine fortress on the outskirts of Gori. I urge him to run harder, faster. His hands grip my ankles. It is market day and there are many tongues I do not understand. Sergei and I race through arguments and negotiations. I ride high on his shoulders, eye-level with men dressed in chainmail and helmets. They are the Khevsurs. It is market day and they come down from the higher gorges, remote eyes still fixed on the Holy Land like their fathers before them.

Georgia is wild and ancient but I am new and changing.

I tell Sergei to stop before a stall selling cloth. I climb off his shoulders. I take my time fingering the cloth, finding the best pieces for my father. A huge man in long boots strides up to the stall. He leans over the mounds of material and in one smooth motion takes a short-handled dagger from his belt and slits the throat of the vendor; the cry of a sum of money slashes the sky. I watch the way the blood spurts from the vein, bright red, new blood. We watch the man in the boots stride quickly away. Sergei and I look at each other for some minutes and then begin to laugh. It is the first time I have ever seen anyone killed. A Khevsur rattles past and looks at us and then at the Georgian with the slit throat bleeding over the cloth. He looks right and left and picks up a roll of sackcloth, slipping the bundle under his arm like a child.

Sergei and I run around to the back of the stall and pile pieces of grey canvas on to our arms. Other people come running and hurl themselves on the bales: material reams like flags. The day is still.

The vendor lies twitching on some silk. I have my father's money in my palm. Sergei hoists me on to his shoulders again and I make a cushion of grey canvas for myself around his neck. I look up at the sky. The world looks different. I do not hear my mother's voice, damp and low from all the village washing, urging me to prayer. I do not hear my father's voice, as pointed as a shoemaker's awl, instructing me to trace a pattern twice around a heel.

I am *Koba, the indomitable*, the Georgian outlaw of legend. I am as tall and as old as the Kazbek Mountain. I can see the white chains of Prometheus on the summit. I feel like a man, the smell of bloodied cloth about me. I raise my hands into the air and yell up at the ghost of Prometheus taunting Zeus: *Ja stal*, I cry, *I am steel*.

I ride high up on Sergei's shoulders until we come to my parents' house. He bends forward suddenly, shooting me off over his head, and I land on my bad arm. I curse him, laughing. I am eleven years old. I run in cradling my elbow, where it doesn't bend well at the seam. My mother, Ekaterina, looks up from her sewing machine, the silky material sliding under her fingers. She smiles at me, and then her face changes. *Soso, your arm!* My arm is precious to her. Her triumph. She once saved my arm from a blood infection, the wound cauterised with the hot tip of a shoemaker's knife. I am the only surviving son of four children. I am precious to her.

I came out of my mother's womb feet first, with the small toes of my right foot stuck together; the foot angled out of her like a small calf. My mother thought I was blessed to land on my feet in this way. Destined for great things. My father cursed. For how was he to carve a proper last from a child with a deformed foot? These wooden lasts, curved and clumsy, were based on the feet of my father and mother and, later, myself. From our feet he fashioned cloth shoes, cut patterns and, for those with the money, spread leather over these lasts for all of Gori.

My father was not a good shoemaker: took risks, had ambitions.

My father looks up from his stitching. His demands split the air: *Where is the cloth*? To his right, the three wooden lasts on the table rise up like elk horns. To his left, a small glass lies empty, an opened bottle of vodka beside it.

Here, Papa. I push a roll of thin grey canvas, bloody at the edges, towards him. My father inspects the cloth and asks me how much I paid. Fingering the rouble in my pocket, I lie to him. *All of the money you gave me.*

He eyes me closely: *And from where did this red come?*

From Sergei, he fell off my shoulders. His head cracked.

My father leans back in his chair. *Is this the truth?*

It is the truth.

I am fingering the rouble in my pocket and playing the white-and-red slitting of the throat over and over in my mind.

My father makes a guttural sound: *Somehow, boy, I don't believe you.*

My mother looks up from her sewing, her voice fierce and low: *Believe him.* I stand between them, waiting. But he is distracted today. Returns to his work. Refills the glass next to him. On the grey cloth he starts tracing a pattern. He is agitated. Today is the day that Prince Amilakviri will come to have his boots mended. He is certain of it. My father wants the Prince to think him hard-working. To see that he is not just another shoemaker in the *dukhan*, counting the bottles he has drunk before dawn.

After tracing the patterns he puts the cloth aside and motions me to him. I move towards him slowly, wondering if he has forgotten about the cloth and the money. I watch him now at the wax horn, running the thread through the pot and then stitching the thin leather, showing me how the wax melts as the thread pulls through. After I nod that I understand, I move across the uneven floor to the corner where my mother sits. The Armenian silk for the merchant's daughter billows from her machine needle. She has spent the morning washing the merchant's shirts. She smells as damp and humid as a washroom. Now her afternoons are for sewing. Her hands move quickly, lightly freckled like the inside of a mountain orchid, the fingers swollen at the joints like an old woman's. Her red hair looks dark in the shadows of the room. I move towards her and put my hand in my pocket. *Soso,* she says, looking up from her work. *Come to your old mother, let me look at your arm.* I lift the bad arm, my father at my back, the rouble in my hand. My mother inspects the veins near the elbow and sees the rouble, weighted in my palm, heavy like a stone between us. We look at each other for an instant and I place the rouble in her hand, and my finger to her lips for silence. *The rent*, I mouth at her. Her eyes widen. She looks over at my father, her hand closing over the rouble. When finally he leaves the house to meet his friends at the *dukhan*, she calls me to her.

How? she asks.

I saw a man killed today. I took his cloth. This is the rent for next month. Take it before he drinks it away.

You took a rouble's worth from a dead man?

He won't be needing it.

Is this what they teach you at school? She shakes her head sadly, but puts the rouble in her pocket.

I taught myself, I say. In my head I think of *Koba*, riding down from the mountains, fighting for his family and his freedom. *I'm a man now, Mama.*

My father comes in again some hours later. Anxious, because the Prince will come today, he is sure of it, and he will want his boots mended for the hunt and he will present us with a bag of roubles, enough for half a year. And the Prince will get off his black horse and will praise him, Iosif Dzhugashvili, for his workmanship, and will invite him to the Palace to become his personal shoemaker, and his fame will spread throughout the land.

My father eases his long body through the doorway and slumps against it for an instant. His eyes narrowing. *Soso*. He says my name in a low rumbling way, like the passing of the Transcaucasus train. I plunge into my Bible for tomorrow's lessons.

He moves towards me. My mother looks up from her noisy machine, her arms full of Armenian silk underwear. He stands over me.

What will the Prince say when I tell him that my son is a liar?

Papa?

There was trouble at the market today. The cloth vendor sleeping with his cousin's wife. The cloth vendor's throat slit, like a watermelon. People all over his stall like ants. Did you pay for this cloth?

Yes, Papa.

Where is my money?

I gave it to the vendor.

Somehow, boy, I don't believe you.

Believe him. From the shadows, my mother's voice.

My father's eyes, cloudy with drink, roll around the room. Suddenly he remembers. *The Prince.* He says to my mother, *Has the Prince called for me?*

No one has called for you, Iosif.

No one?

No one.

He staggers back to his chair. His eyes fixed on me. *Come over here, Soso.* The heavy tone in his voice. I look from my mother to my father. She looks away. I move towards him. He beckons me with his left hand, the top of the index finger missing where the leather knife sliced through it.

I could never understand my father. His thoughts as slow and black as the Kura River. I close my eyes and wait for his hands around my neck. Instead he grabs me roughly by the shoulder and says, *You move too quietly. I cannot trust a man if I cannot hear his feet.* He pushes me away from him.

Go, get away from your books and mix me the paste, he says.

I combine the quarter cup of flour, the thimbleful of salt and the cup of water on the stove. The shoemaker's recipe. My father sits and stares out of the small window, a diamond-shaped awl in one hand, a glass in the other, waiting for the paste to be done. Then he will paste the leather together and use the awl to punch diamond-shapes through which he will draw his waxed thread. I have watched him countless times. My mother finishes her sewing and rubs at her eyes. She sits back and flexes her fingers and, from a pot near the machine, rubs oil and salt into her hands to keep them smooth. There is silence, except for the bubbling on the stove and the dry papery sound of my mother's hands. I keep stirring the paste on the stove, counting to a minute in my head. I think of the cloth vendor and the red hole in his throat. I stop counting, remembering the ride on top of Sergei's shoulders, myself as tall as the Kazbek Mountain.

Soso! My mother screams and stops rubbing her hands as the paste boils and a sticky whiteness lips over the pan.

My father rouses himself, shouting, *And you call yourself the son of a shoemaker?*

Yes, Papa.

You want to be a shoemaker?

I take a deep breath. *Yes, Papa.* The lie comes out smoothly. I look over at my mother. She wants me to be a priest.

I want to be as tall as the mountains. I am destined for great things.

He lunges at me suddenly, the diamond-shaped awl in his hand. *He's a fool. The priests and those books have turned him into a fool!*

My mother screams at him. Shields me with her body and puts her hands over my face. My father lunges at us both with the awl, wanting to stamp us into diamond-shaped pieces. My mother picks up a wooden shoe-last, modelled on my father's foot, and hurls it at him, hitting him in the chest. He is winded and falls back against the wall.

My mother hisses at him, *There's only one fool in the family*. And pulls me to her, her rough-smooth hands over my eyes; my eyes stinging with salt and stuck fast with oil. I look up at my father through oil-soaked lashes.

The Prince does not come.

DR VISHNEVSKY'S DIAGNOSIS
MOSCOW
JANUARY 1952

D R VISHNEVSKY LOOKS at his notes. He knows the diagnosis is not favourable and he wonders what to do or say. It is early 1952. The *Khozyain*, the boss, is not in good health, but how to tell him that the slow-moving arteriosclerosis is affecting his brain? Vishnevsky recalls his last session with Iosif Vissarionovich; the overturned chair, the foul language, the disbelief. After all that he had lived through, the *Khozyain* could not believe that *time*, the most arcane and frightening of enemies, was now against him. Stalin's bad temper was becoming more pronounced; the moods oscillating between extremes of suspicion and delight. And now, forming in the frontal lobes, tiny cysts, oystered over each other, gleaming strangely, like the inlay of a Fabergé egg. Vishnevsky knows that time will deliver these deadly bursts in the frontal lobes and that things will never be the same again. For the past few years he has cautioned his boss about the hypertension and arteriosclerosis, urging him to rest for the sake of his health. Each time Stalin has resisted the suggestion. But now, with Stalin's latest medical report in front of him, Vishnevsky feels uneasy. This report indicates disturbances in the cerebral circulation and the massing of cysts in the frontal lobes – the area of the brain governing complex forms of behaviour. It is an irrefutable fact: Comrade Stalin needs close attention.

Vishnevsky now knows that the days for Iosif Vissarionovich are marked; oyster-coloured spheres marked one out from each other; this dark massing at the front of his cerebrum.

Vishnevsky frets. He swears. And then he decides that the best course of action, indeed the safest, would be for him to issue instructions for treatment through an intermediary. Then he would be spared the tantrums and caprices of the *Khozyain*. He looks at the Bakelite telephone gleaming blackly on his desk and resolves to ring the one man who could possibly help him in such a delicate situation: Lavrentiy Pavlovich Beriya.

That night in the Kremlin apartments, after everyone else has gone and Stalin has emptied two bottles of pale Georgian wine, Beriya enquires after his health.

'Fit as a bull,' Stalin asserts.

'Vishnevsky does not seem to think so.'

'Vishnevsky is a foul dog. Don't listen to him.'

'He says you are very ill.' Beriya presses on. 'He urges complete rest from public life and a prolonged period of medical treatment. He is very worried about your health.'

'He is a cur, trying to get rid of me.'

'Maybe,' Beriya acquiesces. 'Maybe he is . . .'

Stalin thinks of all the physicians who have complied and surrendered. It had begun many years before. He remembers the business with his wife – her death registered as appendicitis. How many deaths registered in this way? The men in white coats were not to be trusted.

Stalin aims a glass at Beriya, misses, and the glass shatters against the wall. 'Tell those white coats to go to hell. Tell them I'm in my prime.'

'Of course,' says Beriya, exiting quickly, his trouser-legs splashed with wine.

S TALIN SLEEPS UNEASILY. He is preoccupied with the shadow of the enemy. What does the enemy feel like? he asks himself. What is the texture and shape of the enemy?

Was it the pale slumbering shape of his second wife in the next room all those years ago? Was it the slope of her handwriting on ivory notepaper?

Was it the man in Mexico, *the Jew*, his skull crushed with an ice-axe?

He asks himself: Is it in the colour of the iodine water that I sip for my blood pressure? Is the enemy the colour of ash, the last butts in the ashtray, the last cigarettes I will ever smoke?

Where is the enemy?

At night in his sleep the enemy presses on him so heavily that in the mornings he wakes flushed and his head throbs strangely. His vision blurs first in one eye and then in another.

He reaches for the blood-pressure pills that Vishnevsky had prescribed for him, months ago. He still trusts the pills, dissolving pinkly on his tongue.

He no longer trusts Dr Vishnevsky.

Stalin looks at his nicotine-stained fingers and runs his tongue over his yellowing teeth. He resolves, after some fifty years, to stop smoking. His health these past years has not been good, although he is loath to admit it. Terrible headaches assail him for days, have him shattering the crockery in the cupboard at Kuntsevo, searching for remedies stashed behind gold-rimmed plates and fluted soup bowls, riven by pain in the early hours of the morning. The pain starts up after he has sent his colleagues home, after they have dined with him and drunk his wine, after he has observed them getting drunk, after they have gone and left him to himself.

An old man, alone in his chair, with terrible pain blanketing his vision.

He consoles himself with the accolades from his seventieth birthday, repeating them back to himself: 'The Great Philologist, the Genius of Economics, the Great Gardener, the Transformer of Nature, the Best Friend of Soviet Gymnasts.'

This mastery has not come easily. It has been hard-won. Nature had not showered him with riches. He has triumphed over his defects.

He has never enjoyed the natural advantages of his contemporaries. Trotsky and Zinoviev, for example. Both tall, handsome, assured. With their cosmopolitanism and words coming at him like knives, he could never compete. But he has outlived and outwitted them all.

All his life, he had to fight his way out of the shadows.

Even Lenin had trouble seeing him clearly.

Lenin, in the early days, appreciated the money flowing in from bank raids in Georgia. Stalin clearly remembers the Erevan raid of 1907. The twist of it. How he had planned it and it had not gone according to plan. Where onlookers were shot and people trampled. But the Party got the money and *every revolution must have its victims*, as Molotov once said. Lenin had recommended that Iosif Stalin – *that splendid fellow from Gori* – be shifted to Moscow. Six months later, after the audacious raid in Erevan, after finally arriving in Moscow, Lenin looked at him blankly, could not place him. Could not remember his name. He still winces at the humiliation of it.

Then Trotsky's pronouncements: *The greatest mediocrity in the Party. The gravedigger of the Revolution.* He had never forgotten, had never forgiven, *that Jew.* Had made him pay.

His whole life has been testimony to the transformation of base nature; the moulding of his life to his will. And he will not let go of life so easily.

He studies the reports by Ukrainian Professor Bogomolet on

rejuvenation. He finds that, occasionally, sight fails him in his left eye. In recent years he takes the baking-soda baths recommended by Dr Lepeshinskaya. He wonders about the *vital substance* linking everything, and, if he ingests it, whether his life will be prolonged. There are enemies everywhere wanting to see his life extinguished. Wanting to destroy everything he has built up.

He has more locks installed on doors, buttressing his life against the enemy. He carries a huge metal ring on which the key to every door in every room in every dacha is kept. For the past four years he has employed a food technician who can give him a scientific breakdown of every item of food served up by the cook who has been with him for twenty years. He demands that the food technician taste the food, that he does so in the presence of a doctor. In the evenings, surrounded by colleagues, he urges them to eat first, monitoring their reactions before he dares to bring a fork to his lips.

He dismisses the doctor. He dismisses any employee wearing soft-soled shoes. *He cannot trust a man if he cannot hear his feet.* He has a deep distrust of anyone who puts a hand inside a trouser pocket. He does not trust what he cannot see. He tries to keep one step ahead of the dissimulators and the flatterers, who no longer reflect him accurately to himself.

He wonders how it has come to this.

He wonders why he feels so empty in a crowded box at the Bolshoi on his seventieth birthday, surrounded by admirers. 'They open their mouths and yell like fools,' he later tells his daughter. 'I despise them.' He longs for one good man to tell him the truth. He cannot find one good man. He acknowledges the applause and the blood starts to pound in his head; he feels dizzy and falls back against his seat.

He remembers watching the evergreens at the Kuntsevo dacha thunder to the ground. The pleasure he felt at bringing nature to its knees. No longer from every window to be confronted with the secrets of longevity and the inevitability of his own death, hidden in the whorls of trunks, the regeneration of leaves on branches.

Nature, always keeping something from him. Something had to be done.

In 1948 he had launched The Plan for the Transformation of Nature. Rivers to be re-routed. Forests tamed. The march towards the future entailed the triumph over natural forces. When man could bring nature under his control there was no limit to what could be achieved.

Such transformations.

He had transformed himself. The terrain and topography of his body bore the scars of the land of his birth. And he had overcome such defects. Conquering all but the accent, he had carried Georgia with him and through him and had borne it all up to Mother Russia – the most exacting of all mothers – and she had pronounced it good.

His own mother had died in 1936 at the age of eighty. She was a devout old whore, he thought, who never understood him. At the end of her life still lamenting, 'What a pity you never became a priest.'

His father. But it was better not to remember his father. Drunk and bleeding to death outside the *dukhan* after a brawl. His father had never lived to see the young Koba become Stalin. Never lived to see his achievements.

Looking back, he believes the Great Patriotic War to be his finest achievement. He strokes his moustache, remembering Hitler, their confederacy, and then Hitler's betrayal. It stung him still.

In recent years, he thinks more and more of Gori, of Georgia, and of the death of his second wife. Her betrayal. He sometimes looks at a shellac mirror she used to keep on her dresser. It is the only remnant he has kept of their life together. She, too, had been interested in taming nature. Her enthusiasm for plastics. He understands her now much better than when she was alive.

In a cupboard at Kuntsevo, there is an old coat from Georgia; squirrel on the inside and reindeer on the outside. He often retrieves the coat and his reindeer fur hat and sits on the Georgian sofa, trying to distract himself from the pain in his head. He sits there inhaling the warmth of the fur and watches the memories swirl past. In particular, he likes to recall a short film from the time of the Great Patriotic War. A film by Arnshtam and Kozintsev. The film consists of one short scene repeated over and over. Napoleon is at the telegraph office, trying to get a message through to Hitler in order to warn him of the danger of invading Russia. *I have attempted it*, says Napoleon. *I do not recommend it.* Stalin leans back in his old reindeer coat and laughs at the memory of the scene. *I do not recommend it.* He repeats this to himself many times, the images of Napoleon and Hitler blurring in his mind, laughing himself to sleep in his chair, laughing himself into his Georgian dreaming.

THE WALLS OF the seminary are prison-grey. Iosif Vissarionovich, also known as Soso, is puzzling over a question:
How many languages did Balaam's ass speak? Balaam, the
angel and the donkey. Balaam's ass pleading for leniency from the
prophet before the angel of the Lord. Soso searches his memory.
The voice of the donkey: *What have I done to you, that you have struck
me these three times? Am I not your donkey on which you have ridden, ever
since I became yours?*

A miracle, say the monks. A fairy-tale, thinks Soso. One thing is
certain. If the donkey had spoken Georgian, it would not have
been a question for examination. He smiles to himself at this, bites
the end of his pencil, and starts to write.

Just that morning, while he had been in the washroom, the
monks had been through the dormitories, confiscating reading
material, listening for the sound of Georgian, the forbidden tongue.
The only Georgian that echoed around the walls was the memory
of a nationalist's curse and a Georgian bullet felling the principal
some years before.

At night under the blankets, the boys whisper in the forbidden
tongue.

At home in Gori, his mother Ekaterina sews the clothes of
wealthy merchants and sews crucifixes from the silk remnants for
the walls of her house. She kisses the silk crucifixes and prays that
God will look after her clever son, her *Iosif*, her *Soso*, in the
seminary school in Tiflis, seventy miles away. She prays that he may
one day be the greatest priest the village of Gori has ever produced.

Why, thinks Soso Vissarionovich, must everything be in Russian?

Whisperings on the way to chapel. There – the hole in the wall from the assassin's bullet in 1883; the principal killed by a student expelled for anti-Russian activities. There – the loose brick under which letters from the expelled students are placed. Soso composes verse in his head to be published later in the liberal newspaper *Iberya* in Tiflis. He is already a revolutionary. On his days off he distributes SDLP leaflets to the striking factory and railway workers in town. In chapel, with bowed head, his dark hair falling over his eyes, he reads the first of Darwin, concealed in the pages of the hymnal. Soso raises up his voice and looks around the dank walls and thinks of those animals that survive through everything to propagate and grow strong as iron, strong as steel. The lesser organisms who fall behind. In this life, he will not fall behind. He is determined not to. He reads:

Thus from the war of nature, from famine and death, the most exalted object which we are capable of conceiving, namely the production of the higher animals, directly follows.

He listens to the reedy voices of his companions, raised in exaltation of a God few believe in. Even if you believed before you entered here, thinks the boy, such belief could not survive the beatings and incriminations, the dank smell of fear that permeated the walls.

What are they so fearful of?

Hermogenes, the Great Russian monk, principal of the seminary, fears for his life. He fears that a disgruntled student may try to slay him, in the same manner as his predecessor.

Police Inspector Abashidze fears an anti-Tsarist plot which could spread out from the bright young students in the seminary and then to the workers' circles just forming. The railway workshops are the centre of agitation. The new industrial workers are drawn to Tiflis. The Russians had built the railways, had seen Georgia as a bulwark against the Ottoman Empire. And Georgia had always seemed not to resist. To welcome Russification. Tiflis was the main junction on the Transcaucasian railway line. But now things are turning, changing. New ideas challenging the existing order. Dangerous ideas about independence are spreading out from the railworkers. The Chief Inspector fears the negation of all the privileges which he, the son of a Georgian peasant, had striven so hard to achieve. Why didn't the Georgians learn to accept their lot – even to do well out of it?

Brother Pavel fears the boys and most of all himself and the unnatural desire the boys arouse in him.

Many of the boys fear that things are not changing quickly enough. They are nationalists. They fear reprisals for their resistance.

Within these walls, there is enough fear for everyone.

It is the monk Pavel whom Soso fears and hates most. Brother Pavel is thin as a wolf with the instinct of a wolf for the kill. Brother Pavel can wrap himself around doors and windows. His breath can snuff a candle under blankets at night. Pavel's dominion is over the fetid dormitories and he reports direct to Hermogenes and Chief Inspector Abashidze. He confiscates copies of Darwin and Mill and Chernyshevsky and denounces the student-readers to the Chief Inspector. There are jokes, soft and muffled, which do the rounds of the dormitories and which Soso Vissarionovich finds vaguely amusing.

Why does Brother Pavel have ears?
To hear better from the Secret Police.
Why does Brother Pavel have hands?
Because God was out of whips.

Once Brother Pavel caught Soso Vissarionovich reading *Ninety-three*, Victor Hugo's novel of the French Revolution. He found the boy reading under a stairwell. The boy was supposed to be cleaning the stairs. Soso looked up to see the monk coming towards him. He pressed himself tight against the wall, to avoid the mop-handle swinging above him, crushed against the wall, like Balaam's donkey, away from the Angel's sword.

Brother Pavel confiscated the book at once. He hurled the bucket of water over the boy's feet and beat him around the head. He made as if to lift the boy's tunic, to force the mop-handle inside the boy. This was Brother Pavel's favourite punishment. The boys feared this punishment more than the feel of Brother Pavel's stubble on their skin. Already that month, two of Soso's friends could not stop the bleeding after Brother Pavel had found them with forbidden books, and had used his special crucifix, skewering them; blood all over the bedsheets, blood all over the back of brown tunics when they sat down.

But the shoemaker's son was too quick. He backed himself against the wall at the exact moment when Principal Hermogenes appeared around the corner to see the boy wet and shivering in his tunic and the monk smirking his triumph, the novel crumpled in his hand.

Well done, Brother.

Brother Pavel nodded and bowed low. He put down the mophandle. The two men marched the boy to the cells at the far end of the seminary where he was kept for three days. Finally Soso confessed to membership of the lending library in the town.

What other books do you read? What other sedition have you brought back here?

Soso kept the memory of Darwin's organisms competing, dying, being born, in his head.

'Nothing,' he said. 'I read only the books of the Lord.'

Only? And the other boys?

Suddenly another path opened up for Soso Dzhugashvili, the shoemaker's son. He thought of the other boys in the seminary. The boys from wealthy families. Sons of wine-makers and wheat merchants. Boys with smooth skin and soft hands. Boys who judged his pox-pitted skin and weak elbow as the mark of an inferior.

> *All organic beings are exposed to severe competition . . . the struggle almost invariably will be most severe between individuals of the same species, for they frequent the same districts, require the same food and are exposed to the same dangers . . . Owing to this struggle for life, any variation, however slight . . . if it be in any degree profitable to an individual of any species . . . will tend to the preservation of that individual.*

Suddenly, he knew what had to be done. That night there was to be a study circle at the rail workshops. In his pocket was a crumpled page from *Kapital*, handcopied from the only Russian translation in Tiflis. He wanted to discuss these ideas. Tonight, a diversion would be needed.

'Tonight,' he said without flinching, looking into the pale eyes of Brother Pavel, 'you will find Leonizde and Sylvester at the lending library in town.'

Brother Pavel laid aside the pointed crucifix, carved for special punishments, fingered the boy's filthy tunic and released him. Thinking of the soft white buttocks of Leonizde and Sylvester, he smiled a yellow smile.

FOR TWENTY YEARS, Vishnevsky had been Stalin's personal physician, Moscow's most eminent surgeon, addressing Stalin privately as *Khozyain* in the deferential tone of all Kremlin employees. Vishnevsky rarely saw Comrade Stalin. The doctor knew that his most illustrious patient had a peasant distrust of the medical profession. Stalin's eyes slatted over every time he came into the surgery. 'You people kill more than all the generals put together.' Stalin had volleyed this at him on their first meeting all those years ago. Vishnevsky, young, new to the position, had smiled nervously. 'Only when required.' Iosif Vissarionovich had looked at him approvingly.

Vishnevsky had not known what to make of this first encounter, but it had become apparent to him some months later when a call came from the Kremlin at a strange hour. A taciturn Iosif Vissarionovich had led him into the room of Nadezhda Alliluyeva, his second wife, and motioned to him. 'Clean this up.' The bloodstains on the carpet and the heart-shaped mess on the floor and later the death certificate, signed by Vishnevsky in an uncertain hand. Cause of death registered by the young physician at the Kremlin Hospital: *Appendicitis. Acute.*

For twenty years, Vishnevsky had lived with the knowledge of a signature that had changed his life. He'd lived well since the time of Nadezhda Alliluyeva's death. There had been swift promotions. The privileges of office: the four-room apartment; the chauffeur-driven car; the prestige accumulated since a hieroglyph at the bottom of a page had confirmed an improbable cause of death, the gentle pressure of Comrade Stalin's hand on his deltoid as he signed, that voice in his ear: *You are a good and loyal comrade.*

His family had lived well off that signature.

There was no crime in that.

Vishnevsky had enjoyed striding the streets of Moscow; the thrilling murmurs of recognition, he felt them vibrate to his fingertips. He enjoyed his summers spent in the wooden dacha provided for him in the best location out along the Kazan rail line.

Now he sits in his Kremlin apartment, rolling a small wooden pipe between his fingers, the pipe engraved with his name, a birthday gift from Comrade Stalin, some ten years before. Today, the 6th of November, is his fiftieth birthday. All day he has sat by the fire, rolling the pipe in his palms. He expects telegrams of congratulations. He expects at any moment for the telephone to ring and to be summoned to a dinner in his honour.

It is nearing midnight.

Moscow's most eminent physician sits alone on the evening of his fiftieth birthday. There is a knock at the door and his maid answers and Vishnevsky moves anxiously towards the sounds of late-night voices; the telegram presses into his hand, presses into the unease of his fiftieth birthday. He stares at the stark assemblage of letters on the page.

COMRADE DOCTOR.
REGARDS.
COMRADE STALIN.

The doctor turns to a drawer in which his private correspondence is kept. He compares the brevity of his fiftieth-birthday telegram with those from the past twenty years. Vishnevsky's eyes shift down the years: the words 'esteemed', 'revered', 'valued', 'inestimable' recur. Now that he is fifty, this praise-flow has halted. Vishnevsky's slippered feet agitate the carpet. For weeks now he has had a pain in his right deltoid; the pressure of twenty years paining him at night.

He now knows what needs to be done.

Vishnevsky goes to his cupboard and pulls out a small leather workbag with heavy black handles. It is the bag he has used for twenty-four years in his calls to Kremlin apartments. He removes crêpe bandages, syringes, headache remedies and sedatives. He piles the tools of his life's work on the floor and repacks the bag with two sets of underwear, a vest, and two pairs of socks. He removes the photograph of his dead wife from its simple wooden frame beside his bed. The photograph, taken in the first year of their marriage, shows her eyes frank and seductive. He looks into those young eyes from a different time, and can now only see the swirlings of his own signature; the life it bought them, the unspoken between them, her hand over his, their secret. He turns the photograph over, so that he does not have to face those eyes, snaps the bag shut, pushes the bag underneath his bed, and waits.

Vishnevsky had fantasised about his fiftieth birthday for months. He had daydreams in which mercury-flashes from 1949, the year of Stalin's seventieth birthday, came to him. The image of Iosif Vissarionovich projected from an airship high above the Kremlin, illuminating Moscow – the image caught in convergent spotlights above the city. Comrade Stalin orbing down upon his people. Government buildings in the city lit from within and without; functionaries at their desks, unable to sleep, waiting for a call from the man in the image hovering outside their windows. Most *apparatchiks* dozed at their desks, worn patches where their heads rested night after night in anticipation, awaiting an instruction from the man who never slept. The night of Stalin's seventieth birthday was the night no one slept in Moscow.

Vishnevsky fantasised often about the Zeppelin-projection of his own image: Moscow's healer, beaming down upon the city.

For months the doctor had practised his reactions to such a suggestion – which he was sure would come – of throwing his image across the Moscow skyline. He practised the shake of the head in disbelief; the flattening of the palm to indicate that no, under no circumstance could such an idea be countenanced. Then his favourite part: the resignation shift of the shoulders, the eyes lowered, the mouth-tremble of gratitude as he acceded to the wish of the Politburo that all Moscow celebrate his birthday. The inevitability of it. Vishnevsky, after practising his repertoire of responses in the mirror, had then chosen the perfect photograph of himself at fifty: head and shoulders, stern-gazed, full-haired. Darkly handsome. Order of Lenin medallions burnishing his collar. As he would like to be remembered. He imagined this image beamed out over Moscow. What did it matter that in reality his own hair was thinning and grey? That he had sent the photograph to be professionally retouched? In 1949, the image of Stalin aerostatted over Moscow bore no resemblance to the ageing man with the white hair, the low forehead, the pocked skin, the man Vishnevsky had tended for so long. Of course not. At the time, Iosif Vissarionovich had appeared less frequently in public. The people did not need to see the stooping, the gradual blanching, the gravity-pull on facial features. No.

The people wanted the strong face, the dependability of the dark moustache which had bristled their decades. A face they had come to recognise as their own.

Posterity was a severe judge. One wanted to be presented in the best possible manner. Vishnevsky approved of his own retouched image at fifty: strong, full-haired, erudite.

This was how he wished to be remembered.

He now contemplates the horror of being remembered differently. Of being forgotten. Or worse, of being remembered for an action that had tormented him some twenty years earlier, but with which he had made a memory-truce. What course at the time was open to him? What choices were available? To have it revealed that Comrade Stalin's wife died at her own hand; or even at the hand of another? Vishnevsky had never been certain. No fingerprints on the gun had ever been taken. Such revelations would only have weakened the gains of the Revolution. *There had been no other choice*. He had played a noble part in protecting not only Comrade Stalin, but the entire Soviet population.

For this he had been rewarded.

Now he sits with his small bag ready-packed. There is no vision of him, Moscow's healer, floating benignly over the city. Government functionaries are slumped at their desks, offices heavily illuminated as usual, nothing to disturb them. Vishnevsky packs away the photograph of himself as he would like to be remembered. The day has gone. The photograph was not displayed in *Pravda*. His name was not proclaimed on *Radio Moskva*. Something has gone horribly wrong. He consoles himself with the thought that at least he is not Jewish. But he fears that perhaps he has over-reached himself, wanting to be caught in the blimp-beam of posterity. He feels that perhaps he is being punished for his fantasies.

Comrade Stalin's most loyal physician sits on his bed, waiting.

It was simply a matter of waiting for someone to tell him exactly what had gone wrong, and what could be done about it.

On the 9th of November at 2 a.m. Dr Vishnevsky is escorted, with his small leather bag lightly packed, to a windowless room at the Lubyanka. He is charged with administering wrong medical treatments to Soviet Party and government officials and of spying for Britain. He is charged with alleged Trotskyite sympathies in his past.

He slumps forward in his chair facing his accuser, his whole life slumping forward. For the first time, there are no studied gestures, nothing he can plan for. He remembers the uprooting of cypress trees from around Stalin's dacha, on the occasion of the Great Leader's seventieth birthday. The triumphal note in Stalin's voice when he described the thunder of branches. He did not care for evergreens, he said. Those constant intimations of his own mortality.

Vishnevsky feels the felling of himself, the internal crushing. As he is handcuffed to the chair, he branches over like a cypress against a wooden shutter, the scent of fermented citrus pervading his senses.

ANNA SOLOMONOVNA MARKISH
MOSCOW
4 MARCH 1953

A T 4 A.M., the telephone shrills at the Ministry for Internal Security. The officer is surprised at the call. Even more surprised at his orders. His grey eyes blink rapidly. The situation appears unstable. The unthinkable. That Comrade Stalin . . .

The unthinkable.

He calls for a chauffeur and ten minutes later finds himself at the door of the last specialist physician outside of the Lubyanka with any experience: Anna Solomonovna Markish.

He assails the door. He kicks at it with his boot.

Anna hears the knocking at her door; a decisive four-beat hammering. Through the slices of wall between the apartments, Anna can hear other doors closing like box-lids; people shutting themselves in against the beating on her door, because such a sound at such an hour can only mean one thing.

When she answers the door in her nightdress, the man in the regulation blue collar stares at her. Her strong face disconcerts him.

'It is urgent.' He pushes her roughly back into the room. 'Dress.' Anna puts some clothes on over her nightgown and moves to pick up the small bag, lightly packed, near her bed.

'Leave it,' the man says. 'Where you are going there is no need.' Anna pushes the bag underneath her bed.

This is the moment, it is upon her. With her colleagues at the Kremlin Hospital gone, first Vishnevsky and then the others, it seemed inevitable that her turn would come. She starts to feel the sliding of her past. The waiting is the worst. This is what people say.

She tries to prepare herself. She has heard of the dark basements of the Lubyanka. The execution cells, the walls blackly painted and pitted with quicklime, which conceals the mess of internal organs that regularly spatter the room.

For those cells, she knows, no one needs a bag lightly packed.

The car smooths past the worn buildings and familiar façades, the dawn hovering over. The car speeds past the Metropole Hotel. One of her favourite buildings in all Moscow. From the back seat, Anna looks out at the façade and longs to touch it one last time, Vrubel's shell mosaics curving the gables. The high period of Russian art nouveau. She loved the architecture of that period. The dissolution of boundaries between beauty, utility and decoration. Her whole life, drawn to the dissolution of boundaries. In life. In art. How she had dreamed of such a future.

As the Metropole Hotel falls away behind her, she holds its beauty inside her. The perfection of form and function, that impossible unity, like a secret, heavy as a child in her lap.

They drive past the Foreign Ministry and the Maly Theatre. With a shock she realises that they have also passed the eight-storeyed looming of the Lubyanka.

She does not understand. Is this a reprieve? Is this a game? Her skull fragments. She imagines a bucket of quicklime marking the spot. This image remains with her as she sits in the back seat. Her companions are quiet as they approach a winding driveway leading to a dacha on the outskirts of Moscow. In the early light she notices evergreen branches, freshly cut, bundling all along the driveway; helix-shaped bundles waiting to be burnt.

Inside the dacha there is fear dampening walls and quickening breath. Fear emanating from an old man on a bed, from young people in white coats.

She recognises the man on the bed as someone she has known all her life. He looks so familiar and yet so different. Smaller, frailer, whiter-haired than the image has suggested. She is motioned to his bedside. She sees the face blackening, hears the laboured breathing. With a shock she looks into the face of Comrade Stalin, dying.

All around her there is the sense of activity, but no one is moving. She sees young interns that she recognises from the hospital. Faces as white as their coats. She sees them looking dolefully at respiratory machines that they have never used. Waiting for an order. Everyone is looking in her direction. She understands from this that she is the most experienced doctor present, the only top physician still practising outside the Lubyanka.

She looks at the faces around the bed. Beriya, Khrushchev, Molotov. Famous men. How small they seem. How vulnerable in the face of a power draining away on the sheets in front of them.

Stalin's breathing fills the room, a rasping, an uneven rhythm like speech.

Beriya says to her, 'You are a doctor. Do your job.'

'But I am a gynaecologist,' Anna protests. 'I am not a specialist in such things.'

'It is not a time for specialists.'

Anna knows that all the specialists are in jail. Most of them Jewish – *assassins in white coats* – accused of trying to poison top members of the military and Politburo.

Anna bends over the old man on the bed.

'He is dying,' she says.

'Do something,' says Beriya.

Anna unhooks the respiratory machine, newly gleaming in the corner. She hooks it up to Stalin's bedside and covers his face with the mask. Everyone watches her silently.

'There is nothing I can do.' She looks around at the men. 'It has gone too far.'

No one can believe that it has gone so far.

That it should come to this.

H E STUMBLES OVER the uneven ground towards the bathhouse. He has tamed and extended and built over the land here for years and yet still there are roots so thick that he stumbles. It is just past midnight. He looks at the land around the dacha with the eye of a *muzhik*; taking its measure, thinking of all the things he can do to the land. He still has many plans for the dacha.

He longs to hear the hot coals hissing as the water lashes over them, to lie down on the slatted boards and feel the blood pump around his body and his lungs expand. Briefly, he wonders what his doctor would say about a man with high blood pressure taking a steam bath. He takes two of the pills in his pocket as a precaution before entering the room. It is so long since he spoke to a doctor. But they are all in league. He knows that now. An American-Jewish conspiracy against him. If he can eliminate the doctors then he will eventually find the source of it.

For there must be a source.

He lies back in the steam and remembers with satisfaction the startled looks on the faces of the Presidium when he passed around the charges against the Kremlin doctors. Beriya had looked sullen. The others were subdued. He could almost hear them thinking. They were so weak that he had to do their thinking for them.

He had berated them. He had railed at them. 'You are as blind as kittens. The country will perish if we do not identify the enemy.'

'Like kittens,' they had echoed.

He had turned on them. He had their attention. He smiled at

them. 'Do not worry, comrades, the Jewish-American conspiracy will be cut off at source.'

He thinks of this as the steam rises up around him. How the enemy must always be cut off at source. About the enemies he has faced in his life. His wife. Trotsky. The Opposition. Hitler. He thinks of the triumphs also. After an hour he stumbles out into the chill of night. He feels weak and dizzy. He makes it to his room and falls to the floor. He is thirsty. His tongue feels too big for his mouth. He tries to speak but cannot form the words. He tries to move to ring the bell, to summon someone, but his left side will not co-operate. There is a loud sound in his head, like a million volts of electricity shorting. He flails about on the floor, as if he is a fish accustomed to a large ocean, suddenly caught in a net. He tries once more to call out. But there is no one to hear him. *Someone has caught me in a net*, he thinks, as fluid floods his brain and thought leaves him.

After the first stroke, young interns apply leeches to the back of Stalin's neck. Others take X-rays of his lungs and monitor his heartbeat. A nurse in a blue apron gives him injections. The dacha at Kuntsevo is transformed. All around him are student doctors, their white coats pristine in the room's shadows. They are waiting for a sign to act. Stalin gasps for air, his lips black. He summons his daughter and the Central Committee to his bedside. He smiles weakly. On the opposite wall is a Georgian pastoral scene – a young girl in peasant costume feeding a lamb with a spoon. How Stalin loves this picture! For that is how it has always been. The lamb is his country. He is holding the spoon. Now it is all mixed up. He tries to joke with Khrushchev, to tell him about the lamb, but the words do not come. Now there is only this pressure in his head and he feels confused about the identity of the lamb. He wonders who is holding the spoon.

Now some days later, when the woman doctor enters the room, there is no movement, only a laboured breathing. Stalin realises it is his own. He opens one eye; the other does not seem to function. He looks around for Beriya who has slipped out of the room to slide along the polished floors of his new dacha. Beriya touches everything he can, like an animal marking new territory. The feel of it all. He is delirious with pleasure. His pince-nez gleam. When he returns his arranges his features into a look of grief and anticipation. He stares straight into the face of his beloved leader, shaking his head and mouthing entreaties. Every time Stalin comes to consciousness he sees the blurred pince-nez waiting for him. He looks agitatedly around the room. No one else can see the look in Beriya's eyes except himself. It is a look he knows well; a look that functions like a mirror.

'The bleeding has spread to the rest of his brain.'

'It is constricting his chest. He is suffocating.'

'He is choking to death.' The doctor hears her own voice above the others as Comrade Stalin lies rasping on the bed, trying to tell them something.

Things come flooding now . . . I smile to myself and raise my glass . . . They mouth at me and I mouth back . . . try to tell them, but the words do not come . . .

It is Moscow, 1939. The gramophone handle is small and hard and angled in my hand. I turn it slowly, cradling my bad arm at the elbow where it doesn't bend well at the seam. All around me, men in uniform are waltzing. Alexei, my bodyguard, glides past and his lips are full and red and parted. His boots shine. The measure of a man is in his boots, the fit of them, the cut. Alexei is enjoying himself pressed against the shoulder of Molotov, who looks uncomfortable. It pleases me to see Molotov so uncomfortable. The generals step past, two by two, and I crank the handle, controlling the tempo. I have the responsibility of a Noah, as learnt from my schooldays. I decide who is to dance and who is to sing. Who is to stand and who is to be pushed. Which animal with which animal.

Alexei. Tall and blond. He will come to me at the end of the evening, a certain look on his face, and I will say, yes, the jacket, and he will press himself close as the jacket is slipped from my shoulders. Yes, I will say, the boots. He will press his face into the shining calf leather: Look, I can see my reflection. And I will allow him to linger there a moment longer than is necessary. And then the upturned face. He has the disturbing beauty of a young woman. And what a gift for humour! He is special, sliding around the Kremlin late at night in slippered feet. Sometimes I think he has slid into my room, is trying to ease off my socks, that his hands are reaching up to where my boots end.

Later, I will have him removed for such behaviour. A man who wears slippers in the evenings, who slides, feline, around corridors, is not to be trusted. How am I to know, when the door handle turns, that it is not the silent tread of an assassin?

I cannot trust a man if I cannot hear his feet.

This, my father taught me.

After the waltzing, the entertainment. Alexei slides in and out of voices and characters. Now he is on his knees, hands clasped as if in prayer.

Guess, he challenges. Guess who I am!

He crawls around on the floor, whining like a baby, a napkin plastered to his head as if it is a skullcap.

Yes, he is special.

Alexei crawls over to me, sinks to his knees, and in a high whining tone pretends to beg for mercy. Please, God, he whines, spare me. Please, don't shoot, don't shoot.

Stop, stop, I say, wiping the tears from my eyes. I look around, helpless with laughter: he should have been an actor.

Who am I? he insists.

He prostrates himself at my feet. He runs his hands up and down my boots and his tongue leaves a wet trace. Who am I? Looking up at me, the napkin at an angle on his head, the tongue-trace, hands moving up towards my thighs. I look into the full of his mouth and feel confused.

Kamenev, I say, laughing, trying to breathe evenly with his young hand on my thigh.

No. Again.

I shake my head. I look around the room. Bukharin! Somebody shouts drunkenly, excitedly, over my shoulder.

Alexei shakes his head and then walks around in a circle on his knees and in the same thin voice cries out, That Trotsky, the swine, he made me do it!

I laugh, recognising the line from the trial transcript. Of course. Zinoviev! I shout, applauding. What a performance! Clapping, cheering. Everyone clapping and cheering.

I crank up the gramophone again. The men are weary but I pair them up and force them on. Rows and rows of boots gleam past, the soles flash up before me. The leather is snug against the calf. Once such boots belonged *only to princes. I urge my men around, faster, harder. The world is very different now. I think of my father, waiting for a prince that never came. I think of my mother, her hand pressed around a rouble. I think of the child who dreamed himself Koba, who in his youth taunted Zeus. The journey from there to here. It all comes flooding now and I try to tell them.*

I smile to myself and raise my glass.

Ja stal, I say to myself: I am steel.

There is a sudden movement beneath the bedclothes and Iosif Vissarionovich Stalin sits up in bed and looks around the room with frightened and terrible eyes – at everyone and no one in particular. He tries to speak. To make himself understood. To tell them about his journey. The long struggle from the shadows. To remind them of vigilance for a final time. He groans and extends his left arm, gesturing into emptiness, and falls back. There is the black sound of leeches cracking on the sheets.

Anna Solomonovna takes two roubles from her pocket to shut the terrible eyes of Iosif Vissarionovich Stalin, the General Secretary of the Communist Party, her face wet and her fingers trembling.

FRIDA KAHLO
COYOACÁN
6 MARCH 1953

O N THE 6TH of March 1953, on the other side of the
world, in a Blue House in Mexico City, the artist Frida
Kahlo wakes from a disturbed sleep and reaches for the
painkillers next to her bed. She is crying. Her amputated leg hurts.
Everything hurts. For he is gone. She takes her red-leather journal
and a pen from the bedside table. She writes:

THE WORLD, MEXICO,
THE WHOLE UNIVERSE
HAS LOST ITS BALANCE
WITH THE LOSS, THE PASSING
OF STALIN.

THERE IS NOTHING LEFT.

EVERYTHING REVOLVES.

THE DIARY OF
LEON TROTSKY IN EXILE
COYOACÁN
AUGUST 1940

T HIS MORNING, I threw open the shutters of our room. The brilliance of the day made me gasp. Natalia lay still. Above our bed the plaster gaped with holes. These days she waits for me to get up first – *to prove that you are still alive*, she says. Only when she sees me at the shutters can her day begin.

For Natalia things are worse. It is worse because the beat of her days are determined by the rhythm of my own. She does not know when she will again have to push me from the bed and cover me with her body. She does not know when the machine-gun fire, the grenades, the assassins, will strike again. She only knows that they must. War rushes towards us, consuming Europe. The biography of Stalin progresses slowly, but it progresses. I am confident that another war will hasten uprisings all over Europe. For each day that remains, the hours are full. The future bells out a promise.

For Natalia, time passes slowly and in a different manner. She tends the household. She reads. She sews. She keeps her needle-work in a round box embossed with Van Gogh's sunflowers. She keeps up correspondence with our friends. She proofs my pages. She feels the threat of time; the space of an hour.

I find the hours too full.

Since the May attack on our quarters, I think of Natalia differently. I notice everything. The hundred small ways in which her love for me is transmitted. And it seems that for most of our life together, I have not noticed. Through these long years, there was never any reason to doubt that she would be there for the next stage, the next house, placing roses in a jar, airing the rooms, fashioning a makeshift cupboard in one corner, sewing a curtain to run along the wardrobe rail.

She has always been there, a heartbeat ahead of me, easing me forward.

But now, after the last attack, we both know that the next place I will pass through to, I will pass through alone. Natalia now has to contemplate the fact of her aloneness. I was always shielding her from it. This was our relationship. In return for her warmth and devotion, I was able to shield her from this fact. I went forth for her. My life set the tempo for her own. And now I look at this pact we made so many years ago, as couples do, in love, thinking that love, and the Revolution, could sustain us.

She has to learn to live without me. To make her own way. She does not like to speak of it. Although she is a materialist, Natalia, I know, has a strong streak of superstition. She does not like to speak of these things.

We have spoken, however, of taking our own lives. On the assumption that I will go first, that she will assist me. If I am maimed in an attack or if the hypertension fells me. If I could not write or speak. She would do her duty.

History has priced my head. That is the fact of it. Natalia understands this. And I am grateful for this understanding. Her love for me is fierce and focused and I love her deeply; I appreciate the fact of her far more than when we were younger.

Since the attack, we have sat on the bed in the mornings, after I open the shutters, holding each other tight. We are no longer young. But the love is there; we hold it in our arms, all its component parts down the years. We hold each other. Each day, a little tighter than the day before. She does not want to lose me, and I tell her that she never will. I know she has her own palaces of memory; that she can store me there safely, waiting for a pencil-beam of light. Sometimes, she does not want to let me go, does not let me out of view.

In dark times, I turn to her and whisper that I am sorry for destroying her life and her happiness, her children, all those close to her, taking her away from her homeland.

I would do it all again, she says. And at once, in a certain light, I see

234

her again, the young married woman in Paris, with the beautiful hair and the *retroussé* nose, willing to abandon her husband, for me and for the Revolution.

You see, for Natalia, the two were inseparable.

At the end of my life, there are two things worthy of the term love. Natalia and the Revolution. In dark times, I whisper to her, *How can I ever repay you?*

And she smiles that slow smile, from somewhere far off, and says, *A life together does not demand payment. You have stretched my willingness to love in the way a child stretches it. And love is that willingness to stretch. You have been my everything. How many people can say that, in a lifetime together? How many?*

Such love is unfathomable. And although I have loved her and still love her deeply, and more each day, I cannot say to her, *You are my everything.*

Should I feel guilt? For in truth, the Revolution was my father, my son, my lover. The revolutionary movement gave and still gives my life a unity. Natalia is a part of this whole.

Love is different for each person. The service of the Revolution was, is, my everything.

At the breakfast table she sits close to me. These past weeks, since the attack, I have almost suffocated with the closeness. Her arm rests on mine at every opportunity. Sometimes I am annoyed, push her away, send her away, demand of her, *What are you looking at?* When I chance upon her in the doorway, looking over me, I say harshly, *I have bodyguards, Natalia.* And she moves away, from the door, from the window, and immediately I am contrite, for how can I ever repay such love? I call her to me then, I apologise. For love is push and pull. This is the dialectic of love.

And often, when Natalia's love threatens to stifle me like a blanket, I find myself turning to a different sort of love, and how my life would be with someone other than my wife, someone more egocentric and capricious.

Frida, for example.

Frida, in our time together, never once appeared at my door, solicitous, to draw back a curtain so that my room would have more light, or to open a window further so that the breeze would reach me. She would not anticipate my needs or plan for them. She was so beyond me, her life was outside my orbit. There was her painting, there was Diego, there were always her friends, her lovers, her legion of admirers.

I was not the only sun in her universe. This I came to understand.

On one level, Frida lives for Diego. On another level, she lives more completely and fully for herself than any woman I have ever met. Men and women are drawn to her for that very reason. She is the most self-realised woman of her time. Like a man in that way.

Sexually, even, Frida seemed beyond me.

With Natalia, in all respects I know who I am. Each morning, Natalia reflects a constant image of myself. We are still intimate and in that intimacy there are certain expectations. I satisfy Natalia. Our love-making can be fierce or tender. With Natalia, I have no doubts. I am, I know it, more virile than men half my age.

With Frida, though, with Frida. Still today, I wonder. I believe that she did not reject me because she found me unsatisfactory. But she seeded doubts. I did not feel master of myself when I was with her. She pulled me towards her and pushed me away. Like a man.

Strange, that such thoughts still come to me. Three years later. My wife clutches at me. And we are closer than we have ever been. And still I daydream of a different sort of love – Frida's reckless, passionate unstable kind of love – without limits and boundaries. And yet I would not have survived such a thing. I know that now.

In Natalia's universe I am the only sun. There is the burden of providing light and warmth. But the security also. Our roles are clear between us.

The affair.

What is an affair but a short excursion from your own life?

Can you love two women at once?

How do you decide between them?

For six weeks in 1937, I asked myself these questions. A tornado across my mind.

Can one person give you everything? Is that not merely a bourgeois notion?

Natalia always opens the world to me anew. Often, she says, *Look at those clouds, the way they move.* She draws attention to the small wonders: the wide-eyed stare of a child, the cheekbones of a person in the street, the press of one young body into another in a passionate embrace. She brings that attention to the details of life that I would scarcely notice. The small things.

Natalia brings artfulness to life, in the arrangement of fruits in a bowl, in the arrangement of flowers on a table.

I recall a recent trip to the desert; one of those rare trips where we lay pressed to the floor of the Chevrolet, covered with a rough blanket. Outside Mexico City it was safer to sit low down in the back seat and Natalia pointed things out to me, as if I couldn't see them, or she wanted me to see these things differently. The car slowed outside a village. There was a small white church set against the mountains, a row of cow skulls and skeletons leading to the entrance. An alleyway ran alongside the church. At the entrance to the alleyway, a woman sat with a bundle of a child wrapped in a grey serape and a red-striped hat. Behind her, three men stood in the arc of the church door, partially opened in the early morning sun. One man stood with his hands low on his back, arching, another man, louche, leant against the doorframe, smoking, one knee bent. The third man stood quite still staring at the woman and the child. They all looked up as our car passed by and then resumed their postures. 'It's as if we walked into something a moment too late,' Natalia said and wondered aloud about the relations between the woman and the three men; who was the father of the child? What were they doing there at that time, in that place? I listened to her musings, and the car soothed me out along the highway towards Taxco, and she spun stories for me, about the woman and the three men, and how I loved to listen to her voice – the deep throaty timbre of it. I fell in love with her voice the first time I met her. Her voice comes from a distance, a place where you do battle with yourself and triumph over a nature that is not gregarious, but thoughtful, observant, full of feeling. Sometimes people mistake this for a certain reserve. But if they listen to her voice long enough, the quality of it, the texture of it, like red, fertile soil, and her laugh, infrequent, but heartfelt and low, if they listen long enough they come to know her as I do.

She could have been an actress, with that voice, our friends used to say. Resonant and memorable. An actress. And Natalia would smile; accepting the compliment because she knew it was true. And in her case, her wonderful voice was the conduit to the soul.

These days, Natalia seldom laughs. Few people see the Natalia that I know and love. She has few reasons, even, to smile. And I notice, after the deaths of our children, that her face has set into an expression of anxiety, of perpetual wariness. The light in her has retracted to some other place.

And lately it occurs to me that maybe I have taken Natalia's life and squeezed it, compressed it, fashioned it after my own. But then, I tell myself, it is a life she has freely chosen and she has never reproved me, never wanted to turn away, to go back in time, before she met me, before exile, before pain and sorrow.

For almost forty years, and especially in this last period of our exile, Natalia has had no home in which to display her everyday artistry. She has known only movement and concealment. In Norway, she packed and cleaned and cooked and filed my manuscripts and letters and stored the photographs of our dead children in a leather box and we were gone from that safe house in forty-eight hours.

All our dead children.

When Natalia has her mind focused, there is nothing she cannot achieve. Great feats of organisation.

At the end of my life, I feel I owe her a testament to our life together, my love for her, my gratitude; I want to capture my love for her in words, like a flower essence in rainbow-coloured glass.

Natalia calls me from the garden. *Look at the sky today*, she says, *a blue duck-egg sky*. For the first time I notice that the timbre of her voice is changing. It is still deep, still resonant, but slightly worn, thinner. It is the voice of someone who is no longer young, a voice spun out of sorrow. It affects me in a way that makes me want to weep. And I think to myself: this is old age; the sound of a voice that once made you smile, the sound of the beloved calling you, now makes you want to weep.

The voice of an old woman. The timbre of it.

Loss has deepened her voice, and stretched it beyond words.

She says to me, *The sky here has become more familiar to me than the sky in Moscow or Leningrad. And summer here is like those summers in the Crimea.*

Yes, I say, *keep talking. I am listening.*

In the worst times, I have always had my work. Natalia has only herself. I could watch Natalia reach into herself, lower the bucket into the well and find that she was able to draw upon her reserves, that she could draw the bucket up from inside, and that it would be full.

This is the measure of character: in dark times, in drawing on the well of oneself, one will not find it empty. But these days, her reserves are diminished, I can see that.

And still, she lowers inside, as she must, to keep going; to keep lowering inside the parched self.

I am plagued with headaches. My ears ring. I feel enervated. In the afternoons, during my rest time, Natalia comes to sit by me, or lie next to me. She places a cold compress on my hot brow, and lies down beside me with a book in her hand until the book slips from her grasp and we both drift into an uneasy sleep.

Natalia always falls asleep with a book in her hand. I always prise it from her grasp. The minutiae of a marriage, a life. In the evening, Natalia always falls asleep with the light on and the book open. The accumulation of detail about a person. How you come to know them better than yourself.

If it hadn't been for Natalia, would I have sustained a personal life? She kept up correspondence with our children. Especially our youngest, Seryozha, of whom she was particularly fond, although he was completely different from me, from the rest of us. He was a dreamy fanciful child, who became a dreamy academic, devoted to his work and completely apolitical. We left him behind when we left Moscow, because he did not want to leave his studies at the Academy, or his friends. His life was so removed from ours. I confess, I never understood my youngest son, and for six years I never wrote to him. I confess that I did not know what to write to him about, for what was my life, but politics? I did not want to draw attention to him, implicate him in my life. We thought he was safe. For six years, Natalia wrote to him, funny, touching letters, full of warmth and concern and domestic detail. She used to read these letters to me before posting:

> *Your father has constructed new cages for his rabbits, how he loves those rabbits – allows no one else to touch them or feed them. He skins them himself; brings them to me, lays them at my feet, like spoils from a hunt, and stands to watch as I boil them for his favourite stew . . .*
>
> *I send you this scarf, I made it myself, remembering the winters. I will think of you wearing it, with your greatcoat and the snow over your boots. Stay warm, stay safe, study well . . .*

But he did not stay warm, stay safe.

Each generation has been touched. Even in 1926, this was foreshadowed. The Politburo meeting at which I turned on Stalin – *Gravedigger of the Revolution* – I charged. I remember, there was soft laughter. Stalin stalked from the room. Later, in our quarters at the Kremlin, our friend Pyatakov turned to me, over the corned beef that passed for meat in those days, over the red Ket caviar, and said, 'He will not forgive you for this, never. Neither you, nor your children, nor your children's children.'

I dismissed his words at the time. The threat seemed so remote. Banishment, exile, fighting to maintain my reputation, all that came later. I did not recognise Stalin's vengeance to be of biblical proportions.

My children were all alive then. Now they are all dead. What does it mean for children to die before the parents?

Sometimes, when I cannot sleep, I open the shutters and stare up at that remorseless sky and ask, *What does it mean?*

And again I close the shutters and return to myself. I pick up my pen and start writing. The course of my life was determined by the course of the Revolution.

My family, from the grave, must forgive me this and understand it.

Without her children, Natalia feels hollow-wombed; I know it, although there is never a word of reproach. But she tends all living things with a ferocity that makes my heart break. She notices children and young adults in the street. 'That child moves like

Seryozha at that age, tumbling like a circus acrobat. Do you remember, Lev Davidovich, how much our youngest loved to tumble? The bruises on him!' Or: 'That young man, the smile, the breadth of the shoulders, the walk, he reminds me of Lyova.'

For myself, each night I close the shutters on our dead children. I go forward. There is no other way.

Neither of us speaks of Zinaida, my eldest daughter by my first wife. Although we speak of the exile and the death of my first wife. The sorrow of it.

I never wrote to Zinaida, my Zina. Although she loved me, idolised me – they both did, the daughters of my first wife – Zina was unstable. All her life, unstable, especially after the death of her sister, she became depressed, wanted more than I could give, in truth, more than I was prepared to give. The times she came to visit Prinkipo were difficult. She resented Natalia and that feeling was reciprocated. She wanted all the attention from me that she had missed as a child. But I could not, would not, give it. She was emotionally unstable. Anyone could see that.

We sent her to Berlin for treatment. We now look after her son, our grandson, the remaining child of our life. This grandson, whose mother was found in a cold Berlin flat slumped beside the gas oven, the thunder of Nazi boots outside in the street.

Her son, our grandson, has more resilience than the mother. My poor Zina was not strong enough for the times she lived through. And the times we lived through claimed her in the end.

So many dead.

Your children and your children's children.

There is a struggle for death and there is a struggle for life. My life is contained in these opposites. I have asserted myself against *Thanatos* time and again.

And there was that time in my life when *Eros* triumphed briefly over *Thanatos*.

That is the only way to explain it.

To explain my infatuation for her.

Frida. The harmony of the opposition of *Eros* and *Thanatos*.

In Mexico they form one principle. The seeds of one contained in the body of the other. A relationship with death as intense as a relationship with the living.

Fri-da.

I call her name slowly. In those two syllables, the unity of opposites.

How does something start? The beginnings of an attraction that can for a time rule your life. Almost ruin your life.

I would wake in the middle of the night and go into our bathroom and I was a teenager again, rubbing myself to the images in my head. Worried that Natalia might wake and come looking for me, or that the bodyguards would notice the light under the curtain and come to check.

And for a time, I didn't care. I would climax into my hands, my hands full of myself. My head full of her.

Amor y dolor, Frida says to me when it is all over. *Love and pain*. After weeks of furtive notes in books and furtive meetings at her sister's house, Frida arrives at my hill retreat with a green *rebozo* over her shoulder and a panatella between her lips. She has grown tired of me, she says. 'Your life is like a metronome, but you cannot control the heart.' Her husband doesn't know and she wants it kept that way. He threatened to kill her last lover with a knife. She has proved her point. She has now evened the score with Diego, who had put her through torment when he slept with her sister – *This is for all those months when I cut off my hair and I could not lift a brush.*

It is over now.

I watch her numbly. She moves away from me. She feels strong again, she says, once again yearning for the flaccid warmth of Diego.

I remember returning from the Taxco hills to the Blue House, heavy with shock. Picking up books and articles only to put them down again minutes later. Natalia comes in to see me, pleased that I have returned to her. 'You look ill,' she worries at me. 'You need rest.' I look at my wife. Her pale drawnness folding in on itself. 'It is the manuscript,' I lie. 'There is so much still to do . . . it is my blood pressure . . .' Natalia comes over to rub the back of my neck. She kisses the top of my head as she has done for almost forty years. 'If you need me,' she says softly, 'you have only to ask.' Her slippers scuff the bare boards. She looks back at me, and I know she is thinking: maybe it is over now, this time of hurt between us.

I take it badly, this rejection from Frida. Overnight, I feel all energy draining away. I wake up feeling aged and empty and without appetite. I tap around the yard in the morning and tend the rabbits like a man wounded. Natalia pleads with me to eat.

How I long to see Frida's uneven bootprints on the gravel path as she lists gracefully ahead, to smell the frangipani in her hair.

Amor y dolor. Frida could capture a life in a few words, as she could in her canvases. I remember her slim, slight elegance. An unusual beauty, even with one leg slightly thinner than the other, the downy hair over her lip, the heavy brows; how these irregularities drew the attention to her, made her even more alluring. As the crack in a Grecian urn draws attention to its beauty. As the flaw in the glass draws attention to its clarity.

And if I compare these two important women in my life, I would say that Frida, the artist, and Natalia, who expressed every-day artistry, formed a unity.

The dialectic of love.

In Frida's presence, Natalia seemed to be less herself, felt ashamed of the flowers she had arranged on the table, or the pyramid of fruit on the sideboard. But Frida, in fact, applauded everyday artistry. Lived for it. Surrounded herself with it. Recognised it, I think, in Natalia. But there was too much between them, between us. And Natalia felt small in the recognition of Frida's ability to transmute the everyday in her canvases.

I remember talking once with Señora Rosita, the Judas-maker, about this question. How she challenged me! How she misinterpreted me! For everyone has an impulse to create, to transform; I still dream of a future in which everyone can.

Maybe Natalia, with the voice of a classically trained actress, and Frida, the painter, had more in common than I ever realised? Maybe it is the kernel of Natalia in Frida that I fell in love with?

The thought consoles me. The thought gives me some reprieve.

And maybe that was how it began. Loving the kernel of similarity and delighting in the difference of the other.

5

JOURNEY TO MICTLAN

PRAVDA
24 AUGUST 1940

Leon Trotsky has died in hospital from a fractured skull, received in an attempt on his life by one of his closest circle.

SEÑORA ROSITA MORENO
COYOACÁN
1954

I PAINTED MANY masks in my lifetime. Each Judas–figure, each *calavera*, wore the mask of someone. Señorita Frida also painted masks: each portrait wore the mask of her own face. For the final journey, the journey to Mictlan, Land of the Dead, we wear masks; the mask of our ideal face, as our ancestors believed.

In this life I was not born beautiful and my life was not easy. I hope one day to enter Mictlan, masked with my ideal face, a face that carries no scars of suffering or sorrow. In old Mexico, the masks were of jade and obsidian. I make my own masks from a paste of flour and water. I mould the features of men, of animals. People hang these masks on their walls. People wear them for carnival. Sometimes these masks are faces on skeleton figures, exploding the streets during *Semana Santa*.

There was a death mask for Señor Trotsky. Bronze. I supervised the making of it. I made a cast of the hands also. What they revealed. The stories they held.

There was a death mask for Señorita Frida. A pink *rebozo* wrapped around her death mask.

After death there are many places; many roads to travel. It is not the manner of living that determines the destination. It is the manner of dying. If you are fortunate, you are chosen for a paradise. For women who die in childbirth and men who die in battle, their destination is the Southern Paradise, the House of the Sun. For those who die by drowning, are struck by lightning or die at their own hand, their destination is the Eastern Paradise, ruled over by Tlaloc, god of rain. For those who die of old age, or other causes,

249

the destination is Mictlan, a place that joins heaven and the underworld. In Mictlan the oppositions between life and death disappear. As in this life, the journey is long and difficult and full of trials. For this journey we wear a mask, our ideal face. We are led across swift rivers by red dogs. We climb mountains which tear at our hands; we endure icy winds, we survive arrows and savage beasts until we at last come to the ninth hell, the deepest hell, and find rest. In this place there are no vents, no openings. We do not return.

The Spanish friars took our Mictlan, used it as a weapon, as a Christian hell to punish our ancestors at the time of Conquest. But Mictlan is not a Christian hell. It is not a punishment. It is a release, the end of wandering and trial. For the journey to Mictlan we wear masks; the mask of our ideal face. For my ancestors believed that in death we are offered this chance to enter the new life with a new face, the face for all eternity.

I look into my obsidian mirror. In its rainbow surface, held up to the light, I see many things. I watch the dead carried on the back of the dog Xolotl, guardian of the underworld. Each evening he carries the dead strapped to his back like the sun, glowing across the Ninefold River and down into Mictlan, that place of warmth and humidity.

The *señorita* journeyed to Tlaloc, the Eastern Paradise, ruled over by the god of rain.

Señor Trotsky died a warrior. He journeyed to a special paradise, *Tonahtiuhlhan*, to become a *companion of the sun*. For my ancestors believed that the sun demanded blood sacrifice. They believed that death in battle purified the soul. Such a destiny made the person desirable to the gods.

And the chosen wear their own faces into eternity; the mask of themselves.

I SIT HERE now, after it is all over, and I look up at the sky, the clouds of a Mexican sky. And it's another sky I remember and other clouds – the snow clouds in Alma-Ata – at the time of our first exile. The clouds massing above the hut.

Snow clouds. Grey membranous pieces floating loose, soft and heavy and shot through with gold and the silence of those times, a huge sky hanging soft and heavy and silent.

A row of tiny birds gathered on the telegraph lines. Small and dark against the silence, beaks pointed at the clouds. Lev Davidovich at his desk. Myself at the door very still. I remember calling him to the window to show him these clouds, how they presaged something, the heavy moment and the two of us in our isolation. He stood up wearily and took off his glasses. He rubbed his eyes and stretched his arms and then looked up at the sky. He stood there a long time, at the window with his pen in his hand, not wanting to return to his desk and miss the sky. And then he folded his arms about me and said, *Thank you, thank you for those clouds, for I would not have seen them without you.*

On the day of his death, I woke early, lying there in the heat of a Mexican summer, waiting for L.D. to stir, to open the shutters. As he pulled back the shutters and light screened into the room, he noted the clouds massed over Popocatepetl. *Seems like rain*, he said, and I murmured drowsily to him, feeling the heat of the day already in the dampness of the pillow.

Now, thinking of that day and his attention to the clouds brings back every other day of our life together when clouds massed at the edge and we did not notice. And it strikes me, now that he is gone, how the sun casts a shadow, how each day is different, sorrow edging a day like pink thread in a snow cloud. The shadows and the clouds at the edge of a day. And maybe how, if we did notice, the day would seem precious, special, because the clouds threatened but did not pour. These things come later. Such realisations. When every day seems clouded and the sun does not come.

In all our life together my husband thought on a grand scale. His thoughts roamed epochs, and continents and revolutions. Without him, I feel the contraction of my mind's horizons; now that the broad strokes on the canvas have gone there is only the cleaning of the brushes to distract me. Now that the future cannot be called forth, cajoled forth, summoned by sheer power of will and skilled oratory, what is the good of this future? What is its measure? How will I know when this future arrives, if he is not in it?

In his papers I come across things I wish I had never disturbed, because the power of shifting those papers is disturbing. All our life together, the pieces of it now like broken crockery on a wooden floor. And here it is, after all these years, Joffe's suicide note, words preserved, and I ask myself, why did L.D. keep such things? As a record of the times? As a testament to the first year of our exile, the harbinger of the Terror?

Joffe's funeral. A grey day. Thousands of Opposition supporters lining the streets, singing on their way to the Novodevichi cemetery. Stalin's wife there, pale and drawn. The militia at the cemetery gates, trying to stop the crowd from entering. L.D. at the funeral, delivering an oration, in memory of Joffe. Pledging in his memory to follow the Revolution wherever it might lead. And now Joffe's final note addressed to Lev Davidovich crumples across time and continents in my hand:

If I may compare great events with small, I would say that the immense historical importance of your expulsion and Zinoviev's and the fact that, after twenty-seven years of revolutionary work in responsible Party posts, I have been forced into a situation where I have no alternative but to blow my brains out – these two events, one great and one small, I would say that these two events are now characteristic of Party rule.

Two events. One great and one small. How typical of Joffe, to place the taking of his life below that of the expulsion of his great friend, the expulsion of the Idea.

Joffe saw his life as insignificant compared to the life of the Party, the struggle for the future. All of us saw our lives that way. In 1930, Lev Davidovich wrote:

And what of our personal fate? I hear you ask. I do not measure the historical process by the yardstick of personal fate . . . I don't recognise personal tragedy. I recognise only the replacement of one leader of the Revolution by another.

Of course, later, when personal tragedy consumed us, when we lost everyone, Lev Davidovich, in private, would rest his glasses on the side table and fold his face into his hands. He would stand at the window and look up at the moon. He would pack the dead away inside himself. So many spaces for the dead inside. We spoke often of our palaces of memory. In these rooms, our children still played. Friends still embraced; we clinked glasses in rooms full of light. But some rooms were closed. It was our memory game. Some rooms, after we had endured too much, could never be opened.

Six weeks ago, when the fortifications to our villa were almost complete, I heard L.D. after his siesta, pacing the paths in the late afternoon, thirty paces in one direction, thirty paces in another, tapping the walls, as he had learnt in his first prison in Odessa, and I heard him talking to someone, and I came upon him gesticulating, addressing Joffe: 'And if you had not gone from me then, would things have been different? You went without turning against me and I have to thank you for that, my friend, the only one . . .'

I could see him wheeling and turning and whispering and inching back in time. I did not interrupt him in these conversations with former comrades. It was important for him to conduct such conversations, to address the historic questions that these deaths and turnings had left.

An old man talking to himself in the garden.

You see, there were no longer people alive who were his equal. You must understand that. People who had lived through his times, shared his experiences, they were gone, taken from him or voluntarily distanced from him. These conversations with the dead were a way for him to bring history to account.

In our lives together, did I dream, all those years ago in Paris, when I left my first husband for Lev Davidovich, that the means would involve blood and sorrow, such blood and such sorrow, and that the end would come to pass and myself still here?

If I had such foreknowledge, would I have embarked on the journey?

Lev Davidovich can no longer look me in the eye. He is young again, buoyed by passion. He hears an argument in the kitchen at the Casa Azul – myself and the kitchenmaid. He comes upon us – I am shouting loudly in Russian, pulling the kitchenmaid by the wrist – furious at her slow movings and refusal to obey orders. I confess, I am not myself. Fear of losing him has turned me into someone else. The young kitchenmaid is crying, rubbing at the bruise starting to form on her wrists. I look at the floor. At the liquid from the upturned stew seeping through the yellow floorboards. The stew is his favourite and I want it to be perfect. The young kitchenmaid is careless, drops the saucepan, is not clean. I look up to see my husband in the doorway. I am wretched, I know; my face is wildly colourless and worn. I am ashamed at how I must seem. He is angry at the disturbance and moves to inspect the kitchenmaid's bruises. He turns a cold even eye on me.

We must separate, he says. And who am I to argue?

He retreats to the hills to work. Frida follows a few days later. She comes by the Casa Azul, the house she was born in, to get some things for the trip. I watch Frida move around lightly and deftly, despite her bad foot. I watch her with the cigarette in one hand and the green *rebozo* slipping over her shoulder as she retrieves a few rugs and old sketchbooks from a wooden trunk in the hallway.

Frida is vague about her travel plans. As she gets into the car, before she closes the door, she spits on to the clay ground, like a *kulak*, I think with disgust. Then Frida looks up quickly to smile, remove something from her tongue, and, pointing at the cigarette, mouths 't-o-b-a-c-c-o'. She waves at me, an old woman framed in the red windowsill, tending the herb garden. I stare hard as the car grows smaller and, as the dust blows up to the window, I say to myself, *A boulder stone is as arid as I*, and turn away then, surprised, after all these years, to find a line from Mayakovsky colliding in my head.

I sit here and I remember the aloneness of his sixtieth birthday at Coyoacán. The discussions we had. He said, 'Natalia, things came easy to me in my life, things came early. Perhaps too easily and too early. At the age of twenty-eight, leading the Petrograd Soviet! Sometimes, I think, things flowing like that should make one suspicious. Maybe later in life, if things are hard-won, less can be taken from you.'

He was in such despair, I couldn't answer him.

'And my death, perhaps, would have saved our sons, our daughters . . .'

'Don't speak like this,' I beseeched him. 'There is nothing more that you could have done . . .'

These moods swept over him in Mexico like the wind over the desert. Each time he recovered. Each time I waited for such recovery.

Such powers of recovery he had.

But with war at our back and the assassins at our door, on his sixtieth birthday his powers of recovery were tested.

It is one month since his death and I stumble around his study, waiting for him to appear. I sit at his table. I lean back and look up at the high ceiling. From the desk I lean over to the bookcase and run my fingers along Lenin's *Collected Works* bound in red-and-blue cloth. Light fills the room from the leadlight windows in the door leading to the patio. The map of Mexico and all the journeys we took press upon me from the wall behind. Sometimes he would stand up and stretch and open the double doors into the garden and tend his collection of cacti. He delighted in the hardiness, the savage survival of the cacti. He drew strength from them.

In these last years, he appreciated the world of the senses more fully. For every day was a new day. Every day was a reprieve. He was by nature an optimist.

I had enough foreboding and pessimism for the both of us. Now that he is gone, I have no buffer to save me from myself, no one for me to draw attention to the snow and rain and the magical passing of a day. No one to share with me the scent of the eucalypt tree in the garden, releasing itself in the humid fading of summer.

I see him leaning forward slightly to hear a visitor at his desk. His focus on a person, on a subject, on an idea, as intense as a heat lamp.

Did he change, over the years? How does exile alter the balance of a person? I write these questions for myself. In substance he did not change, but the form softened, the outline became less sharp. Yes, in some ways, he softened with people.

For the man who closed the doors to latecomers in 1918 became the man for whom doors were closed. The sound reverberated around Europe. The only open door was in a Blue House, in a small town outside Mexico City.

I am the wandering Jew. He said this to me in 1937 when a copy of *Pravda*, three weeks old, arrived on his desk in Coyoacán. *They never let me forget it.* He pointed to the caricature of himself as a murderer and a hangman, squeezing the body of the Soviet Union. Trotsky with the face of Judas.

And then the heart was trammelled with the deaths of all those close to him.

Confronted with a closed door, a person is forced to open the heart; comes to know the many chambers of it.

Above all else, his great love was the Party. He never lost his love and faith in the idea of the Party. At the thirteenth congress of the Bolshevik Party, he had said:

No one wants to be right against the Party. We can only be right with the Party because history offers us no alternative. The English say 'My country . . . right or wrong', but we say 'My Party . . . right or wrong'.

When the Party rejected him, he had no alternative but to create something new. A new international party: The Fourth International. To challenge Stalin from outside. And people often asked why he wasted his energy on this small grouping, ineffectual, beset by divisions from the beginning. And my only answer, the answer I always give: *He was a revolutionary. He knew no other way.*

I USED TO watch Natalia watching him. How she was as still as a hawk. How she swooped to anticipate his needs. How when she was nearby he was visibly more relaxed because Natalia attended to the detritus of living, while his business was to think, to agitate, to polemicise the future into being.

It was an August day, fourteen years ago. Already the past.

I sit here, with the newspaper open in front of me, the photograph of Frida's coffin. I sit here tracing the arc of my life – from participant to witness.

That morning the rabbits were agitated. Lev Davidovich could not get them still; they ran over and around each other; they would not eat. He had been up since six, grinding the grain himself. The August heat was stupefying, although it was only early morning. Maybe it would rain. He looked up at the sky, still in his blue-and-white pyjamas, trying to understand the agitation of his animals.

Visitors always marvelled at Lev Davidovich's passion for his rabbits; the care he took, the fact that he would let no one else feed them or touch them. They were equally amazed at the ease with which the Old Man could snap the neck of his favourite rabbit and consume it in a stew at dinner. With a wave of his hand, the Old Man dismissed their objections: *One can easily devour what one loves.* There was nervous laughter around the table and the Mexican guests always nodded politely and pointed to the moon. *The rabbit moon,* they said. For the Aztecs believed that a rabbit was thrown in the face of the moon at the point of creation – to blunt its brilliance, to distinguish it from the sun. They understood the sacrifice of the rabbit, in stories passed down through generations. The year Cortes invaded was Year 2 Rabbit according to the Aztec calendar. Signs and portents.

The rabbit was not to be consumed lightly.

Every day the Old Man walked around the yard at Coyoacán, after he had fed his rabbits, tapping the walls of the garden with his stick. When asked why he did this, he laughed and looked surprised at the question, saying, *It is an old habit from prison days*.

We had been working hard, weeks without sleep, after the May raid on our quarters. The fortifications were complete. We were tired. Tino, one of our Mexican drivers, described a dream he had partially recalled from the night before. It had alarmed him. In the dream, he said, the walls of the Casa Azul were no longer blue, they were red, dripping red, like an artist's palette that had been knocked to the floor.

'It was like blood,' Tino insisted. 'I don't like it.'

'It's no concern of ours.' I was irritable that day, with the heat and the waiting for rain. Annoyed with the Old Man and the break with Frida and Diego and what it had meant for me. The loss of her. 'The Casa Azul no longer affects us.'

'Mmmm . . . I remember,' Tino smirked. 'The trouble with the Old Man's *pinga*.'

And we laughed then at Trotsky's expense. The safety-valve of laughter.

It was late afternoon when the man appeared at the gate. There was the sound of a motor turning over up the street, but he appeared on foot. We saw him at the gate in the same suit as the week before, the grey raincoat over his arm. We were playing cards, and we were tired. Our shift was almost over.

Tino looked up at the man at the gate. 'It's Jacson.'

'Jacson, Sylvia's lover boy?'

'The very one.'

RAMÓN MERCADER
MEXICO CITY
20 AUGUST 1940

I T IS 2 a.m. Mercader feels it to be the correct time without looking at the bedside clock. A group of journalists are singing outside his door in the Hotel Reina. They are drinking rum and throwing mock punches, hurling each other on to the glass-bricked floor with the light coming up from the foyer. Mercader gets up to complain. He needs his sleep. For tomorrow, of all days, he must be alert. The *maître d'* takes a long look at the man on the floor play-punching and laughing, the others taking photos of him. 'But they are Americans,' says the *maître d'*. 'Nothing can be done.' He winks at the journalists. He likes these Americans, likes them a lot. The tips they leave. Mercader scowls at the man on the floor. '*Chingado*,' he says, and shuffles back into his room. Sylvia is asleep, as usual. He climbs back into bed. In his mind he rehearses what he must do. He lulls himself to sleep by playing the scene over and over: the placement of the raincoat on the chair, the point at which the Old Man turns to look at the manuscript, the point at which the weapon is eased from the pocket of the raincoat. Over and over he plays the scene. He tests himself. He is prepared. But he cannot sleep. He moves to the writing desk and rolls back the cover. He turns on the desk lamp. He writes a note claiming to be a disaffected member of Trotsky's circle. How he once admired the Old Man but how he feared the direction in which Trotsky was moving. How the Old Man had threatened the life of Comrade Stalin. He folds the paper and places it in the inside pocket of his raincoat, next to the *piolet*. He returns to bed and tries to sleep. He imagines the *piolet* smashing a block of ice. The arc of his arm. The angle of

261

movement. The veins pumping, visible in his forearms, in his hands.

To lull himself back to sleep he imagines the white spaces of climbing. When he is out climbing, he feels the empty glow of it; nothing comes close. He remembers his trips to the mountains, days in the Pyrenees or the Alps, he and another comrade, days without conversation, of concentration on the mountainface, on the movements of hands and feet. Chalk on the fingertips as they reached for crevices, felt for the next direction of movement. And he had sensed, as many climbers do, a third presence, something at his back protecting him. One night, he had a dream that something was wrong. He had woken up shivering on a ledge at 3,000 feet, not clipped into his safety harness. He had clipped himself back in and thanked the dream. It had been on that trip that he first realised his skill with the *piolet*. How easily he handled the ice axe. How he could split a block of ice in one movement. He had felt sure, then, that he could crack a man's skull with one blow.

He hopes that tomorrow, the third presence, like the dream at his back, will again protect him.

His mother had always been convinced of his special abilities. Had imbued him with belief in the role he would play for a better future. If he fails, his mother will suffer. The *Khozyain* will order her back to Moscow. He will not, cannot, fail.

Preparation. He thinks back through these months of preparation.

On the streets of Mexico City, large blocks of ice were often delivered in the early morning and left on street corners. Later the café owners and street vendors would break up the ice and put it into refrigerators and buckets. In preparation over these past months, Mercader has tested his skill against these blocks of ice slowly melting on the street. In the early hours sometimes he would take his long-handled *piolet* and offer his services to the café owners and street vendors. And they would watch him raise the long-handled axe above his head and smash the block even before they had rubbed the sleep from their eyes. Some even offered to pay him for his services. He always declined. It gave him great satisfaction to see the blocks of ice gorged through in the cool of the morning.

Preparation.

Last week had been the rehearsal. Quite by accident. He had been waiting for Sylvia outside the gates at the Avenida Viena, smoking and talking to the guards, trading cigarettes with the gardener. Natalia had seen him and invited him in for tea. He had looked around the small kitchen, at the pale-green walls. At the sagging shelves near the sink, at the blue and yellow pots along the shelves, at the metal tea canisters that Natalia had assembled: *Earl Grey, Prince of Wales, Assam*. He had stared at the old copper samovar in the middle of the table. He noted the collection of outsize tea-strainers on hooks. Had noted the bars on most windows, but not all. Seen the rooms leading off the kitchen to the library and Trotsky's study. From the kitchen table he had a view of Trotsky's desk, the wicker chair pulled back. The inkwells half full. He could see a round straw hat and Trotsky's walking stick on the day bed. The details were clear in his mind. In the kitchen they sat on wicker chairs around a large table with a gold tablecloth. The ceiling was high. The floors dark red. The kitchen was quite dark. He had felt heavy in this kitchen, a weight upon him. There was a recent photograph of Natalia in profile with a black hat and black netting over the hat. He asked her about it. Complimented her. In the photograph she is pouring tea from a white kettle, the netting from the hat shades her face. She nodded at the photograph, smiled faintly. 'My widow's hat,' she said. 'We were out at Paseo del Campo.' Trotsky smiled also. Mercader noted the three large bullet holes in the wall of the kitchen. He had noted several larger bullet holes on the walls of Trotsky's study as they walked through the double doors from the garden. He suppresses a smile. He had glimpsed some titles in the glass-fronted bookshelf. Lenin's *Collected Works*. James Connolly's *Labour in Ireland*. Jack London's *The Iron Heel*; D.H. Lawrence's, *The Plumed Serpent*. He had spoken to Trotsky about some ideas for an article; if he brought it soon, would Trotsky check it for him? Trotsky had agreed. Surprised and flattered at this new-found political interest from the Belgian. How it was always possible to win someone over. Mercader had looked through to the study and imagined where he would place this manuscript. Where he would stand to get the correct angle of movement. How, if that did not work, the revolver would finish the job.

As he was thinking all this, Natalia poured the tea and Trotsky handed round a plate of biscuits. Mercader had taken a biscuit. He remembered Natalia watching him as he dipped the edge of the biscuit into the steaming cup of tea. She had watched him bite into the biscuit, smiling at him. He remembered how suddenly he felt self-conscious, felt a need to be gone, kept looking at his watch. He waited for Sylvia to finish typing in the next room; he could see her through the leadlight windows in the door which led off the kitchen into the library. He could see her at the wooden filing cabinet, one drawer open, taking out papers. Natalia saw him looking at his watch. She called Sylvia, who came with papers in her hand for Trotsky to sign. Sylvia smiled at him shyly, surprised to see him sitting there. And Natalia had looked at the young couple. She had turned to him and said, 'Go – do not let us stop you. Go and do what you have to do.'

Preparation.

In bed, he flexes his right arm. He tenses his muscles and then relaxes them. He works down his body. Flexing and tensing. Outside his door he hears the laughter of the journalists fade as they move off to their rooms. He tries to sleep.

This time tomorrow, his mother will be waiting for him, the motor ticking over. After it is done, they will drive to the airport. This time tomorrow they will be crossing the Atlantic, new passports in their hands, heading away from Mexico, towards a new life.

THE POLICE INTERROGATION REPORT
SEÑORA FRIDA KAHLO DE RIVERA
22 AUGUST 1940

A S FRIDA IS led into the police station she passes a small wooden crucifix by the door. The Christ figure looks down at his rough-cut feet, his head hanging, mouth open, as if surprised at his own outstretched abandon.

Frida knew every corner of Coyoacán. Every street stall, and every street vendor. She knew where to find the best and brightest wooden toys, the best *tamales* and *quesadillas*; the juiciest chillies. On this day however she does not notice her surroundings. She does not notice that she is outside the best stall for cloth in all Coyoacán. Sateens and striped cottons flap in the breeze. She pays no attention. On this day, the familiar is no comfort to her as her hair hangs down her back in a long braid the shape of a question mark.

She has come to answer questions about two men. One, a man she had met only once in Paris. The other man, long estranged, had once professed love for her. She is confused and uncertain. The man who had once loved her is now dead. *The Old Man is dead.* In this death, the police tell her, there is a connection between the two men.

For all of life is connection.

She will answer questions. Testify to someone and something from long ago. But the interrogation, she reasons with herself, is nothing to do with the fact of the Old Man's death. In her head, the interrogation is about revenge and betrayal, the cycles of it, the vertigo of it in the life of a couple. A million things. Things that can only be felt. Or painted.

What does it mean, for a husband to go with your sister, who is your best friend?

For your best friend, your sister, to go with your husband?

A double betrayal. A double revenge.

A pistol for revenge, thinks Frida. *A gunshot from my vulva.*

And in the revenge, to take another woman's husband, just because you can?

How these decisions, taken years before, rippled to this moment. How they led her to this moment, in a police station in Coyoacán, awaiting interrogation.

In my sister's house we played at making love. In the house my husband bought for her, we played with the danger of falling. We advanced and retreated. And the Old Man was so much for falling. Even now, when I think back, it surprises me still, how much he was for falling.

Frida watches these thoughts form, the shadings in her mind, as she is led into a small room and, behind her, Señora Rosita Moreno is led into another. As Rosita is led into the adjacent room she turns around, shrugs her shoulders and raises her eyebrows. Frida tries to smile back.

But inside she feels abandoned. She longs for Diego to walk through that door, past the policeman dozing on duty, to call her name, to save her. But she is also estranged from Diego. He is at that moment in San Francisco in the arms of a *gringa*; she has no doubt about it. Frida sits there, waiting on a hard wooden bench. Beside her a man lies stretched out and stinking of *pulque*. A *campesino*. He is deep in a drunken sleep, stretched out on the bench, a piece of cardboard across his chest, one leg underneath him. She thinks of his life. She inhabits the story of the poor *campesino*; all those stories of pain and loss, those everyday stories of Mexico, are within her. She thinks of the hours he spends sliding up gravel mountains, against gravity, to find a place to sow corn. And how the rains come. Or they do not. How his luck holds. Or it does not. If the rains fail to come, fail to reward his efforts, the *campesino* cries into a hot wind, *Es muy triste la milpa.* The corn is very sad.

How if the rains do not come there is always the *pulque*, the milky messing with his mind, how seasons without rain send him drifting to the city, a piece of cardboard in his hand on which he pays someone to spell out: *de alquiler.* For hire. And he stands day after day at the edges of the *zócalo* in Mexico City, along with the other men with cardboard signs: *Electricista. Plomero*. And they jostle for shade as the sun awns high above them and the shadows grow shorter. Frida has seen them, burning, desolate, at the fringe of the *zócalo* near the Presidential Palace. For the city is another country, and he wakes up one day, the piece of cardboard across his chest, drunk, stretched out in a police station, his beard covered in vomit.

Frida knows this story. She knows what the man has left behind.

She knows what it is to slide up against the gravity of life, her hands full of promise, to slide back down again, with nothing. Her spine broken, her leg withered, in her hand a fistful of brushes.

How all of life is contained in the sliding.

The Old Man is dead. She makes a phone call from the police station. She rings Diego, in the States. She is full of sadness and fury. '*El Viejo* is dead . . .' She cannot finish the sentence. She puts the receiver down. Diego is far away from her. She is unable to reach him.

El Viejo. She does not like to think of him gone.

The wife. Natalia. She remembers the wife at the windowsill that time. A grey shape against the red frame. How she, Frida, had looked back and waved, spat some tobacco out on to the ground, watching Natalia watch her as the car spun away from the Casa Azul speeding her towards that final meeting with Trotsky. She remembers Natalia's face in the window. The story on that face, like a *campesino* when the rain has failed and the crop rots in the ground.

Es muy triste la milpa.

And Frida had felt her youth and beauty blazing against the woman framed in the window. To think of it this day, three years later, while sitting in a police station, the triumph she felt, and the evanescence of that triumph, shames her. It makes her want to take it all back, relive the whole moment, to step towards the wife in the window and make her peace.

For she knows what it means to suffer a husband.

The interrogation is not about Trotsky. It is about the life she lives with Diego. It is about Natalia. It is about an alliance once formed with a husband that almost destroyed a wife.

The policeman taps his pencil on the desk to get her attention.

How well did you know the deceased, Señor Trotsky?

Frida looks up at the pencil in the man's hand. 'He was a guest in my house for almost two years. His wife also. At the time, we knew them well.'

We knew them well. I think of Natalia and I think: no, I did not know her well. With Natalia there was always a barrier, something invisible and cold between us, and I blamed her for it. But the barrier was Trotsky. Next to him, I saw his wife as tired, sad, lesser in every way. But she had a way with colour and flowers, a way of arranging things. For me it was an adventure. For the Old Man it was serious. One step more and he would have forsaken everything. I was young. I could recover. My heart was more tensile than Trotsky's. Who would have thought it? This power over him, a power I could no longer exert over my husband, and I could see his hold on Natalia and together we exerted power. Against us, she could not win.

And for what did we compete? An Old Man who liked to watch me bathe. Who liked to watch me dress. Who liked to touch my hair. An Old Man, who could bring himself to fuck me only once, who plunged into me and kept plunging, as is the way of such men who prove virility by their display. Afterwards he lay, straight-backed, away from me, with his head in his hands, weeping.

For what?

For whom?

For Natalia? For himself?

He would not say.

And yet. He came back. But physically, I felt nothing for him. As is the custom of men who have had their way all their life, he did not understand. How I did not want to fuck him ever again. No matter if he could wield his pinga like a man half his age. He sawed into me for an eternity. This relentlessness was sex for him.

The Old Man, El Viejo. The Great Revolutionary.

The most selfish man I have ever fucked.

But at the time, his intensity was overpowering. The desire.

He had a great mind. But it was as rigid as the tracks that carried his famous train during the Civil War, all those years ago.

Enough, I said. Let's go back to the beginning, be close comrades, muchachos.

But it was an insult to his manhood. Didn't he have the virility of a man thirty years younger?

It made me angry. I said, If stamina equals sex, then I am sad for you.

But what else is there? he said. It is important.

For whom?

He failed to understand.

And at that point I said to him: It is over.

And the World's Greatest Revolutionary, as I said, the World's Most Selfish Fuck, collapsed at my feet.

How well did you know the accused?

The policeman repeats this question.

Frank Jacson, how well did you know him?

'Not at all.'

He claims to have met you in Paris.

The policeman holds a photograph of a clean-shaven man with horn-rimmed glasses. He pushes it over. The man has large clear eyes behind the glasses, dark hair.

Try to remember.

'Paris?'

And I go back to my first exhibition in Paris. A man admiring my earrings. The earrings Picasso had given me – long silver fingers hanging from each earlobe, tiny hands pressed in an inverted supplication. And this strange young man moving towards me, engaging me in conversation on everything from Picasso to Trotsky. Asking me if I knew Trotsky well, if perhaps I could arrange an introduction, as he was a great admirer . . . and at that time I had completely finished with el Viejo, could not believe that the subject of him could arise at the time of an artistic triumph for me, at a time when Vogue *magazine featured the rings on my fingers and a commentary on* La Mode de Madame Rivera . . .

'Maybe, maybe at the Paris exhibition of my work,' Frida says to the policeman. 'Maybe that is where the man claims to have met me. But I assure you, we were never formally introduced, there were so many people there, my first exhibition in Paris, you must understand . . .'

What were your relations with Señor Trotsky in the period before his death?

'We had lost contact. Señor Trotsky and my husband had disagreed about the political situation in Mexico. In truth, I had not seen Trotsky for two years. He moved out of our house and into another on the Avenida Viena . . .'

Relations between us were nonexistent. For a period, he longed to see me. But I refused. Then there was the break between Trotsky and Diego while I was in Paris. I admit, I felt a residual affection for the Old Man. I feel it still. The sort of bemused affection you feel when you look at a photograph from long ago; the people in it and the memory of them stir the affection from that time, but you have lost contact, you now live different lives. Or maybe it was only the trace of a feeling, based on his desire for me? Once, I saw him in a car. Low-down in the seat. Surrounded by his bodyguards. It was early in the morning. He did not see me, I felt very sorry for him . . . the prisoner in his car. I often ask myself: What had he wanted from me? What had he failed to understand? His effect on people. In some ways he was very conscious of his effect on people, believed that no one was immune from the power of his words . . . But in other ways, his understanding was opaque, as if he saw his effect on those close to him through a cloudy glass of pulque.

But this house was not far from where you were living . . .

'No, it was not far, *señor*. But in ideological and personal terms, yes, it was very far . . .'

Do you believe your ex-husband to be involved in the murder of Señor Trotsky?

'No. Absolutely no! My ex-husband is an artist, *señor*, not a murderer.'

My ex-husband is a helpless womaniser. The obverse of this is that he cannot bear me to lie with another man. This is the way of the womaniser. He has threatened my male lovers several times. But the women in my life . . . well, that is another story . . . If Diego had ever guessed the truth of the Old Man's feelings for me, and I believe he glimpsed it, there would have been more than a piolet in the skull, señor, I can assure you.

And yet, Rivera has vanished?

'I do not keep a track on all my ex-husband's movements. If he has vanished I can only presume it is because he believes that suspicion will fall on him because of his strained relations with Trotsky.'

In truth, señor, *my ex-husband is fucking two women at present, an American film actress and another. He is painting their portraits. How the* gringas *flock to my husband, to be painted and then to be fucked! If my husband has vanished, I suggest you start with them, in California, the* gringa *movie star and the other . . .*

In an adjacent cell, Señora Rosita Moreno studies the plasterwork on the walls. In her mind she works her way through the process of making a wire skeleton. She listens to the police officer, but drifts away from his voice. She is modelling first the jawbone, shaping the wire, fixing the line of it, ensuring the hinge allows movement. Then she starts on the head, using small springs for eyes and pieces of wire woven together with tweezers. On the small skeletons only the jaws move. She then focuses on the dark jaw of the policeman in front of her, the skin under the jaw like a heavy sheet hung to catch the features as they drop. She wonders how to get that effect on a Judas-figure, a jaw disappearing into flesh . . .

The jaw in front of her is moving quickly and she realises it is speaking. Questions. Rapid-fire questions.

And it now becomes clear, now she understands why she is here. The *señorita's* relationship to Trotsky. And politics. The political views of her husband, Alberto. Every miner and miner's wife in town is hauled in for questioning. Every Communist is suspect.

'My Alberto came and went. Went to Spain at the time of the war and came back. Went to the mines and came back. That is my understanding of politics, *señor*. It takes them away. It brings them back. And when they come back they are different – hard, like plaster drying in the sun. I know nothing of the politics of my husband, *señor*. And of Señor Trotsky? I met him once, maybe twice. He came to visit me some years ago with the Señorita Frida. They were friendly then. I read the palms of the Old Man. Once he visited my stall. But I never met the killer of Trotsky, I swear it.'

Her Alberto hated Trotsky. She knew that. Remembered how furious he had been to learn that Trotsky had visited his house in his absence. She knew, after the fact, that her husband had been involved in the first attempt on Trotsky's life, had come home exhilarated by the rounds of machine-gun fire pumped into the bedroom. How he had burnt the police uniform he had worn in the attack, and buried the fragments in a hole in the yard. How desolate and angry he had been to hear that Trotsky had somehow survived.

How happy Alberto was now.

But she will defend her husband against the police. For a bad husband is better than no husband, and this time he is innocent, she knows it.

She thinks of the terrible palms of Señor Trotsky. The life she had seen in his hands.

She will remain silent. She looks again at the policeman's jaw moving in front of her. Imagines a Judas-figure fashioned after his image, packed with explosives, fit to burst.

BLUE WAS HIS favourite colour, the shadings of it; even as a child, he told me, he was drawn to that colour, brushing lint off his blue trousers, always just so, with that exactitude that was my life for many years, an exactitude I remember as I removed the blue twill jacket from his body and placed my hand over his heart.

I would like to say that we never crossed words, that our life was harmonious, but this would be wrong. Even now, days after he is gone, I am tempted to reconstruct, to fashion it after my own desires. I want to say that life was never grey with him. But when I think about the years in exile, the sudden journeys, the subterfuge, I need to say that it was not easy.

But it was my life, bound up with his life. How strange to write these words. He, never without a pen in his hand, the pen as sword, the pen as comfort. His preoccupation with the tools of writing; the perfect shade of blue ink, the taper of the perfect pen nib. After the deaths of our children, after the time of muteness and trays passed under the door, he would find energy to emerge from our room and move to his desk and pick up a pen and start to write.

The pen as solace.

He was my life and my comfort. With everyone else gone, I too, turn to the pen, feel his spirit around me, urging me on.

His *spirit*. He never liked that word. Too insubstantial. A term, incompatible with materialism.

Am I wrong to say that the deaths of our children: our youngest son in exile; the daughter in Berlin by her own hand; our eldest

Lyova in a GPU clinic in Paris; am I wrong to say that these times of shuttered rooms and open conversations are the times I remember, the only times when he was fully there, with me alone, with the feelings that went beyond grief or pity, when we sat silently for days on end. Is it wrong to say that I recall these days as some of my happiest moments? In his death, I am selfish. When he was alive, there were too few times without the intrusions of others, of the world outside us, the world that Lev Davidovich strode into as if it were his.

And now it is myself, some weeks after, with the pen in my hand, the pen she gave him, inscribed with a facsimile of his signature. The pen as comfort, as I sit in this chair, with *that* portrait, her gift to him on the wall of his study. And it is that pen I hold now, the facsimile signature strongly curving, the strength of it flowing up into me, as I try to recall our time together, inscribe it for myself, so that I shall never forget.

I force myself to sit in this room. The walls and floor freshly scrubbed, the bloodstains no longer visible. The portrait of Frida Kahlo on one wall. I sit here writing of everything that led us to this place.

Our first day in Mexico. 9 January 1937: walking down that wooden plank into the warmth and safety of the port of Tampico. Lev Davidovich in tweed breeches and tweed cap, myself in a dark wool dress with white stitching, dark stockings and high-heeled shoes, for it was a special occasion. Our warm arrival in Mexico, our new place of exile, after the rest of the world had refused us. We always dressed for the occasion, L.D and I, and we looked well together. My handbag was heavy against my hip and I walked carefully, one arm through his, and he was slightly ahead of me: he always seemed to know exactly where he was going, he had a resolute tread. Lev Davidovich Bronstein walked as if he were still the leader of the Red Army, dressed in a leather suit with a red star on his cap. He walked as if he were leading an army of a million instead of our small group: myself, the bodyguard, three American supporters and the artist Frida Kahlo representing her husband.

In our first exile abroad, in Prinkipo, there was the time of the telegram from Berlin, in the weeks before Hitler became Chancellor of the Reich. We had been expecting a telegram telling us that the Communist Party had failed. That their refusal to ally themselves with the Social Democrats, 'the social fascists' as Stalin called them then, had brought about the destruction of the entire German Left. We spoke about this constantly. My husband isolated, the only voice in the world, calling for a movement, an alliance against Hitler. The West too worried about Communism to listen. The Stalinists too concerned with their fiefdom to listen. Installed on Prinkipo with a fishing boat and a hunting gun and a Greek fisherman to row us out beyond the villa, my husband wrote out his horror of what was building in Europe.

On this small rocky island, the fate of Europe rocked us, preoccupied us. Prinkipo, the Island of Princes. A fitting place for our first external exile. Now we were treading in the footsteps of those earlier exiles, the Princes of Byzantium, sent to Prinkipo when they had lost favour with the Emperor. The Princes, bound and blinded and set sailing from Byzantium to this tiny outcrop of stones, now Turkish territory.

Ourselves, bound and silenced, sailing away from our homeland and everything we had struggled for. But we were not blinded. This was Stalin's first mistake.

And I recall Lev Davidovich fuming over a new pen nib which had arrived by post from Istanbul, which ripped holes in the paper as he wrote, and then the telegram circulating through the house, L.D. upstairs muttering over his pen nib, myself in the kitchen gutting fish for dinner, and the silence then and his face as he led me by the hand up into our bedroom and I said to him immediately, 'Hitler.' And he said, *No, not Hitler*, and showed me the telegram which said that his daughter Zina had gassed herself in a flat in Berlin, and what was to be done about her boy? And L. D.'s face as he took off his glasses, I was the only one ever to see him without his glasses, and the sadness in the eyes behind them this day, as we shut the door, took off our shoes and sat side by side on the bed.

Not blinded, as I said. We both saw all too clearly.

The pattern repeated, years later here in Coyoacán, after news of the death of our son Lyova. Myself in the kitchen, L.D. coming for me, leading me by the hand, the glasses off and the news beyond anything I could ever have thought.

And I had many dark thoughts.

By the time we emerged, he was again Trotsky with a pen in his hand and I was somebody other than myself. After each blow he had somebody to return to: someone ravaged and older but still Trotsky, himself. And I had only the stranger, the unfamiliar person I became, each time a little greyer, a little older, a little more wary.

And it strikes me now, as I put my hands over my eyes and imagine how our fortress here must have seemed, and how it actually was, that next door, rising above the towers of our house, is a sign in white curved lettering: *Instituto Óptico Científico*. I have never been into this building, but I have the remnants of his glasses in my pocket, with one lens broken, and the thought comes to me that I can get the glass replaced in this building. That he need not be without them for long and the thought soothes me until I remember that I no longer have to worry about such things. For he will never again stride through that door and take off his glasses and look at me with affection in our private moments, the look that no one else has ever seen. He will never stride through, place his glasses on a side table and sit with me on a strange bed in a strange land mourning the death of everyone dear to us.

I remember suddenly that the building next door has been vacant for many years. That the sign is an old one.

Fragments of glass line my pockets, and my hand digs deeper, closing over the frame of the glasses that I can never repair or return, for he is lost to me now.

LEON TROTSKY
COYOACÁN
AUGUST 1940

I T IS A few weeks after the violence of Election Day and the gun battles in the street. Finally the results have been announced. Trotsky thinks of the articles he should write about this election. He is still annoyed that *Life* magazine wanted to interview him, wanted Capa to take photos of him, and yet they had refused to publish his article on Stalin a few months before, claimed it to be libellous.

Twelve months earlier he had argued with Diego Rivera about the election candidates. They had fallen out over Rivera's support for Almazán; the bourgeois candidate who had the backing of American oil interests.

It had been an accumulation of things, this falling-out.

One time, early on, Diego thought to help by feeding the rabbits for him at the Casa Azul. Trotsky came upon Diego at the hutch and launched into an attack – what business did he have with the rabbits? No one knew the rabbits like he did. No one was as well qualified to feed them. How could Diego know their particularities, their peculiar needs? Diego had crossed the line of friendship. This was exactly the sort of behaviour that was the ruin of the Mexican section. 'Stay with your walls,' Trotsky told him. 'That's how you serve us best.' The Old Man tantrumed, threw down his gloves.

Diego was bewildered and hurt. He shut the mesh door, his short fat fingers (*like sausages*, said Frida) carefully bolting the rabbits in. 'To hell with your rabbits,' he muttered *sotto voce*, but loud enough for the Old Man to hear, and gathered his hippopotamus body about himself and moved away, fiercely stroking the green-and-red parrot on his shoulder.

It was a prelude to the break between them.

Ah, the incident with the rabbits! Lev Davidovich reflected on how right he had been about Diego's rampant individualism. There had been Diego's insistence that he have a key role in the Mexican section of the Fourth International, a role for which he was ill-suited. Diego did not have the discipline to be an organiser. He was an artist. It was as simple as that.

Then of course there had been the unstated – Frida – between them. A memory from that time returns, before the split with Diego . . . *A few months after the affair* . . . Frida sits in Diego's lap laughing and curled up like a kitten. She blows at the red feather in Diego's felt hat and looks over at Lev Davidovich with her chin upturned and her eyes half closed. He feels the feather vibrate and looks away from the memory of the full red mouth and the red feather, falling momentarily into his own sadness.

He draws himself back. He does not want to think about the Mexican elections, about the break with Diego, about the refusal of *Life* magazine to accept his article.

Instead his mind turns to his last visit to the market with Frida.

It was the Day of the Dead. Frida had parted the crowds before them. They had approached Señora Rosita's stall. Mountains of sugar skulls rose up. A child lay on a rough blanket next to the stall; she held tiny sugar skulls up to her eyes like looking-glasses, elbows right-angled.

Señora Rosita welcomes them warmly, remembers him from the time when she had read his palms. She searches through a large bag of metal objects at the back of the stall. She draws a small rectangle from the bag, which he recognises as a *milagro*, a small square of tin, a devotional object. Frida and Diego have hundreds of such objects hammered to their walls. Señora Rosita presents him with a small square of tin embossed in the shape of a heart. *For your protection.* Frida smiles. Two bodyguards flank them. Trotsky laughs and remonstrates with Rosita. 'Thank you, thank you,' he says and then points at the bodyguards, 'but you can see, I have enough protection.' But he keeps the *milagro* in his hand, undecided. He is suddenly reminded of André Breton's visit – Breton prising old *retablos* and *milagros* from the walls of village churches around Mexico, pocketing them. How this had outraged Trotsky, the disrespect of it. At the point of declining the gift from Señora Rosita and therefore declining superstition, Trotsky accepts the gift, on impulse, moved by Rosita's concern. He accepts her gift because it affirms something about his stay in Mexico, the warmth, the hospitality; Frida. It is his way of repaying something, a cultural debt. He accepts the *milagro* that day, and Señora Rosita smiles hugely, halfway around her face, the gold teeth that Frida had paid for gleaming in the sunlight.

With the *milagro* in his hand he is reminded of a heavy gilt cross that once lay in the vestibule to his Kremlin office. It was 1922. He had chaired the commission to requisition valuables from the Church. They had eventually sold off the cross to a German banker. It had been a necessary act, to obtain money for the Treasury; to sell off, melt down, destroy Church artefacts, to put pressure on the reactionary clergy.

At that time, and later, there had been excesses. Over-zealous comrades. Of course. In a revolutionary period, there would always be excesses.

Sixteen years later, he holds the tiny *milagro* in his hand as firmly as he had once flung the ornate crucifix on to a pile in the Kremlin.

As he remembers this trip to the market with Frida, he rehearses, still, over and over what he would say if ever they met again by chance. Although his world is less and less governed by chance these days, every moment accounted for, everything organised, no random happenings.

Such thoughts about the recent past preoccupy him. He gets out of bed, tries not to disturb Natalia and goes through into the study. On these sleepless nights, he turns once again to the biography of Stalin. But he has no passion for it. His heart is split, like a tree hit by lightning. In these last days, he is as preoccupied with questions of love and friendship as he is with questions of the coming war. More and more he turns back to such questions and their meaning. He remembers a chance remark at a meeting of the Politburo, when Lenin was still alive, and someone – Rakovsky? Could it be? – someone had declared Engels to be superior to Marx.

Trotsky, intrigued, had demanded, 'As a thinker?'

'No,' came the reply, 'as a human being.'

The remark stayed with him. Engels and Marx. The two of them together greater than the sum of their parts produced one of the most resonant first lines in political history:

A spectre is haunting Europe, the spectre of Communism . . .

How that line still thrilled him. And it was a line born out of shared experience, out of friendship. There was now no one alive who shared his memories of the Revolution. Of the Civil War. No one alive from the time of his most intense friendships and collaborations. Rakovsky, once his dear friend, had denounced him. Trotsky remembered a beloved photograph of his friend. It showed Rakovsky relaxed, looking straight at the camera, arms folded, face open and intelligent. It was a photograph that had accompanied Trotsky everywhere in his exile, but after the news of Rakovsky's trial, he shredded it and handed it to one of his secretaries to dispose of.

And if it *was* Christian Rakovsky who had made that statement about Engels, Trotsky wonders, perhaps it had been intended as a veiled attack on himself? Was Rakovsky saying all those years ago that Trotsky, like Marx, neglected those closest to him? Made intolerable demands upon them? Maybe it was a fair comparison. Maybe he had no talent for love or intimacy. Maybe Rakovsky was telling him this, thereby laying the grounds for betrayal years later? Such thoughts tormented him in the early hours. It was preposterous, Trotsky knew. But insomnia made his thoughts turn, unexpectedly, down paths of fear and confusion and hurt.

Beriya, Molotov, Khrushchev . . . Sometimes he intones the names of the members of Stalin's Politburo, over and over, in an effort to lull himself to sleep. But in his head this night is *her* voice lowly calling those names, calling her xolotl dogs, seven of them named after Politburo members. He shakes his head at the memory of those dogs, the way they always growled at his approach and how he would turn helplessly towards Frida, as the dogs circled him: *It's as if, with those names, they know* . . .

'Yes,' Frida said, 'dogs know everything.'

Lately, all his thoughts begin and end with Frida. His internal compass is awry. He can no longer distinguish between true north and magnetic north. Natalia and Frida. The red arrow of desire pointing in Frida's direction. The pull of her too great for him.

He had once said to her, his mind full of his rival, Diego, 'I could take you away from him.'

Only if I want to be taken away. She had looked at him then with a mixture of pity and challenge in her eyes, head thrown back, arms folded. Maybe it was his statement that had sent her away, had the opposite effect from the intention?

In the weeks with Frida, time had slowed down as it slows down when you travel very fast or sit in the presence of a strong gravitational field. The gravitational pull of the young woman bent time out of all known shape, and there were no longer days and weeks but only moments between one kiss and the next. In Einstein's physics, he knew, the future was out there waiting to be stepped into. The splash of a stone on water already ordained, the reflection of yourself in the water already contained in space-time. All times co-existed. His time with Frida was out there still. And memory could touch it.

It was a mystery to him, how Frida could prefer her philandering frog of a husband to someone like himself. The mystery of attraction. The mystery of friendship. And sometimes he felt the cold shadow of the future touch him, prepare him for a time when there were no more mysteries.

Of all the emotions he had ever allowed himself, this longing was one of the most difficult. It confused him. He woke at night when the nembutal wore off, his body held taut around his wife like a picture frame. And yet it was Frida who preoccupied him, not even in a sexual way, as he lay there, his arms enfolding Natalia. He was preoccupied beyond sex, beyond love, beyond the life he had built with his wife over half a century. Maybe he would never enjoy again that feeling of losing himself in the eyes of another, of seeing himself reflected larger than he was in a look that contained the appreciative roar of a crowd. A look that contained the steel hum of a train on its tracks, he in a blue carriage at the height of the Civil War. A hero to himself. It was a half-century of appreciation that his wife carried within and was, if he looked closely, reflected in her actions every day. It was expressed in her concern for him, the way she poured his tea, the extension of her arm opening a window, her caress on the back of his neck. It was there in gestures so familiar. But it was not new to him; it was not fresh; his life sometimes felt as if it had shrunk to an audience of one – Natalia – and he was not always enamoured of this audience with its predictable responses, its singular clap.

In truth, he hankered for that larger audience, the unpredict-ability of the first night, emotion undulating and uncertain. In Frida he had sensed such an audience, an audience he had to work hard to convince, but not so hard as to find it tedious. Yes, in his private life sometimes he longed for an audience beyond Natalia, and in his brief time with Frida he had glimpsed it. He had seen himself new, had felt as if all the accumulations of his past had been rolled back in the body of a person much younger than himself who knew only the grandeur of him and none of its fading.

For Natalia knew the lustre. She knew, also, the efforts to maintain it, to polish. The effort, sometimes, to keep going.

The younger woman saw none of this, and this cheered him. Made him forget how much effort it took to rise again in the morning, preparing for battle, wondering if that day would be his last and, if that were the case, how best to live it.

He had seen himself reflected in Frida's eyes: handsome, virile, strong. With a great capacity for living. *Not old.*

Sometimes he saw himself in his wife's eyes. It was not always flattering. The man who stumbled in the half-light without his glasses, the man who required bottles of pills to sleep, the man irritable when things did not go his way.

He had never allowed Frida to see him without his glasses. When he had felt her gaze upon him, he had basked in it, like a seal in sunlight, sleek and glistening.

Natalia had once looked at him like that. And he had responded.

Maybe that was the sum of private life? A reflex to a look from a beautiful woman. Was he so different from other men that he could resist such a look?

Guiltily he lifts his wife's nightdress. He strokes himself as he merges the images of the two women, loses himself in what he imagines is their double gaze of adoration.

And then he turns away in sadness at the realisation that perhaps the best of him is now past. He has lost the facility to stay in the present. He clutches at the blankets as Natalia stirs in her sleep, worried that all that is left of him is a past: of life, of love, of Revolution.

And it was not so much desire that bothered him, plagued him, guilted through him. It was rather the memory of desire, the illicit deliciousness of it, and the loss of it.

The time with Frida had been the last time he had felt alive to his fingertips. Outside the blankets he stretched out his hands – felt the stiffening in the fingers, extended them until he felt what it meant to say lifespan, turned over the palms in the dawn light, felt what it meant to hold your life in your hands.

Was a lifespan really written in the hands, as Señora Rosita had once said? The breadth and the length? The veins weaving through?

He remembers Señora Rosita. The small intense woman with the broad high cheekbones and the green cloth wound through her hair. He remembers her passion for her work. He remembers the conditions of her life: the dirt floor, the hammocks in the corners, the icons of Stalin and the Madonna in tin frames. The obsidian mirror. How such conditions, such a life, always convinced him of the necessity of struggle. How there was no other way.

He remembers desire at his fingertips. He would not feel such desire again, he was certain of it.

One day, there would be bullets and his body would be punctured through. Then he would know the meaning of life and desire. What was durable. What was transient. What his life had been worth.

Natalia lies sleeping. He watches her uneven breathing in the light coming through the curtains, the pallor of her skin grey. He notices the lines forming at the back of her neck. She has become an old woman and he does not know how this has happened. And he gets slowly out of bed and looks at himself in the mirror as a stranger might look at him and he sees himself as if for the first time, an ageing man slightly paunched, his white hair awry, faintly ridiculous in his pyjamas. He slumps back down on to the edge of the bed. He looks over at Natalia and feels confusion and love, her grey hair curling across her head like rainclouds curling across a sky.

He leans over to touch her hair, still soft although the colour has leached from it. He loved a woman's hair most of all. It was the first thing he noticed. The weight and fall of it, the fragrance and texture of it.

Frida's hair had been heavy and straight and strong as twine. He had loved its glossy weight, piled up on her head or curtaining heavily down her back, ribboned, plaited, pleated, braids looped and looped again, like rope on a quayside. Every day her hair was different, and he came to expect this difference, to note the alterations from one day to the next. He had believed that she made a special effort for him. But he soon realised that it was for herself that Frida made such an effort: *Every day I dress for paradise*, she once said.

You are a different woman every day! He had marvelled at her self-invention, the time she took. So many different women! He felt that it would take him a lifetime to possess all the different women she contained. The challenge of it.

He thought of his wife's hair. The chestnut curls that had so captivated him in Paris all those years ago. His wife's hair was always the same. Bobbed and curling around her face, making her eyes seem large and vulnerable. His wife's appearance altered little from one day to the next, one period of exile to the next. It was that steadfast predictability that he so valued, that she would not alarm him with difference or caprice, would be there for him, smoothing his way before him.

How then, at this stage of his life, had he come to appreciate difference, ornamentation, and novelty?

A thousand times a day he enumerated and analysed these differences between his wife and Frida. But the conclusions defied rational thinking. There were no logical explanations. He felt lost. For as enamoured as he was by variety and difference he did not want to go back to a time in which he could not think clearly, had no will to write and felt tormented by a desire to see whether the object of his affection had braided her hair with ribbons that day or flowers.

It was absurd.

All his children had been taken from him. All his friends. He had no one left except Natalia. It did not feel enough. He felt numb. There was nothing except remembrance of desire.

He turned back to Natalia and wound one of her soft grey curls around his index finger. He wondered whether Natalia had ever experienced such guilt and torment, and felt jealousy and shame tear through him at the thought.

NATALIA IVANOVNA SEDOVA
COYOACÁN
SEPTEMBER 1940

AFTER HIS DEATH, I think about everything between us. I think about the time of our separation, the anger crackling down the phone lines across the desert. How I felt as if I might never recover. How, after a lifetime in the service of Lev Davidovich, I knew nothing else.

I once had another life. In the early years of the Revolution, I worked at the Ministry for Cultural Enlightenment. I fought hard to preserve the art of the past – bourgeois art; many comrades opposed me. I once saved a Rembrandt from destruction. I believed that we could not progress as a people without knowing the past. I had my triumphs, independent of Lev Davidovich.

Since then it seems that his triumphs have been mine. His setbacks, his defeats also. As if we had become one organism with one heart, one lung – inhaling the world, attacking, defending and retreating.

A shared life.

In recent times, we felt no need for new people. We were both tired – of struggle, of the endless steps of visitors, of danger. Now that the struggle is over, the tiredness is there, like a blanket around me, and I could sleep for a lifetime. L.D. always had trouble sleeping. At night I would measure out the tablets, enough to lull him under. My life was in the measuring.

I lie on our bed, weeping. Crying hard. The indentation of his head still on the pillow. I should be issuing statements, wielding the pen like a weapon. But I lie here, wondering whether it is all over now.

For we always assumed that I would survive him, outlive him; assist him if necessary in outwitting his pain. And I always went before him, easing his way. And now I am left behind – the survivor of the wreckage of our family. To have your children and your husband go before you . . . after a life of measuring and smoothing the path . . . I now want to put down this burden of survival – this terrible thing.

I could now sleep for a lifetime.

But that is not what he would have wished.

Last night, I took handfuls of nembutal and fell into a sleep in which the past was more real than the present. I dreamt back to my time at the Ministry. The incident that Lev Davidovich threw back at me in our separation.

Was it a betrayal? In the dream, I was in the arms of a tall fair young man, ten years my junior. We had been colleagues some twenty years before and, at the time, he had desired me.

The young man had flattered me; had professed love for me.

And yes, I remember one night working late. I remember the young man leaning to kiss me and I confessed that I, too, felt an attraction, but that my future was with Lev Davidovich.

Those were the facts. But in the dream last night, there was more than a kiss. Indeed, the young man was pushing inside me as we lay on the floor in a darkened room. And then I woke, wondering if it had ever happened like that, if it was something I had desired at the time, and why I should be dreaming of a young man infatuated with me from the past, only weeks after my husband's death? Why should I wake now, over twenty years later, flushed and pleased with the attentions of a boy?

My life merged so gradually with that of my husband.

A shared life.

The expression of these things does not come easily. I write now with difficulty. For myself.

In times of stress Lev Davidovich would often reproach me with the *affair*. And in the past I always fought back: *There was no affair.*

Of course, I knew of his infatuations. He was an attractive man; he became animated in the company of women. I knew this; accepted it. I did not believe him to be unfaithful.

But in Mexico, things changed. The painter came between us. I sat and waited for him. I staked my territory. After all we had been through together, I believed he must come back. After he retreated to the sparse Taxco hills to collect himself, to wonder who and what he wanted, I felt as desolate as the landscape.

He said, *We must separate.* And who was I to argue?

The phone calls. He reproached me – in my grief at the thought of losing him – he reproached me once again with this imagined infidelity. And instead of denying it, I collapsed under the weight of his accusation, convinced that I was to blame, ready to confess to something that had never happened if it would bring him back to me.

He had gone to the hills to be alone.

I remember Frida visited the Casa Azul to collect some things, her face tight towards me. I believed she was going to see him. Some days later, there was a change. His communication with me softened. Something had broken. I never asked him directly. But his desire for me returned. He wrote passionate letters as in the first days of our courtship. How inflamed for me he felt. And I tried to summon up a level of desire for him, but there was only grief and fear at how close I had come to losing him, and it was many months before I felt, deep inside, a passion for him like before.

But the feeling returned. Slowly, slowly. Things were never the same between us. But we found something greater, deeper, calmer. For myself, older, no longer desirable, I felt that I had won in the contest of youth and allure and beauty. I had won. And my victory gave me strength.

After this dream of the young man, I now understand things more fully. Frida, at the same age as I had been when I was at the height of my powers all those years ago, had seduced my husband, simply because she could.

It was as simple and as difficult as that.

I T IS EARLY evening. And all day those newspaper photographs – a grieving Diego behind Frida's coffin – have stayed with me. Early evening always reminds me of that life before, the time of the Casa Azul, and later at the Avenida Viena and the routines of early evening, a sense of the day winding down, like a clock on its springs, and all of us still there as the sun sank in the sky. The change of guard on duty. The evening meal. And later, perhaps, the possibility of release, of trawling the bars in Coyoacán with Frida, listening to her stories of the Old Man, and how guiltily I absorbed those stories; how Frida hated his routines, his pedantry. *But without such routines there is only chaos*, I once argued with her, remembering my father, the noose around his neck, remembering all the reasons I had joined the Opposition.

Embrace the chaos, Frida had said. *There is nothing else*.

Back then, I was unable to do so. I understood too well why the form of Trotsky's days didn't alter – how the unexpected signalled danger.

His routines: the rabbits, the writing, the transcribing. The siesta in the early afternoon. Natalia turning the teapot. Still today I can remember these routines, put out my hand and touch them. The hours we spent watching the street from the tower, anticipating attack. How on *that day*, none of these routines mattered: and I return to that day, already history. The guilty release of that day.

I remember I got up slowly, to go to the gate. I didn't like Jacson. It was just a feeling, but when I'd mentioned it to Trotsky, months before, he dismissed my objections. *Where was the evidence?* Just something about him, I said. I admit that this was the time of tension between us. I could feel myself moving away from the Old Man. I was not as vigilant as I should have been.

Until you have something more specific than a feeling, Trotsky had said to me, *I'll continue to allow him to call on Sylvia.*

And on that day, as I got up to open the gate, Trotsky called out, 'Jordi, Tino, I will see to it.' I watched him press the button and the heavy gate slide open and saw Jacson walking quickly across the courtyard, trying to keep up with Trotsky. I saw Natalia behind the screen door of the kitchen. I watched Natalia watching them. The rabbits clambered over each other in their hutch, agitated, excited.

It was the end of our shift and we were playing poker and I put my cards down as Trotsky and Jacson crossed in front of our guard box. Again I looked at Jacson, at the dark eyes pouched in his face; he looked pale in the heat, overdressed in the suit, with the raincoat over his arm. I heard Natalia with the teapot and the kettle, filling the kettle with water in the kitchen, the water sighing through the old pipes.

Xavier, the Catalan gardener, stood watching the card game, a shovel in his hand. 'He doesn't look too well today,' he said, looking over at Jacson. Xavier leant on the shovel, shaking his head. 'You know, it's a funny thing . . . The day before yesterday, Jacson and I shared a cigarette and he thanked me in Catalan . . . And it was perfect Catalan, I'm telling you . . . But he's a Belgian, no?'

I looked up at Xavier leaning on the shovel. I shut my eyes. At that moment, Xavier's words were like the bullets you don't hear, because it is too late, because they have already burst the skin and entered the bloodstream.

His words hit through to the place inside, the part of me that had always known; that had tolled loudly and had not been listened to. The words lodged there and then I was on my feet, shouting at the others, and the cards fell like ash from my fingers, and no one played their hand because this was it, that moment, and there was no fear, only a reaction . . .

I grabbed my rifle and ran across the courtyard and passport-flashes of people and places and a time past were in my head. Faces in queues, at meetings, imploring, beseeching, angry. Faces from that time in Barcelona. Faces I had seen only briefly; the glint of an eye above a sandbag, taking aim . . .

There were many refugees from the Spanish War here in Mexico. Many Stalinists with the passports of dead *brigadistas*. We all knew that. But some things we chose not to see. We had anticipated attack from the front. Blind to any other possibilities.

We heard a disturbance in the main house. It was precisely four minutes since Jacson entered Trotsky's study. Only four minutes and already too late. We ran, with our rifles over our shoulders, and we saw Lev Davidovich on the ground, bleeding from the head. And I saw the man Jacson differently then: as clearly as if I had passed him on the streets of Barcelona all those years ago. I saw him before me, as I could have seen him months ago if I had looked more closely, this Catalan colonel in the pay of the GPU, clean-shaven, very thin, still clasping the *piolet*. If I hadn't been so distant with the Old Man . . . And then I raised the butt of my rifle, and Jacson's eyes changed, the whites turned milky with the fore-knowledge of pain; the fear was there and I wanted to pulp his face into oblivion. Then Tino and Xavier set on him as well, and there was frenzy and there was blood and there was nothing else, but this frenzy and this blood, and we beat him with our fists and our rifle butts until the floor was red. And four minutes ago none of this was happening, but the moment was always there, that moment in the future, quite empty, waiting for us to step into . . . and Trotsky, his head bleeding into Natalia's lap, said weakly, 'Don't kill him.' And the man from the GPU, the Catalan colonel with the Belgian alias and numerous passports, cried out also, 'Don't kill me.'

Jacson was badly beaten and then the shrill of the ambulance and the prone and bloodied figure of Lev Davidovich was taken away. And none of us had ever seen him without his glasses, and he looked defenceless, smaller, strapped into the back of the ambulance, and Natalia was another person, keening softly beyond our reach, and we didn't even try to reach her and all I could think of was that it was all over.

And afterwards, the things that came back. The illusion of

movement three years before in that short walk from sea to land; from something fluid to something more solid.

I remembered Frida's scent of jasmine and sex over me. I remembered praying to a black saint in a darkened church. How I had wanted my heart to be whole. All the things I had kept secret from the Old Man.

And I tried to pray, but I could not.

Three days later, the funeral. At the crematorium the door to the furnace does not shut properly. There is the smell of burning cloth. *Even in death a resistance*, I think to myself, leaning back in the wooden pew and looking up at the flat white ceiling.

Later, on the evening of his funeral, I went to the Plaza Garibaldi in Mexico City. Each night the Plaza comes alive. The tables are full. I sat in a hard-backed chair in the Plaza Garibaldi, tilting back against the wall, a glass in my hand.

I sat alone. I remember turning to the table of a young Mexican family next to me. There was a newspaper on the table and the headlines announced the funeral of Trotsky. I raised my glass and proposed a toast: '*El Viejo*,' I said. The children at the table giggled and clinked glasses of water with me, unsure of what I had said. Their father understood, he raised his glass. '*El Viejo*,' he said sadly. At that moment, a large old woman with long braided hair and a silver sombrero wandered past. Her mariachi band in tow. She leant towards me. She smiled at me and I could see her solitary tooth green in the gum and her breath steamed of alcohol. She carried a guitar. 'I will sing later,' she said. 'Remember me.'

I nodded and smiled at her. 'Of course.' Later, when the Plaza was full of young couples and their chaperones, serenaded by mariachi in tight white trousers, I wandered around the edges of the square, feeling maudlin, the effects of the day and of the tequila starting to bite. I heard a woman's voice lilting towards me, the clarity and timbre of it made me turn, and there she was, the old woman with the one tooth, her silver sombrero at the back of her head. I stopped to look, amazed that such beauty could come from such ruin, amazed by what life put in my way. And I gave her band some money and they played for me, forming a semicircle, and I sang with them, the way Frida and I used to do in the bars, and I offered up this moment just for her, remembering the taste of honeycake on her fingertips, and afterwards we sat together and they told me stories into the small hours and the woman with the one tooth and the beautiful voice sang in the deserted Plaza, and I gave myself over to it, when suddenly I remembered that the Old Man was gone. And I was surprised to find such joy here, on such a day. And I remember thinking to myself that maybe this was how life was, how it always would be: how you think it is one thing but it is always another.

My wife comes in and sees me looking again at the newspaper photograph: Frida's coffin draped with the Communist flag. She feels my loss. She puts her hand in mine: warm palms and cool fingertips. In the touch of her hand I know how much I have changed, and I remember the young man I once was, how I had pinned a small tin heart to a red felt board; how I had prayed for love to enter my life. How I had longed for a paternal embrace which never came. Always, the longing. And I say to my wife: *Even in our times together, Frida spoke of this death, how she would welcome it. Her health, her Diego, her painting – it was no easy life . . .*

My wife smiles slowly at me. *No life is easy*, she says.

I look up at her then and pull her close.

RAMÓN MERCADER
COYOACÁN
22 AUGUST 1940

I LIE HERE under a rough blanket in a prison hospital. They ask me who I am, every hour they repeat this question. *I am Frank Jacson*, I tell them, *businessman*. I know now that I will be Frank Jacson for many years to come. I lie here thinking of my mother. All of her hopes for me. After months of preparation, when it came to the moment, how things slowed down then sped up, how the moment overtook me. How the Old Man fought back. How nothing had prepared me for that.

I am falling off a high mountain. There is no third presence at my back.

I keep returning to what happened. Playing it again and again inside. The details of it.

He was a man of routine. I knew his routines from Sylvia. Early in the evening, after hours spent working on the Stalin biography, Lev Davidovich would sigh and put down his pen. The pen inscribed with his name, a present from Frida. He would stretch. He would open the leadlight doors into the garden of the house on the Avenida Viena. He would look up at the small guard tower; pleased with the new fortifications. He would move across the garden to the rabbit hutch. He would take them out one by one to stroke their ears and to check them carefully for parasites. His back would be to the gate when I arrived. This I knew.

Yesterday was humid and unsettled and I could feel the warmth of the late-afternoon sun on my shoulders as I stood at the gate. Trotsky heard a voice, my voice, calling him. And I stood at the gate, moving from foot to foot, a manuscript sweating in my hands. 'Sir,' I addressed the Old Man, 'I beg a moment from you . . .'

I was dressed in a loose grey suit with a grey raincoat over my arm. 'Very sensible,' Lev Davidovich said to me, noticing the raincoat as he opened the gate. 'Rain may still come.' He knew me as Jacson, the companion of Sylvia, one of the American secretaries. He slipped off his gloves and he sighed. His evening disrupted. But he was flattered also, I knew. He enjoyed the fact that young people still came to him for advice, deferred to him unquestioningly. *He thought he could win me over.* He ushered me inside, calling out to Natalia and his bodyguards, 'It is only Sylvia's Jacson.'

He strode purposefully through the courtyard and I tried to keep up. 'Those rabbits!' Trotsky shook his head and gestured towards the hutch. 'This weather unsettles them.' He smiled over his shoulder at me. 'You should stay for some stew.' I nodded and looked at the pink noses fleshed up against the mesh wire. I turned away then, feeling nauseous.

Natalia appeared at the screen door as always, to monitor visitors. She was surprised to see me at that hour, but Lev Davidovich reassured her, smiling. 'These young comrades and their manuscripts!' Natalia smiled edgily, nodded at me, proffered tea, coffee, which I declined. She returned to the kitchen to make some tea for the Old Man.

We went through to his study. On one wall was a self-portrait of Frida Kahlo with the inscription: *For Leon Trotsky with all love I dedicate this picture on the 7th of November 1937.* It had been a present for his birthday, he said, also, the twentieth anniversary of the Russian Revolution. I looked up at the painting of Frida swathed in colours of salmon and green, a spray of flowers in her hand, gazing at us like a bourgeois coquette. Trotsky said he was glad he had taken this portrait with him after they moved from the Casa Azul. It pleased him and soothed him to look upon it. 'Ah Frida,' he said sadly. 'She is incredible, no?'

And I looked up at Frida's portrait and it disturbed me. The woman behind the coquette. I felt exposed before her as I had at the exhibition months earlier. Her eyes saw it all, those eyes accustomed to duality. And I stumbled for a moment and was fearful that he might notice. *The man in the too-large suit. Inside someone else's clothes.*

'Yes,' I said, looking away from the portrait. 'Incredible.' I handed the manuscript to the Old Man who spread it over the pages of the unfinished biography of Stalin. As he turned, I placed my raincoat on the chair and raised the *piolet* concealed in the inner pocket. And the Old Man surprised me then, turning back to face me at the exact moment of skull being crushed and blood seeping over the letters. And he turned round, eyes blood-lit blue, to bite me on the hand. We grappled and he cried out to Natalia who heard the wicker chair fall and a dull heavy sound. Blood the colour of Frida's ribbons spread over the Stalin manuscript. The bodyguards rushed into the room.

And I was standing there with the *piolet* in my hand, breathing heavily, unable to move, unable to get at the gun in the other pocket. Already blood was congealing around the wound at the back of the Old Man's head. Blood on the floor. On the walls. On the manuscript like a Rohrshach blot. And the Old Man's round glasses lay in a pool of blood, one arm bent up, as if in defiance.

Nothing had prepared me for such defiance.

COYOACÁN
21 AUGUST 1940

A S THE BLOOD weeps from his head wound, Lev Davidovich looks up from the floor of his study and the portrait of Frida kaleidoscopes in front of him. *Amor y dolor*, Frida had said in 1937, after it was all over. Love and pain.

Three years later, as he lies dying, the details rise up. Not the details of the glorious Red October. Not the details of the Kronstadt uprising, the bodies bloating in the snow. Not the details of all the years in exile, the death of everyone dear to him.

No. It is the small, private details of the end of the affair that he remembers.

Lev Davidovich retreats into the hills around Taxco to restore his spirits. Natalia watches him go. Wondering when he will be back.

He writes Frida a long and passionate letter in which he pleads with her to reconsider. She does not reply.

Amor y dolor. Gradually the words worked over and over in his mind have a soothing, rhythmic quality. In his sleep, Lev Davidovich looks up from himself to see Natalia's large eyes crying in their folds of worry.

He goes for long walks in the hills looking for cacti, and wakes up one morning, realising that he has left behind the one person who is witness to his life. He cleaves to Natalia.

He remembers writing her long letters. *I love you so much, Nata, my only one, my love and my victim.*

Tentatively, she writes back: *I feel so totally alone.*

In private she puts her face in her hands and cries into the mirror at the passing of time, and curses a God she no longer believes in for not making her more beautiful. *I saw myself in the mirror today*, she writes, *and I look much older. My inner state makes me look older.*

Eventually forgiving him. Consoling him. *We are old*, she writes. *We have only each other.*

Lev Davidovich weeps. For what he is not entirely sure.

Natalia watches him return. Walking slowly up the path to the Blue House. A bunch of desert orchids in his hand. That night, they sleep little. The milky scent of orchids fills the room. She lifts her pale-blue nightdress and Lev Davidovich remembers suckling her small dry breast until dawn.

I SIT HERE at my stall. I am well past my Aztec century of fifty-two years. I am an old woman. I have outlived them all. And they flood through me now, these lives, flowing like the stories of oceans and rivers. For what is one life but the record of other lives?

I have outlived my Alberto also, who went into the mines, descended into the frescos of the *patron*, and never returned. An explosion underground, they said.

If not an explosion, the pulque *or the mescal or the politics*, I said.

I buried Alberto these past months, almost twelve months since the death of the *señorita.*

How I loved him, my husband. How I wanted for us to grow old. How I knew it was not to be. For I had seen a vision in my mirror, the goddess of *pulque* – Mayuel – rising out of a maguey plant with a cord and some cups in her hand. The cord bound tightly around the neck of my husband.

In my rainbow mirror I saw how much she wanted him.

And now he journeys to Mictlan, the Land of the Dead. He will journey through eight hells until he finds rest. I set out water for him. I set out his hat, a mask, and a crucifix also, for it is a long journey. And he will greet Mictlantecuhtli, the Lord of Death, like an old friend. My husband will recognise this skeleton figure with his clothes of paper and conical cap; the colour of him a matt Spanish white. For he took shape many times under my hand, stood sentinel in our doorway. Alberto knows him well.

All of these journeys.

The *señorita*. She loved the rain. She was destined for the Southern Paradise, ruled over by Tlaloc.

Drowning inside the flower, she had said.

I placed a dry bough near her funeral urn. It will turn green when her soul arrives in Tlalocan.

How many deaths I remember. How many things I saw in my obsidian mirror. How many things pressed in the track-lines of a palm.

I remember the death and cremation of Señor Trotsky. The wife, her face like stone. Eyes tight. The body of Señor Trotsky wheeled into the furnace. I remember the door to the furnace would not shut. The shirtsleeves of *el Viejo* caught alight. The attendants pushed their weight against the door. The wife collapsed as the cloth started to burn.

I watched, fascinated by *el Viejo* refusing to be pushed into the furnace. I could smell his terrible palms burning.

He died a warrior. As a warrior, he was destined for the Southern Paradise, the House of the Sun. He is now a *companion of the sun*. He plays at battle each day with other warriors. I see him rise every morning with great energy to greet the dawn, his sword clashing all colours of fire against his shield. With the other warriors, he carries the sun on the first part of its journey.

The souls of warriors return as humming birds or butterflies. The *señorita* loved to paint them.

How the warrior becomes a butterfly.

Red flashes in the sky because of it.

ACKNOWLEDGEMENTS

This book could not have been written without a grant from the Literature Board of the Australia Council which enabled me to travel to Mexico and bought me the time and freedom I needed – my heartfelt thanks. I am also deeply grateful for the Literature Fellowship to the Varuna Writers' Centre in Katoomba and to Peter Bishop and Tracey Ann Rankin for making my stay so memorable.

I would like to thank my family and friends for their support and encouragement during the writing of this novel. In particular, Gaby Naher for her belief in what I was doing and her comments on an early section and Ivor Indyk for publishing my short story 'In the Blue House at Coyoacán' in HEAT 9 (1998). Peter Bishop at Varuna – for his wonderful insights and unfailing support; Pam Wardell at BBC Radio Scotland for her warmth and enthusiasm; Ramon Arumi for his boyhood remembrances of the Spanish Civil War; Esteban Volkov for our chance meeting in Coyoacán and for sharing with me his recollections of his grandfather's life. Responsibility for the interpretation of events and personalities in this novel is of course my own.

I want to thank Liz Calder and Rosemary Davidson for their ideas and support; Mary Tomlinson for her patience and skill with the line editing; Marian McCarthy for her help with the finer points and everyone at Bloomsbury for their hard work and generosity.

Finally I would like to thank Francis Cassidy – for everything.

I am indebted to many sources in the writing of this novel; in particular the biographers of Leon Trotsky, Joseph Stalin and Frida Kahlo and the various commentators on the Stalin era. Trotsky's own writings were also very important: *My Life: An Attempt at an*

Autobiography (Pathfinder Press, New York, 1970); *Trotsky's Diary in Exile 1935* (Harvard University Press, Cambridge, Mass, 1976); and his unfinished final work – *Stalin: An Appraisal of the Man and His Influence.* (Harper & Brothers, New York, 1941).

The following were invaluable:

Isaac Deutscher's trilogy, in particular *The Prophet Outcast: Trotsky 1929–1940* (Oxford University Press, London, 1963), and his *Stalin: A Political Biography* (Oxford University Press, New York, 1967).

Serge, V. and Sedova-Trotsky, N. *The Life and Death of Leon Trotsky* (Wildwood House, London, 1975).

For further reading I am grateful to:

Alliluyeva, S. *Twenty Letters to a Friend* (Hutchinson & Co, New York, 1967).

Colton, T. J. *Moscow: Governing the Socialist Metropolis* (Harvard University Press, Cambridge, Mass, 1995).

De Sahagun, B. *The War of Conquest: How it was Waged Here in Mexico: The Aztecs' Own Story* (transl.) Anderson, A. J. and Dibden, C. E. (Univeristy of Utah, Utah, 1978).

Don Levine, I. D. *The Mind of an Assassin* (Weidenfeld & Nicolson, New York, 1959).

Herrera, H. *Frida: A Biography of Frida Kahlo* (Bloomsbury Publishing, London, 1998).

Kahlo, F. *The Diary of Frida Kahlo* (Bloomsbury Publishing, London, 1995).

Van Heijenoort, J. *With Trotsky in Exile* (Harvard University Press, Boston, 1978).

A NOTE ON THE AUTHOR

Meaghan Delahunt was born in Melbourne and lives in Edinburgh. She was the winner of the Flamingo/HQ Australia National Short story competition in 1997, and is working on her next novel.